Out
re The

Out
re The

**FREIGHT
BOOKS**

First published in the UK September 2014
Freight Books
49-53 Virginia Street
Glasgow, G1 1TS
www.freightbooks.co.uk

A CIP catalogue reference for this book is available from the British Library.

ISBN 978-1-908754-68-4
ISBN Ebook 978-1-908754-69-1

Typeset by Freight in Garamond & Gotham
Printed and bound by Bell and Bain, Glasgow

the publisher acknowledges investment from
Creative Scotland toward the publication of this book

About the editor

Zoë Strachan's most recent novel, *Ever Fallen in Love,* was shortlisted for the Scottish Mortgage Investment Trust Book Awards and the Green Carnation Prize. Her opera *The Lady from the Sea* – composed by Craig Armstrong – premiered at the Edinburgh International Festival in 2012 where it won a Herald Angel Award. She is a Director of Glasgow Women's Library, Patron of the Imprint Festival in East Ayrshire, and teaches Creative Writing at the University of Glasgow. Sexuality – her own or imagined – is a major theme in her work, although not necessarily the most important. She lives in Glasgow with the writer Louise Welsh.

Zoë Strachan

Preface

A few years ago I did a Sunday morning event at Ullapool Book
Festival. The moderator joked with the audience about the order
of service and lack of communion wine, but the final statement
of the session came from a woman who said she thought that in
some respects we'd done what a church congregation might do:
communicate, share ideas, compassion and empathy. The higher
power that had brought us together was Literature, and I'm not sure
that gay people need compassion so much as equal rights and freedom
from persecution worldwide, but I appreciated her sentiments.
I'd been reading from what was then my work in progress, a novel
called *Ever Fallen in Love,* and the questions and discussion had
circled around gay themes, gay characters, gay identity, being gay and
Scottish. Ullapool is a very particular festival, friendly and intimate
but with a high level of discussion that builds over the weekend.
There were writers and critics in the audience whose work I admire
greatly, including my partner Louise Welsh, who was sitting beside
my mum. Like most authors these days, I'm used to public events,
but this was different. It was a coming together of professional and
personal, of fictional and autobiographical, of political and artistic; I'd
hesitate to say it was a spiritual experience but it was certainly quite
an intense and thought-provoking event for me. It raised questions:
about the unpublished manuscripts that might be mouldering in attics
around the country; about the lack of gay male counterparts for the
generation of world-class Scottish women writers who are lesbian;
about whether we can talk meaningfully of gay or queer fiction; about
how new writers will embrace, subvert and reject such labels and
themes. In a fit of enthusiasm, I said that I would love to edit a new
anthology of contemporary LGBT writing from Scotland.

Well, here it is. And if it answers any of the questions that occupied me, I hope it poses many more. I approached a wish list of established writers, all of whom responded positively and warmly. I invited submissions from writers who considered themselves LGBT and Scottish by birth, residence, inclination or formation. Editors often use a euphemism about the standard of submissions being very high, but in this case every single piece I received was worth reading. Amongst those that I could not include here for reasons of space or technical accomplishment I found some incredibly revealing and moving pieces – not to mention many that were entertaining and risqué.

At Ullapool I said that, if I edited such an anthology, I'd call it 'He Hung a Good Washing' after an anecdote from another audience member. I haven't done so, I'm afraid. This collection was edited in referendum year, and went to press before September 18th. The independence debate has focussed very strongly on place, on what it means to be here in Scotland and how we might change the way in which our political and social structures function in this country. LGBT Scots will have to wait until after the referendum to exercise their right to equal marriage, while the first same sex couples tied the knot in England in March. Some churches will be dismayed – as will those gay people who see marriage of any kind as outmoded and patriarchal – while other religious groups will celebrate with the openness and humanity of that Sunday morning audience in Ullapool. Not all of my contributors are resident in Scotland, but all of them share a kernel or more of Scottishness at the heart of their identity. All of them are both here, and out there.

I owe a few acknowledgements, first of all to the Ullapool Book Festival audience for spurring me on to create this anthology. Toni Davidson's *And Thus Will I Freely Sing* was the first such book from Scotland, and when I discovered it on a low shelf in Glasgow University Library it was an inspiration to me in many ways. The author Kevin MacNeil kindly helped me by reading the Gaelic submissions. *Out There* was largely realised with the aid of a Cultural Commission grant from

LGBT History Month Scotland, for which I am extremely grateful. An Arts & Humanities Small Grant from the Royal Society of Edinburgh contributed to production costs of the book. The anthology would not have been possible without the enthusiasm of everyone at Freight Books, in particular Adrian Searle, Keren McGill and Robbie Guillory.

Berthold Schoene

Foreword:
This Queer Affinity

When I arrived at the University of Glasgow as a new postgraduate student in 1990, acclimatisation was not at all straightforward. I had spent time in Scotland before, during my intercalary year in 1987/88, but then I had experienced the country very much as a visitor might, or a tourist; this time round I had come to stay. As expected, I struggled familiarising myself with a new language (English) and a new culture (Scottish), but as a young gay man, who had recently split up with his first-ever boyfriend back home in Germany, I also faced the entirely unanticipated challenge of having to come out all over again, and this time under quite different, far less hospitable circumstances.

1980s Germany had not exactly been greatly advanced in its attitude towards gays and lesbians, but what I experienced in Scotland was definitely a step back in time. Especially disconcerting to me were people flaunting their homophobia in places where I least expected it, namely among supposedly enlightened and intelligent folks, in the university, on campus. Back in Freiburg it had just about become acceptable for same-sex couples to walk around hand in hand on campus, and it had become quite chic among students to have gay friends; at Glasgow, by contrast, the University's Gay and Lesbian Society had to meet in complete secrecy to avoid homophobic abuse. On coming out to my supervisor in an aside, I was promptly transferred to another member of staff whose 'sensibility' ('He's from Edinburgh!') was deemed much better equipped to accommodate my 'cosmopolitan' airs. Off-campus, I found a buzzing gay subculture, yet this was strictly confined behind closed doors. Scotland would not celebrate its first Gay Pride March until 1995, and that, it has to be said, turned out to be a rather muted affair. I found myself not only in another country, but beamed up to another time as well. (Clearly, Scotty had a lot to answer for!)

As I only discovered quite a while later, Scotland was indeed lagging behind, by about a decade in fact. Whereas male homosexuality had been (partially) decriminalised in England in 1967, and in Germany in 1969, Scotland only followed suit in 1980.

For me, then, it was back into the closet, for the time being at least, back to leading a double life, with my gaydar switched to the highest alert level lest I misjudged my company and naively assumed too much of a tolerant attitude. Only much later did it dawn on me that this upsurge of paranoid self-consciousness was in actual fact the best possible initiation to Scottish culture I could have hoped for. Duality – superimposed as well as self-inflicted – has traditionally been a major, pervasive trait of Scottishness at so many different levels. In terms of class, culture, religion, gender, language, nationality and location, in pre-devolution Scotland self-dividedness ruled, often mixed with an awkward inferiorism and acute lack of self-esteem, resulting in a highly volatile blend of national pride and self-loathing. This emotional cocktail of extremes is of course not entirely alien to gay culture either, but at the time Scotland seemed too resolutely homophobic to realise, let alone explore, this queer affinity. Scottish masculinity seemed particularly expert at projecting queerness invariably onto the other, be they actually gay or just 'foreign'.

As a PhD student in Scottish literature, what brought me much comfort at the time, and considerably renewed my delight in irony, was the discovery that the Scottish word for 'book' was *quair*, and that Lewis Grassic Gibbons' *A Scots Quair* (1932-34) was one of Scotland's most iconic texts. To my foreign eyes and ears, this struck me as a poignant *double entendre* or *trompe l'oeil* if ever there was one. I wanted it to suggest that literature provided an inside/out home for the queer, both as a refuge and a hiding place. The more I became acquainted with it, the more Scottish literature in particular revealed itself to me as a place where queerness was more than a visitor or fleeting presence, where indeed, in manifold fits and starts and retreats, both the resemblance and the enduring incommensurability of the Scots and queer conditions were playing themselves out. Scottish literature told it as it was, recording and reflecting what was wrong with the given status quo. At the same time it also set out to re-imagine society and the nation, thereby allowing potential alternatives to take shape and unfold. As the Chinese-American literary critic Pheng Cheah encapsulates in his reflections on literature as a 'world-making' activity, literature 'tells us that we can belong in many ways, and that quivering beneath the surface of the existing world are other worlds to come' (2008: 38). This has always struck me as particularly true of Scottish as well as gay and lesbian writing.

Another eye-opener soon after my arrival in Glasgow was my discovery of the American feminist Elaine Showalter's chapter on 'Dr Jekyll's Closet' in her book *Sexual Anarchy* (1991). Wisely leaving the question of Stevenson's sexuality to one side, Showalter reads *The Strange Case of Dr Jekyll and Mr Hyde* (1886) as 'a case study of male hysteria' and 'a fable of fin-de-siècle homosexual panic', complimenting Stevenson on his insight in 'the fantasies beneath the surface of daylight decorum, the shadow of homosexuality that surrounded Clubland and the nearly hysterical terror of revealing forbidden emotions between men that constituted the dark side of patriarchy' (1991: 107). Clearly, the chapter was originally designed to cause both mirth and outrage in equal measure, as Showalter chooses to draw our attention to the text's imagery of 'forced penetration through locked doors into private cabinets, rooms and closets' (110) as 'a series of images suggestive of anality and anal intercourse':

Hyde travels in the 'chocolate-brown fog' that beats about the 'back-end of the evening'; while the streets he traverses are invariably 'muddy' and 'dark,' Jekyll's house, with its two entrances, is the most vivid representation of the male body. Hyde always enters it through the blistered back door, which, in Stevenson's words, is 'equipped with neither bell nor knocker' and which bears the 'marks of prolonged and sordid negligence'. (113)

Showalter's mischievous queering of a Scottish world classic proves particularly pertinent with regard to how it links the *doppelgänger* motif to masculinity and male sexuality, as well as Scottishness. The much bandied-about critical trope of the 'Caledonian antisyzygy', which has traditionally been employed to describe the recurrent interplay of the realist and fantastic modes in Scottish literature, becomes expressive of the Scottish male's abject horror of his own intrinsic self-and-otherness, or 'effeminacy'. In my own reading of Iain Banks' *The Wasp Factory* (1984) I developed this issue further by introducing a deliberate postcolonial twist. 'Within the imperial framework of English-Scottish relations', I argued, 'the Scottish male is already feminised as a disempowered native (br)other' (134). While at home in Scotland masculinity might be aspiring to patriarchal domination, within a broader international context it was assigned a position of marginality because of its Scottishness. This awkward duality inevitably serves to unsettle Scottish masculinity's sense of natural superiority, while at the same time necessitating a commitment to subversion and resistance that could easily be identified as 'queer'. The same inherently queer quality of Scottishness is also invoked by the novelist, poet and critic Christopher Whyte in a short piece on 'Gender and Nationality' published in 1991:

We live in a state where everyone is English until proved otherwise, where English identity is natural and axiomatic, while Scottish identity is the result of a conscious choice whose artificiality we cannot deny. It is voluntary and, in terms of existing political power relations, unnatural. The analogy with the experience of gay men and lesbians is not hard to see. Heterosexual by default, they experience a sense of difference for which no external validation is offered, and which they can live fully only as the result of an act of will, of self-definition. It looks as if nationalists have a quite a lot to learn from them. Far from being at opposite ends of the spectrum, nationalism, feminism and sexual liberation have the potential to create a formidable alliance. (46)

Whyte's hope here is for fruitful intersectionality to facilitate a mutually beneficial coalition between gay and lesbian liberation and pre-devolution Scottish nationalism, with the desire for emancipation, independence, and recognition of equality in difference as the common denominator. Whyte reasserts this hope several years later in his introduction to *Gendering the Nation* (1995): 'Precisely because in small, minority, emergent cultures, national identity can never be taken as given, these are privileged sites for the study of gender and its interaction with other factors in the formation of identity' (xvi). But by then doubts had crept in: whereas such a coalition might be a no-brainer for gays and lesbians, it was perceived as an unsustainable compromise and embarrassment to Scottish nationalists. The two subordinate identities are far from on a par with regard to their subordination as minorities. Irrespective of its subnational status, Scottish society remains heteronormative, leaving Whyte eventually to concede that 'to be gay and to be Scottish, it would seem, are still mutually exclusive conditions' (xv). Even many years after devolution, the problem of gay and lesbian Scottishness appeared to remain unresolved. In her contribution to *The Edinburgh Companion to Contemporary Scottish Literature,* Joanne Winning writes that even though anthologies of queer writing such as Toni Davidson's *And Thus Will I Freely Sing* (1989) and her own *The Crazy Jig* (1992) both 'established that there was indeed a space where Scottishness and same-sex desire might intersect' (283), 'it is clear that a strongly nationalist agenda might actually work against the articulation of a gender-specific voice marked by sexual difference, be it gay, lesbian or simply female' (284).

We are now firmly ensconced in the twenty-first century and despite the war on terror and ongoing austerity, we seem to have managed to make some genuine civilisational progress, especially with regard to minority rights. Following the Civil Partnership Act of 2004 Britain has recently witnessed the legalisation of gay marriage, and with the referendum on Scottish independence now imminent, it seems tempting to say that whatever rifts and tensions there may once have existed between gay and lesbian liberation and Scottish nationalism, they have now either been resolved or simply ceased to matter. If a final reconciliatory seal of approval was needed, then it was provided in spectacular fashion by Edwin Morgan, gay and Scotland's first poet laureate, who posthumously bequeathed £1m to the Scottish National Party. Yet perhaps we should not too quickly yield to complacency. We might be very well-advised to stay alert to Scotland's proclivity for somewhat delayed development, if only to counter the ever so slightly deceptive story which, as David Torrance explains, 'most Scots like to tell themselves, of a more liberal, tolerant and – perhaps most flatteringly of all – egalitarian land than our larger southern neighbour'. As Torrance reminds us in no uncertain terms, Scotland's 'legislative time lag was in line with public opinion. For until relatively recently, when Scots were asked for views on three key social indicators – homosexuality, divorce and abortion – their responses were significantly more conservative than those in England'. Neither an independent Scottish nation, nor a nation entirely composed of lesbian and gay citizens, is likely to be the best possible place on earth. Neither queers nor Scots are naturally equipped with a stronger moral fibre than everybody else. An independent Scotland is unlikely to put an end to ever-increasing neoliberalisation just as queer culture is unlikely to suddenly denounce the glamour of consumerism and return to politics. If literature does have a clear-cut purpose, then it is to help us keep our eyes peeled for the way things really are, not just where we live but in the world as a whole. It is also to help us remember that there remains always room for improvement.

Torrance finishes on a high note by celebrating James Robertson's *And the Land Lay Still* (2010) as the first straight-authored novel featuring a gay protagonist. I am inclined to agree that the character of Michael Pendreich is as close as Scottish writing has so far come to portraying the nation through a gay lens. But, having said that, does Robertson seriously attempt the launch of a 'Mike Caledonia', an entirely new, if not so very different kind of Scots *quair*, mirroring Grassic Gibbons's creation of Chris Guthrie as 'Scotland herself' and 'Chris Caledonia'? Be this as it may, Robertson's novel has various other precursors. It seems only fair to mention in this context the achievements of Alan Warner and Irvine Welsh for what Zoë Strachan has called the 'normalisation of homosexuality'. In addition, there are major queer-authored works that represent milestones not only in Scottish literature but in world literature as well, and these certainly made a big difference to me personally. They include Simon Taylor's *Mortimer's Deep* (1992), Jackie Kay's *Trumpet* (1998) as well as Zoë's own *Negative Space* (2002).

I am very excited by the project of *Out There*. It strikes me as extremely timely to revisit the previous anthologies of Scottish queer writing – Davidson's and Winning's pre-devolution collections and Joseph Mills' post-devolution *Borderline* (2001) – and to continue the sequence by adding a brand-new pre-independence specimen.

Bibliography

Cheah, Pheng. 'What Is a World? On World Literature as World-Making Activity.' *Daedalus* 137:3 (2008), 26-38.

Schoene, Berthold. 'Dams Burst: Devolving Gender in Iain Banks's *The Wasp Factory.*' *Ariel: Review of International English Literature* 30:1 (1999), 131-48.

Showalter, Elaine. 'Dr Jekyll's Closet.' In: *Sexual Anarchy: Gender and Culture at the Fin de Siècle* (London: Virago, 1991), 105-26.

Strachan, Zoë. 'Queerspotting: Homosexuality in Contemporary Scottish Fiction.' *Spike Magazine* (1 May 1999), http://www.spikemagazine.com/0599queerspotting.php [accessed 5 May 2014].

Torrance, David. 'Gay Caledonia.' *Scottish Review of Books* 8:1 (2012), http://www.scottishreviewofbooks.org/index.php/back-issues/volume-8-2012/volume-seven-issue-four/459-gay-caledonia-david-torrance [accessed 5 May 2014].

Whyte, Christopher. *Gendering the Nation: Essays in Modern Scottish Literature*(Edinburgh: Edinburgh University Press, 1995).

Whyte, Christopher. 'Gender and Nationality.' *Cencrastus* 41 (Winter 1991/92): 46-7.

Winning, Joanne. 'Crossing the Borderline: Post-devolution Scottish Lesbian and Gay Writing.' In: *The Edinburgh Companion to Contemporary Scottish Literature*, ed. by B. Schoene (Edinburgh: Edinburgh University Press, 2007), 283-91.

Janette Ayachi

Dandyism to Debauchery
For K.L

Women laugh and spill their drinks
   dissolving after midnight
      when everything is jocular
         glasses are refilled in circuits
as smoothly as the songs play
like spider-string tumbleweed
        crashing against our ankles
     a crenellation of waves over rocks.
   Comfortably the background blots
and my gaze centres on you
straight rum stinging my throat
   my intemperant tongue
      eager to taste you
         dancing for the first time
we swing ourselves in patterns
kissing for the first time
   we wield a shoal of sparks.

In the two hours that we slept
   I dreamt we faced the sea
     like a cinema screen
        drinking from the projections
but nothing could quarry
my thirst to touch you
      burrow between the coastlines
   of your shoulders
   as if you were the first boat
I had seen for miles

ſpent from drifting from green to blue
    bed to bed, ſtreet to alkaline sky.

The hotel room was ugly, small and yellow
    so we took to the waters
        mascara tracing trains across our faces
        one blink and time slowed down
under shower-ſpray we kissed
filled our mouths with chlorine and ſtars
        and ſpat them out like mermaids
        on a Bernini fountain in Rome.
    You reached for the slope
of my inner thighs and found
    where I ſtored my surrender
        the veins in your hands pulsed
            as my climax filled the pockets
                between your knuckles
your eyes as blue as Bunsen flames.

Gravity

For P.C

Every comet throws an arc
And scars our vision 'cross the dark
(Shirley Manson, Beloved Freak)

When two comets collide to stain
         the white sheets of the Stratosphere Hotel
                where tequila talks, cocktails listen,
cheap champagne blurs even bionic vision
         machine-dark of the dance floor fixes our gaze
                on artificial smoke swallowing outlines of its prey
like staring at constellations from the trenches
this place for queer Utopia to rise from the ashes:
         fags, dykes, trannies, cross dressers, clowns,
                lost snow queens in stilettos, sulphur-crowned
with energy and bar mirrors where lips stick
         behind curtains of the Baronial towers of toilets
                where all the beloved freaks of society circuit colour
into disjointed rainbows, shooting arcs of neon
and the love that dare not speak its name is screaming
         and everyone is dancing or talking about dancing
                like spirits self-rooted under the arm pits of trees
gossip stirs a timber boom across a frieze of speakers
         couples at tables warm their hands on the undertow.

Digits on screen before the dial and waving holographic smiles
         echo where this is supposed to be a love poem
                the undeniable crush and kismet of connection
when parallel with my virtual doll for the first time
         her long hair like a serpentine midnight river
                tracing its glorious way over my face and down

to where butterflies transformed into a cage of stars
        her laugh so potently desirable I trapped it in a bottle
               with solar-strength ion tails of ice and dust
close enough to the sun now to be nucleus with our lust
        all urgent pulse and streaming jets in our wake
               from the internet ether to real-time orbit
we carry our mystery, our weight, depend on the magnitude
        of gravity to pull us closer in or further away.

Demolition, Banshees and the Beginning of Love

The day we watched the demolition, walking to stations
from our Glasgow hotel, the carcasses of offices
dissected for post-mortem in the morning rain
its electric skeleton of wires crossing scrap-metal
under x-ray ether, bone-structure bent
against the energy of sky, all silicon and felt
where songs of pylons wavered like harmonica reverb
our hair static with the stygian gloom of the streets
wind lashing our faces like the last eager flap
of a bird's broken wing and I wanted to hold her hand
stroke the differences between the confessional
and the cautious, but she was the girl who
had giddy banshees on her side
and I let her stun them with her absurdities.

Star alignment trodden, we teased out our own common element
water became our beacon; she emptied the taps of the Clyde
on my drunk nakedness, the sheets we slept on
tricked puddles into orbs as an orphan storm tapped the glass
her hair a star-choked river as we chatted through the night
from one length of a coastal haar to another
to join under demolition, banshees and the beginning of love.

Perfect Alchemy

For D.M

She stepped into my life with the stamina of gold-leaf pressed into
tempera
shuffled the pack of me and challenged my hand to unravel in the dark
– it was fire on fire, a banquet for any Queen, a perfect alchemy.

I left her in the garden with the detachable stars
her topaz eyes flashed steel-spun silver with wonder.

Her scent was of camphor and oleander, I climaxed
in her mouth like a storm testing the boreal pull
Minerva in sight calling all the shots
toward a masquerade of voluptuous surrender
in a place where time tumbled, anything was possible.

So I returned from sea suspended in that space
where land and water kissed, spoke only in tongues
followed the pheromone trail that spilled like petrol.

Our territorial disputes over who was on top
sent us rolling in circles like the juggernaut tide
but I was always hurricane drunk and she was a Celtic dream
slick as Velcro with a bag of talismanic tricks that threw me blind.

She French inhaled in my bed and was aware only of her mouth
the ghettoes of my blood chortled and burst like red halogen

– I have yet to have my heart broken.

Damian Barr

The Man in the Mirror

Now I see me, now I don't.

Steam nibbles the bathroom mirror – orange plastic framed and plate-sized, the only one that's not brought us seven years' bad luck. It's survived every hurried flit, every Friday night. Now it's propped tipsily on the back of the sink. Like its cold cousin, frost, the steam creeps from edge to middle disappearing me as it goes: first my ears, then my chin, then my eyes, then my nose. My lips linger for another moment and I swear out loud as they go – my Mum's not here to catch me and I'm old enough now anyway. I wanted the place to myself for this so I waited till she dragged my wee sister up the road to Streaks Ahead Hairdressers.

Shaving is harder than it looks in the Gillette adverts. I can't believe I've got to do this every day forever or maybe every other day. Is this really the best a man can get? It's a mega-waste of time and hair. Like Flash Gordon putting his hand in that hole in that tree, I reach into the darkness under the sink where my Mum stashes her *women's things* feeling for what I know is there. My fingers find the treacherously crinkly bag and I quickly pull out a bright orange Bic Safety Razor fringed with white plastic. I wonder if she counts them? A Lil-Let escapes and swells in a splash on the floor. I bin it to save us all a redneck, lifting it carefully by its tail like a dead mouse.

I'm a couple of driving lessons into being 17 and I'm off to uni at the end of this summer – my mum's told the whole village. Twice. Edinburgh, she boasts to them before warning me it's full of snobs and yuppies. It's not actually Edinburgh, it's Napier – the ex poly. But I don't care. Over and over I keep adding up the days, hours and minutes to try and make them go faster. I give dirty looks to every clock I see. I thought she didn't want me to leave but this last fortnight it's like she can't wait to get me out the house.

Because Logan's back.

I can't believe it. Can't believe she took him back after all these years, all he did. He's the man she walked out on my Dad for – the red-faced Rangers fanatic that wanted her but not her weans and definitely not her son. I was eight when she pulled her wedding rings off. I was ten when she left Logan. It was Christmas Eve and she sneaked in to my room bringing cold night air, whispering that she'd got me my Millennium Falcon. She saw the bloody pillow and my ear hanging from my head and it all hit her at light speed. Straight away she marched us out into the snow and out of his range. I should've told her everything then but we were away already and it's too late now. I'll pack all my secrets when I go: three weeks, two days and too many hours and minutes.

I try wiping the mirror with my hands and imagine I'm rubbing Logan away but I skite across its smoothness. Two weeks ago I came back from one of my last days at school and he was just sitting there drinking tea in the living room with my Mum. Side by side on the burgundy leatherette Chesterfield she's only just paid off, them both acting normal. The worse bit is he's not stopped smiling. I catch a corner of the towel I've wrapped twice round my waist. There's nobody in and the snib is on the door but I'm still careful. I turn to the side. Is this how I'd look in a skirt?

I remember my Mum wrapping me head to toe in this towel when she was still with my Dad and the steelworks were still open and everybody had jobs and it was just the three of us. Now the big orange sunflowers have faded and it's so thin it goes see-through and I'm the oldest of three and when my Dad makes his custody weekends I'm up past his shoulders. Gro-Bag, he calls me. I never want to be taller than him.

Wipe complete I can see myself again. I'm still getting used to the face peering back. I should probably be wearing the specs I've only just caved in to because who wants to be lanky and spotty and bent *and* speccy. And you never see a man shaving with specs on. They'd steam up.

I remember the tickly tufty brush my Dad used to foam his coal-black stubble and him picking me up with one hand and grizzling the back of my neck with his chin and me giggling and kicking and screaming and him not letting me go because he knew this was all I wanted really.

I bought my can of Gillette Gel at the big Boots in Motherwell, 20 minutes away on the number 44 so nobody in the village would see. The razors cost too much but I remembered my Mum's orange ones. I keep the can in my pant drawer. It's black with luminous green lettering and it stays cold no matter how hot the bathroom gets. It's slippery with condensation but the lid pops off and I press the button on top. A crazy string of gel the same neon as the writing shoots out swelling and wriggling as soon it hits the wet air and it puffs up in my palm when I catch it. About twenty pence worth, I reckon. I close my lips tight as I follow the instructions on the can and apply it where my beard is supposed to grow. It's surprisingly minty cool and reminds me of when I put toothpaste on my spots after I heard at school it kills them. It doesn't.

Lips pressed tight I breathe so hard through my nostrils I accidentally suck some up. Twitching my nose like a rabbit doesn't get it out so I just snort over the sink. I've still got loads in my hands and don't want to waste any so I cover the rest of my face just in case. Straight away it avalanches down my forehead into my eyes. More swearing out loud. Blind and burning, I reach for the cold water tap and my hand slips twice before it turns. Relief.

I look like a snow man and my skin is tightening as the foam dries. I pick up the razor and start just below my left sideburn. The single blade immediately clogs as I catch a chunk of hair. I better even up the other side. Soon I've shaved to the top of both my ears and I'm glad I've left school because I'd never live this down. Maybe at uni it will be a look.

The can isn't clear about technique so I try holding the razor still and turning my head. This works until I hit my chin where it catches on a spot and the foam blooms red and it nips and I think how easy it would be to cut my own throat. I turn my left wrist over and look at the knot of veins pulsing purple and blue just below the skin. Above them sit two scars, two hole-punches whiter than even my library-white skin. I remember getting them.

I was eight and had a pair of grey plastic handcuffs that I used to play soldiers with. When another boy nicked the keys I marched back home like a prisoner of war with my hands out in front of me and managed not to fall. When I got there Logan promised to get them off. I kept my arms held out while he turned the poker in the fire. I watched the tip go orange then red and when it was white he took it out and told me to stand still. I've never been stiller. A whoosh of bitter stink as he melted the chain between the cuffs then heated the poker up again. He took my right hand in his. My skin shrank away as he melted through the cuff. I shook it off rubbing my freed wrist. Then he gripped my left hand. Too tight, the plastic pinched. I pulled away. 'Be. Still,' he snapped bringing the poker closer. Too close. I try to pull my hand from his. He won't let go. From plastic to skin the smell changes. I remember letting my wee sister pick the scabs off.

I start shaving the other side of my face, plastering on another twenty pence worth of foam, and manage not to cut myself. It's going quite well now. The fiddly groove that goes from your nose to your lips and which I remember from Biology is called the philtrum, is surprisingly easy if you just pout. With my buck teeth this is all too easy. My Dad's not old enough for a hairy nose but I think his Dad had a few whiskers poking out so I do my nose too. It's a short swoop from there to between my eyes. I finish with a single swoop of my forehead nicking the top off another spot as I go.

Done.

Except, I've missed a bit near the love-bite shaped birthmark on my neck. The bathroom is starting to cool down so I fill the sink with more hot water. Hot water is the only good thing about Logan – he used to work for British Gas. The first day he was back he bled our radiators and programmed the timer that baffles my Mum. But I can't breathe the newly warm air, open my windows wide at night to let it all out.

More steam swirls. The mirror clouds. The corner of my towel is sploongin so useless for wiping. Without taking my eyes from the mirror I twist round, reaching with one hand for the snib on the door and racing with the razor to get the bit I missed before my face disappears completely. My towel finally slips but I let it fall shaking it free of my hips. My fingers find the snib and the bolt clicks and the door opens and the steam rushes out and up the stairs. I'd not realised I was boiling until now. I get off that last bit of bumfluff and foam, mostly foam, and I'm keen to see the results. The mirror clears quickly as the bathroom cools. I lean over the sink for a closer look and there I am.

And there is Logan.

I didn't hear the back door go and nobody comes in the front so he must have been in the house all this time. But where? He stands there in his blue boilersuit, his always red face getting even redder in the heat from the bathroom. I still have the razor in my hand. Safety razor. I tighten my grip. I refuse to turn around or bend over to pick my towel up off the floor. I stand as tall as I can. He makes no move. He just stands there smiling like he just found an extra biscuit in the bottom of the packet. He watches me watching him in the mirror. Just watches me. And I watch him back.

Paul Brownsey

The Kreutzer Sonata

Carrying a violin-case, she limps into Philip's sitting-room. On each limp her long plait of grey hair jerks. On each limp, too, she says, 'Fuck.' She says it, Philip judges, automatically, because a pattern has been set up: limp, *fuck*; limp, *fuck*; limp, *fuck*. She doesn't know she's swearing.

She halts by the grand piano that dominates the room. 'The minister's lovely wife is always available to assist a promising young musician in the parish.'

She turns to scrutinise Philip. Her face takes on the cunning look of someone who has tumbled to a secret being kept from her. 'The meeting for the buggers is in the minister's study.'

'No, Catherine,' coos the Reverend Moira Dinnett, as though the old lady had made the most natural mistake in the world. 'Philip isn't one of the...' She swallows the last word. 'Mr Boyes is the kind gentleman who was so sorry you couldn't play your violin in Fynloch Lodge and said I could bring you to play with him. He is an *excellent* pianist.'

As if you'd know, Philip thinks. At that point his mobile rings and when he sees who it is he is nothing but need, almost out the door before he says, 'Excuse me, I'll just take this in the hall.'

'I got your text,' Philip hears in the hall.

'Thank you.'

'All right. We'll talk. Get it over with. I'll come round right away.' Already, Philip is telling the old lady and Moira they must leave at once, *this instant*, it was the hospital, a relative mown down by a car, sorry, maybe we can re-arrange...

'Not now,' Philip replies. It is definitely heroic, how right conduct, forgotten when Philip saw who the call was from, has now re-asserted itself; though, of course, things turn out well for people who do the right thing. 'She's just arrived. The old lady, the violinist who's not allowed to play her violin in her care home. I *told* you.'

That he can not only honour his appointment with the old lady but even imply criticism of Malcolm for forgetting shows that Philip is definitely not needy, oh no. He adds hopefully, 'She'll be away by eight.'

'Because of the buses I'll need to hang outside your place for around forty minutes,' says Malcolm, as though the inconvenient bus service were another of Philip's failings. 'Symbolic. I'm always hanging around. Until your family let go of you long enough to allow you to fit me in. You're 37! Think about that while you're tickling the ivories. I was always second fiddle.'

'Thank you, thank you.'

'You placed too much on me. Expected me to be an entire new family. I am not substitute father, mother, sister, brother.'

'You're right, you're right,' says Philip, exhilarated because there would be no point in Malcolm's saying all these things again unless as a prelude to giving their relationship another go, break-up rescinded. And note the encouraging present-tense of that *I'm always hanging around*.

The door to the sitting-room has opened a crack and closed again. 'Right, see you at eight,' he says heartily.

The door opens a crack again. 'You're finished,' Moira whispers, informatively, but also as though she might still be interrupting. She slips into the hall, shutting the door behind her. 'I wanted a word before you came back through. I think she thought for a moment she was back in the manse and someone was trying to find a meeting. The memory for people and so on, the short-term memory, is all over the place. She can be a bit of a potty-mouth, too. But she'll be all right. Deep down she knows exactly why she's here, and I know she's *very* grateful.'

How do you know? he thinks, then is surprised by a huge surge of anger on behalf of all oppressed people everywhere. This awful treatment of a helpless old woman by awful Fynloch Lodge, denying her what's most precious to her! He pictures the place going up in vengeful flames, though is scrupulous to script a safe transfer of all the residents to a nicer alternative.

He leads the way back into the sitting-room, away from the anger. 'You'd think,' he says with a calm maturity Malcolm must think well of, 'there'd be a day-room, some out-of-the-way corner where she, you could play the violin.'

Catherine Mackie stands just where she was before.

'Well,' says Moira, professionally seeing both sides, 'I suppose it could be a disturbance, people living in these little rooms, no sound insulation, everything done on the cheap. And some of the old ones can be a bit snappy.' She lowers her voice in token inaudibility. 'It was the cheapest home we could find. Alec didn't leave her much. She just sits in her chair all day staring...' Normal vocal service is resumed. 'But when I heard that in our own congregation there was a real, trained pianist, I couldn't help trying to arrange *something* for you, Catherine.'

'It will be a pleasure to play with you.' Malcolm would approve of that, too. 'I don't know how I'd cope if I couldn't play the piano.'

She doesn't acknowledge this remark. She hangs on to her violin-case as Moira helps her off with her coat. There's a stain, pure care-home, on the front of her limp floral-patterned dress. When Moira makes as if to undo the violin-case, the old lady whisks it away with surprising energy and takes out the violin herself. Without change of personnel in Philip's sitting-room, someone arrives. Catherine plays a few notes, manipulates the pegs that tune the instrument. Philip plays the A she needs for tuning. She opens the score of the Kreutzer Sonata he's placed on a music stand for her and murmurs, 'Ah, the Henle Urtext edition.'

She announces, 'The minister's lovely wife makes a long-awaited return to the concert platform.'

'Ready?' says Philip.

He learns that she is indeed ready, though he could not say whether it was from a flicker of her eyes or a barely-perceptible nod. She begins the slow sequence of chords for violin alone that opens the first movement.

The sound is in quest of something, there is uncertainty in it.

Oh dear.

With a leap of the heart Philip realises that the questing and the uncertainty are entirely within the music, not at all in the performer. He plays the answering sequence for piano alone without thought of her age and infirmity, and the ensuing dialogue of two-note phrases between the two instruments establishes a bond of trust between them that allows the subsequent *Presto* to take off with exhilarating brio.

'Oh, excellent,' cries Moira like a primary school teacher inducing self-esteem, and without missing a beat or a note Catherine growls, 'Quiet, you silly!' Philip grins to himself: he and the old lady have forged an alliance in music and in other things, too. Everything is going to be all right – at least, as far as the music is concerned.

As regards Malcolm, who knows?

For all its difficulty, the rest of the first movement fulfils the promise of a happy collaboration: they are nothing but two dedicated musicians losing and so freeing themselves in their music. Its two concluding chords, in perfect unison, express the triumph of her undiminished ability and hopefully presage a different triumph for Philip after eight o'clock.

'The lavatory.' Catherine lays her violin on the piano.

'Oh, yes, of course... I'll just show you.' Philip leads her into the hall. There's no swearing now. He's proud that their music-making restored her to normality. He indicates the lavatory door, moves to open it for her.

'This is something in which I need no assistance whatsoever.' That could have given lessons in rebuking to Lady Bracknell, but then Catherine peers at Philip in her secret-fathoming way again. 'What are you doing in this part of the house? The meeting for the buggers is in my husband's study downstairs.'

Philip retreats to the sitting-room.

'She's good,' he tells Moira.

'Well, she could have had a professional career, she won prizes at the Academy, everyone said she was brilliant, but – '

'She's a *wonderful* player.' For a moment there he forgot Malcolm.

' – but, well, Alec's career always came first and she just followed him around.'

'That's a *travesty*!' He is so familiar both with the phenomenon of family members crushing the life-blood out of you and with the modern mis-use of *travesty* in which it is curiously shorn of anything to be a travesty *of*.

'It was what women did. The husband's career was what was important. And a minister's wife was expected to be the minister's full-time unpaid assistant. Sometimes there'd be some part-time school-teaching, perhaps some local amateur players to play with, but... It didn't help that Alec was so outspoken in support of, you know, lesbians and gays' – does she sound like someone trying to be non-alarmist about a diagnosis of cancer? – 'in the Kirk at a time when hardly anyone else was; one of the newspapers called him the *poofs' pastor*. I did my final placement with him when I was training, and people looked at *me*!' She laughs heartily. 'He tended to get out-of-the-way parishes where no-one else wanted to go. Difficult ones. She was never on the spot long enough in somewhere like Glasgow or Edinburgh to build a musical career. Sometimes, down in the Borders, she'd play in orchestras for amateur musicals just for the pleasure of performing with other musicians. Way below her level. *Hello Dolly!* and things.'

'Really, she's completely out of my league,' says Philip.

He has used the same phrase of Malcolm.

They hear her limp along the hall. The accompanying swearing seems to be back, but Philip can't make out the word.

'Sh, here she is,' says Moira.

Limp, *buggers*; limp, *buggers*; limp, *buggers*.

'Drawing attention to themselves,' she says severely. 'Here in a hospital.'

'No, no,' Moira soothes. 'This isn't the hospital. Catherine had an operation – didn't you, Catherine? – and two of the male nurses were rather, well, I think the word is *camp* – and they had a double act, I suppose you'd call it, that many of the patients found very entertaining. They cheered people up, which can be so important in hospital, but let's just say that they weren't Catherine's cup of tea. Were they, Catherine? But this isn't the hospital. It's Philip's flat!'

To resurrect the musician and sweep away the alarming possibility that he has a manner that reminds Catherine of the camp pair at the hospital, Philip plays the theme that begins the second movement. It's gentle, almost dreamy, and there's a defiant pleasure in imagining it as 'our tune' for himself and Malcolm, though first he'd need to change Malcolm's musical tastes. The sound of the piano does what he hoped, silences the old lady, refocuses her, and the violin entry comes just where it should. They unwind the andante in perfect yearning amity.

'That's lovely,' calls Moira.

Catherine says something – a reply to Moira?

Philip realises it is again *buggers*. She emits it from time to time. When 'our tune' begins its first variation she calls *buggers* in time to the high triplets on C that feature in the violin's part, *buh-uh-ggers*. She calls it with a kind of mad cheerful trilling lightness.

Things take a more manic turn in the second variation, where the violin part unfolds in continuous sequences of four fast notes, papapapa, papapapa, papapapa, papapapa. Though it's too fast for her to utter the plural, *buggers*, from the start she utters a syllable to every note, *buggerbugger, buggerbugger, buggerbugger, buggerbugger*.

But her voice soon becomes sound without meaning, an idling motor easily overridden by the unimpaired deftness and grace of her violin.

During the later variations her words are no longer confined to *buggers*. 'Disgusting, disgusting, disgusting, disgusting, disgusting,' she chants, and then, 'Buggers in the hospital, buggers in the hospital,' and then, 'Drawing attention, drawing attention, drawing attention.' There's no attempt now to fit the words to the music, and they're so loud and emphatic and persistent that they resist blanking out. The present-tense of Malcolm's *I'm always hanging around* is obliterated by the irrevocable past tense of his *I was always second fiddle* and *You placed too much on me*. Philip's fingers alone, not his heart, take him to the end of the second movement. *Get it over with*.

Moira claps enthusiastically, perhaps a retrospective attempt to drown out Catherine's words. 'Not finished,' Catherine orders, without so much as a glance at her.

Philip's hands are between his knees. It is evident that Malcolm is making his bus journey only because he has the good manners to complete the ending of their relationship face to face, the relationship that he, Philip, shipwrecked by all the awful ways in which he was alternately distant and clinging.

He stares at the keyboard, aware that Catherine is waiting for him to sound the loud A major chord that begins the whirling last movement.

Beethoven changed the dedication of this piece from the violinist he was originally going to dedicate it to because the man made a smutty remark about a lady of Beethoven's acquaintance. Good old heaven-storming Beethoven, fiery, standing up for his principles, refusing to take his hat off to the emperor. Wouldn't it be following in Beethoven's footsteps over this very piece, if Philip refused to carry on playing it with someone uttering such vile words that besmirch Malcolm?

Philip looks up to fathom the hatred in Catherine's eyes and finds nothing but the focused eye of the musician, all ego absent, patiently awaiting his concurrence in the renewal of their musical communion. And before he knows it – against his will, it feels – he's walloped (but musically!) the A major chord and she's launched the violin into the helter-skelter tarantella that dominates the movement and produces out of nowhere an expanding delight. He and Catherine might be dancing together, blending and twining and circling round each other, pain all gone.

She's talking again, chanting, singing, fitting it to the tarantella rhythm, even to its tune: 'Sodomites, sodomites, sodomites, gay! Sodomites, sodomites, sodomites, gay!'

He fights off his anger, tells himself it's just a tic, a verbal tic, and finds that in his head he, too, is fitting words to the tarantella: 'It's just a tic, it's just a tic, it's just a tic, a tic! It's just a tic, it's just a tic, it's just a tic, a tic!'

'Catherine!' Moira calls in entirely good-natured sing-song. 'You'll put Philip off!'

She certainly doesn't put herself off. You could believe her violin is animated by Beethoven's score alone, without any intermediary, let alone a fallible human one. The notes, the rhythm, every nuance of phrasing – all are perfectly in place. There's no faltering, even when, seemingly triggered by Moira's reproof, she recommences her unrhythmic chanting: 'Buggers in my husband's study, disgusting, disgusting, buggers in the hospital, disgusting, drawing attention, drawing attention, disgusting, disgusting, sodomites, sodomites, get out, get out, get out, burn, burn, burn at the stake, buggers, buggers, buggers, my husband's study, disgusting, sodomites, sodomites...'

Just imagine a demon has bored a hole through her brain, making a speaking-tube to broadcast his invective. It's not coming from her. The wonderful musician is her.

No!

This is not, after all, a matter of words gabbled automatically, without meaning. These are clusters of related phrases the old hag is spewing. They add up. She can't be unaware of what they mean. They manifest understanding and intent and a dark hatred for Philip and his kind. Philip *must* defy this abuse; for his life's sake; for Malcolm's sake; for the sake of everything true and lovely Malcolm has shown him but that he has lost forever. He will cry 'No!' He will halt. He will rise to his feet and slam down the lid over the keys.

And all the while his distress, his determination to halt, his positive decision to halt *this very second* – these exist in some separate and irrelevant region of himself, imprisoned there by the music that makes him its unresisting channel and his hands its unwavering servants. The pure stream issuing from her violin is magnified into an immensely potent kindness, drawing out of Philip abilities he didn't know he had. A dozen or so bars from the end there's a high right-hand trill above low triplets in the left hand, and he's never managed this before without a slight but unfortunate slackening of speed, but this time Catherine's own trill in the same bars carries him along with her at her own rollicking tempo. He's safely into the final joyous dash of his fingers down the board to the united A that is so plainly the end that Moira can clap without fear of reproof. 'Bravo, bravo,' she calls. 'Oh, now wasn't that something? Marvellous, absolutely marvellous.'

Catherine bows, but not towards Moira. For a moment Philip thinks she's honouring him, and notwithstanding *buggers* and *sodomites* and *disgustings*, the words reforming themselves in his consciousness in all their venom, and notwithstanding the final doom heading his way this very moment with Malcolm, he exults.

But, no, she's obviously not bowing to him, either. The audience to whom she is bowing, again and again, is somewhere else, remembered, imaginary, perhaps what once was dreamed of.

'The minister's lovely wife has not shamed Max Rostal,' she says.

Moira throws Philip a look saying that he, too, must be wondering what that means.

The cunning look comes back into Catherine's eyes.

She puts her violin to her chin again and begins to play. Philip is intent on identifying something from the classical repertoire – a Bach partita for solo violin, a Paganini caprice? Only when Moira, her face radiant with having a good time, begins to sing along does he recognise it.

... see you back where you belong.
You're lookin' swell, Dolly.

I can tell, Dolly

Surreptitiously he edges his shirt-sleeve back. Seven o'clock. An hour until he knows whether he will be back where he belongs.

There is nothing for him to do but sing along, too.

You're still glowin', you're still crowin',
You're still goin' strong.

You could say that about Catherine, too, at least as regards her violin. Philip's voice and Moira's take on increasing gusto.

...Find her an empty lap, fellas
Dolly'll never go away again!

A cup of tea before she leaves? But Catherine begins the tune again, ornaments it. There are slides upwards and downwards, a wild gypsy spin, jazz inflexions, a bluesy melisma. Suddenly it's metamorphosed into a version of the rondo tune from the last movement of the Beethoven Violin Concerto, and the melody of *Hello, Dolly!* – now left to their voices alone – somehow sits on top of it as comfortably as Dolly on an empty lap.

Perhaps the violin and the voices can be heard in the street outside, in the city where at this very moment in a hospital ward the two camp nurses may be performing their double act, amusing patients and making them feel better; where other women are no doubt regretting lost lives and other pupils of the great Max Rostal may be looking ruefully at arthritic fingers; and where on a bus south of the river Malcolm is getting closer with an expression on his face that Philip tries to read and that he finally interprets as meaning that, like Dolly, Malcolm will never go away again.

Jo Clifford

The Fine Art of Finding a Safe Place To Pee

Ladies and gentlemen and those of a different gender:

This is a true story.

It happened a long time ago and it still happens today.

I was in a temple of high art: the Metropolitan Opera House of New York. I was there to see Wagner's Ring Cycle, so I guess art doesn't get much higher.

You may think the important thing about Wagner's Ring Cycle is the amazing, powerful music; the leitmotifs; the profound and powerful stories of Rhinemaidens and Valkyries and Gods and Nibelungs; or maybe the visionary staging.

But no: the most important thing about Wagner's Ring Cycle is where and how you go to the loo.

The thing about the Ring Cycle is that no-one said to Wagner, Now look Ricky, this is all very wonderful and everything but don't you maybe think it's just a teeny bit long? Is there any chance you could squeeze it in to a wee bit less than fifteen hours?

Maybe nobody had that conversation with him, or maybe they did and he just took no notice, because as everyone knows every opera in the ring cycle is very long and every act in every opera in the ring cycle is very long and the result is that going to see them also involves a very long time queueing for the loo.

Especially at New York's Metropolitan Opera House, because this was an eventuality its builders had somehow never foreseen.

And the queue for the ladies seemed to be full of very thin and rather desiccated looking ladies in expensive dresses with immaculate make-up and intimidating hairdos and I knew if I joined them I would stick out a mile. I knew of transgendered women like myself being ejected from establishments by security guards for trying to use the ladies, and even locked up in prison cells; and even though I had travelled across the Atlantic on a woman's passport it was for the very first time and a border guard had detained me for a couple of hours in the airport and I knew I simply did not dare join them.

At that time in Britain I would use the disabled toilets, because in the UK it seemed that disabled people didn't have to identify themselves by gender.

But in the States they certainly do and I couldn't go there either. So I stood in line at the gents' and people would snigger and stare and occasionally say 'Excuse me, but aren't you standing in the wrong line?'.

Until I couldn't bear it any more and went to the opera house attendants and explained I was a transgendered woman in the early stages of transition and was there somewhere in the building a gender neutral loo.

The attendants were all dazzling and attractive young women in short skirted pink uniforms, immaculate hairdos and helpful smiles that when I asked my question would all immediately disappear.

And they would say No. No. No. And I had obviously asked for something extremely shocking because none of them apologised.

Until the fourth one I asked considered my question for a while and then said she thought there was something she could do and after several phone calls led me down to the lowest basement in the building where, just beside two more loo queues, there was a door marked 'Security'.

She knocked on the door and behind it was a huge retired New York policeman chewing gum who eventually grunted and took out a bunch of keys and led me to another door marked 'Strictly Private' which he unlocked and led me down a long corridor to another door marked 'Medical Centre' which he also unlocked and then he pointed to another door.

Which led to the only gender neutral toilet in the whole of New York's Metropolitan Opera House.

And the Valkyries did their ride and I would go down to the

basement and the guard would unlock the strictly private door and Brunhilde disobeyed her father and was put to sleep in the magic ring of fire and we would make the journey down the long corridor.

And Siegfried forged his magic sword and learnt the secret language of birds but the guard would never talk to me and never look me in the eye. It was a different guard for every journey, maybe because they enjoyed making me explain it on every occasion or maybe because they all wanted their turn to gawk at the freak and I kept my sanity by reflecting on how dangerous an idea it obviously was, in the US of A, to imagine gender non-specific toilets and how dangerous an individual I obviously was to entertain it.

And so it went on for days and days until the very last night of all when Siegfried colluded in the rape of Brunhilde and the world was about to come to an end and I went down to the basement and had to explain all over again and the man looked at me and said: No. The room's in use.

And I knew he was lying. And I looked at him and he looked at me and I saw the contempt in his eye and he said: Go to the men's.

And I had to, trying not to let anyone see my tears.

But when the lights went down in the theatre I could weep in the darkness. Not at the downfall of the gods or Brunhilde burning herself alive or even the death of her beautiful horse but at my own shame and humiliation.

And that was how I enjoyed the high culture of America.

America. The fearless defender of human rights.

America who has killed millions to defend freedom of expression and everyone's inalienable human right to happiness.

America. The land of the free.

Toni Davidson

As the Veneer of Sexuality Begins to Fade

Flash paused, dragged deeply on his Gauloise and then gently placed the photograph of Cecil Beaton on Repo whose naked body was laid out on the coffee table, like a goose-bumped cadaver.

Repo extended his fingers for the cigarette.

'Please, don't move. It's easier if you stay still.'

Repo shook his head, tapping his mouth then parting his lips.

'Ah, sure...' Repo heard the surprise then smelt Flash's smoky breath, the tangs and tones of the stylized smoke was such a familiar smell to him now. Somebody, maybe Ichan in a flurry of self-endorsement, wanted the group to refer to themselves as The Gitanes, a suggestion that earned him derisive rebukes. 'That's so bourgeois...'

Repo opened his eyes and turned his head to one side, 'Actually...'

Flash pulled back quickly, a poem in his hand by Christina Rossetti ripped out of a library book and ready to be placed on Repo's skin, 'I thought you wanted me to kiss you?'

'The cigarette. I was wanting the cigarette.'

'Oh.'

Repo lifted himself up slightly, squinting down at his body through the swirls of blue smoke. Flash had positioned the candles in different parts of the room with the emphasis on shadow rather than light; on angle rather than direction. It was Repo's room and they shared so many tastes but in moments like these, when the others had gone and it was just the two of them, Flash liked for everything to be just right: red filters on some lights, blue on others while the music shifted from the depths of dub into the suspenseful notes of Satie, cut up by the twisted arias of Nomi. In moments like these Flash liked to be art director. He choreographed their pathos.

On a weekday night when the others had peeled off early, Flash fetched dusty bottles of red wine and decided Repo was to be covered in photographs in postcard form or torn from books and then photographed. 'The Naked Tableau,' Repo thought he heard him say and that was fine. Flash wanted everything to be recorded for their shared posterity. 'We are the Bloomsbury Set on acid' he declared and no one corrected him. Thanks to Panache they all appreciated the allusion.

Merrit's *Love Locked Out* was on his right knee while Chatteron lay dying on his left thigh. A still from *Nosferato* lay between his nipples and a forlorn figure from an Odilon Redon sketch stretched across his stomach. Repo was thin rather than slim, his white bones easily visible through translucent, blemish free skin and this was complemented, as it was meant to be, by his dyed hair, darkened to the tone of his clothes and to the imagination his parents had despaired of as they waded through a bedroom imprisoned by adolescent chains.

Flash was watching him, Rossetti in one hand, a new cigarette in the other. Or more specifically he was watching a part of him. Repo looked down and could see the stern gaze of Antonin Artaud looking up at him from his groin, a puckered portrait if ever there was one.

'I wonder what Artaud would do?'

Flash nodded, his eyes widening when Repo's penis twitched and Artaud's grimace changed to a smirk.

Repo sat up suddenly, breaking the moment with brusqueness.

'We need to drink more and then do something else.'

It was probably the only lecture he went to on anything like a regular basis. By the beginning of Repo's third year he had missed an epoch of philosophy and several juntas of politics and while he made it to more English lectures than most, mornings were always about recovery not learning.

There was one class that Repo, Flash and the others always made it to. It was taught by the flamboyant Panseer or *Panache* as they quickly nicknamed him. A forty something *mind provocateur* who ostensibly lectured on Marxist theory and its intersecting impact on culture, society and text but really just provoked, criticized and entertained. Tall, Bowie-esque with winkle pickers studded with ruby-coloured diamonds, he wore a red velvet jacket, with blood streaked ivory buttons and a tarot card sticking out of the breast pocket. Ichan, a keen occultist, was usually the first to spot the day's choice. 'Major Arcana, the Struck Tower... could be in for some wordy detonations today...'

Panache, Repo and friends decided, was a Dali-esque figure, a cocktail of a Buñuel villain and the campest of thespians. They marvelled at his ability to run around the lecture hall to make one point, to then gyrate his narrow hips to emphasize another. The answers to his in your face questions were waited for with ill-concealed impatience as some intellectual lightweight floundered. It was rarely good enough. 'Pah!' would be his dismissal. 'You must challenge your own perceptions, you must deconstruct your cherished beliefs. Just for a day, just for a moment believe in something you don't. With your heart and soul, feel that belief.'

For all the theatrics, Repo liked it best when at the end of the lecture Panache would slump back into the leather chair beside the podium, a spent actor sipping a red coloured drink – Cochineal Claret, Flash named it. For the last few minutes he would become reflective.

'You see me now, as eccentric, mad even but you see the life in my eyes and hear it in my voice? It wasn't always like this. I spent much of my youth usefully miserable. I couldn't get enough of rainy days in old houses, on and bloody melancholy on. I sickened myself when there was no other disease to be caught. No doubt I was difficult to be around, nothing worse than an artistic type without a surging ego, where's the fun? It's a long story from there to here, but if you listen carefully, then from time to time there's always a part of that old me wanting to come back out and you know I always listen to that voice. I am not an ex-melancholic who can't have even one sad thought. Far from it. I have learned that anyone can be good at being busy; it takes skill to be still.'

After this trademark finisher, Panache would lift himself up somberly, put the wilting, brown fedora on his head and walk slowly out of the hall. It was Repo that started the trend to applaud at the end of these lectures. It goes without saying that nobody did this in the political history lectures.

In the art house cinema, he chose the cheaper matinees to see the films everyone needed to see. If the modern classics were to be discussed, emulated, called upon for life guidance then one needed to be versed in *120 Days of Sodom, Hiroshima Mon Amour, The Damned*... The friends would sometimes watch films together, a line of unpopcorned seriousness, disdaining the trailers and adverts as distractions from Art but Repo liked the time alone, to sink into cinema seats and suspend everything.

For the third afternoon in a row he was one a few solitary men at the matinee, all of whom looked up when he walked in. As the film began, his skin was painted by the metallic colours of *Querelle,* a sunset, like a slick of burning gasoline, spread across the stagey backdrop. It was just right for him, his distracted mood. For the third afternoon in a row he missed parts of the film as he replayed intense conversations, refelt intimate touch. This group of friends had known each other since the Freshers fair when the six of them – Repo, Flash, Ichan, Morte, Espers and Violet – all tumbled out of the student union, holding hands like a search party fanning out across the leafy road home.

It was always back to Flash and Repo's. They had the biggest flat and both had spent time couturing their environment. 'You step in here,' Flash would say with the design braggadocio he loved to use, 'you leave the outside world behind. You don't just live here, you escape here.' And so the walls were painted dark flecked with gold paint, black silk roses weaving through empty frames sometimes trailing like the ivies he arranged over the mirrors. While there were two battered chaise longue for the friends to drape themselves over with gnawing self-consciousness there were also chairs not for sitting on – an old dining chair, covered in William Morris fabric, its springs sprung and extended into the incense air, a sheep's skull bobbing like a Jack in the Box.

Jeanne Moreau was singing her torch song on the screen while the man two rows in front of Repo was dabbing his eyes with a stained handkerchief. It was moving. It was a tender, laden moment and while Repo could see it, cite it, he could not feel it. Just like so many nights with the Bloomsbury Set on Acid.

There was a routine even if no one wanted to acknowledge it. Post-club, they would collapse into a buzzing, busy heap – Morte rolling joints, Espers fixing drinks, Ichan and Violet arguing over the choice of music – 'New Age Steppers,' Violet would demand while Ichan went for the more lewd Lee Scratch Perry. Flash would be buzzing and lighting candles to darken the room. And Repo? Repo would be waiting for it all to start; for desire to emerge from friendships; the cocoons of restraint kicked aside as black clothes flew like crazed bats and another session of pale on pale action began. Indeed, in the sprawled aftermath of their orgy, Ichan declared they had invented a genre. *'Erotic Gothic. Hot Action With Death Warmed Up.'* They all laughed as they reached less energetically for last joints and last sups from drinks that still glowed in the dark.

Repo tightened with both fear and joy when it came to these nights. It wasn't every time they went out of course; there were quiet trips to a local bar and all of them had some other commitments from bedsit bands to working in cafes, the jangle of change and chains ringing in their customers' ears. But on big nights such as these, Repo knew what was coming later and he spent too long in front of himself before going out, the mirror fattening his skeletal form.

Now the fire was on. Flash liked to build a pyre in the grate.

'To roast our souls.'

'Just close your eyes,' Espers whispered to him as she unbuttoned his black shirt, her too cold fingers making him flinch. 'And open your mind,' Ichan intoned as he kissed Morte, his light kisses becoming feverish quickly as Morte stroked Violet's thigh.

There was just one rule. 'Nobody left out, everyone always included.' Violet – far from shrinking, Ichan usually chimed – was careful to assert this. A couple of years older than the rest, she seemed like a veteran of something. Of open sex? Perhaps. She had a pedigree of nuanced understanding, a willingness to infuse proceedings with humour. 'We are sexual revolutionaries, don't forget that. This is our frontline. The RCP, SWP, they march for their freedom but they all go home to the missionary position.'

When she stood amongst them, tall, strong, flinging off her dyed clothes, pushing her hands through her spiky red hair, it was as though she was in charge of them until Flash would rise up beside her, a quiff of arrogance and they, like the leaders they were, pushed their bodies closer and became cheerleaders for expression. This was how to do it.

The coward does it with a kiss, the brave man with a sword.

Repo lingered with the Director's cut on the taut, attractive body of *Querelle*. Ichan was dismissive of the film. 'It's so full of stereotypes acting up. What's the point?' Flash agreed as they all left the cinema together. 'Too cloney, too stagey, too repressed.' Repo had said nothing, hearing that he was the only one to lust after the unartful.

'We are all desirable,' was Violet's usual declaration, her heart felt manifesto. 'I desire therefore I exist.' She quoted head nodding truths as if they were her own, her strong words and a tightening grip on Morte's penis were all part of the struggle. 'None of us should deny any of this,' she warned, as if someone was about to go Judas.

And midst the throbs and throng, where was Repo? 'It's okay to be shy, we all accept that.' Espers reassured him as she stroked his flaccid hope, her small, sinewy body curling around him. And Flash whispered to him, 'I can help you,' as he waved his large erect penis in front of them all.

Some do the deed with many tears, and some without a sigh.

In the cinema, the man who had been crying turned round when the house lights cut through the thick layers of film they had all been wrapped up in. Repo's throat was dry, he needed a smoke, he wanted to be Querelle. All of it. The man stared at him and smiled; a nice smile, inviting, friendly. Repo walked out into smothering grey weather.

On the big nights out, it was best for Repo when everyone was spent; as the candles reached their quick, the night reached its slow, inevitable end. There was dawn outside the shuttered windows as the friends curled into crescents, back to back on sofa cushions dragged to the floor. Repo would sandwich between two of his friends even though his own bed was just next door. No one wanted to break the mood with the selfish need for comfort and so he lay awake to a dawn chorus of snores as desire finally caught up with the moment now gone.

Flash's voice carried above the mayhem as Morte convulsed in rhythm with the bass line and Violet writhed, arms swirling on top of Ichan's broad shoulders. Espers was lost, eyes tightly closed and she reached out for a hand. Repo offered his.

The director clapped his hands, warmly if not enthusiastically. Earlier, he had auditioned for a play the Gaysoc was presenting, an adaptation for the stage of a coming out best seller, *Fear and Loathing in a Smalltown*.

'It was good, I liked your voice. There was some feeling in your intonation.'

Repo hadn't felt a thing.

'It's a demanding part. A lot of dialogue and a fair bit of simulated sex. You, eh...'

The director hesitated as though uncertain to apply the label which was on all the posters, leaflets and lapels in the room. '...okay with that?'

Repo thought he had been simulating sex ever since he had first orgasmed, white string hanging like confetti from flock wallpaper, his rite of passage celebrated alone.

Violet hugged him at the gig, as Sonic Youth launched into the first song of their set. She shouted confidently into his ear.

'You can talk to me, to us, about anything, Repo. Anything.'

Repo answered the Director with a bright yes but the audition had been a mistake, a knee jerk response to identity.

He laughed at himself. He'd be better off at the society next door. *Goths Anonymous*. The only difference from this lot was that there would have been more black than pink.

And it was laughable. Everyone else in the group seemed pretty comfortable to flutter like sexed up butterflies. Why couldn't he?

'Could you take off your shirt for a moment please?'

'Okay.'

Repo pulled his *Love Will Tear Us Apart* t-shirt over his head and smiled when he caught the Director's double take as he took in the blood tears dripping from his right nipple - a present from his friends on his last birthday. 'One from each of us,' Ichan said as he wiped away the blood from Repo's skin.

'You're rather thin,' the Director laughed, sounding like someone who had already chosen someone else. 'We would have to fatten you up for the part a little.'

Repo looked at other members of the Gaysoc, taking notes, looking at scripts, preparing a promotional poster. One of them, a mature student, camply, paternalistically trying to organise two younger members into guillotining leaflets to the right size, glanced over. Repo couldn't decide if his look held contempt or desire. He never could. There was no radar.

The director thanked him. 'And listen, and I am saying this to everyone who auditions, please come back to the group. It's not just about the play, the Gaysoc is very active.'

Repo managed a wan smile but had already put on his headphones as he walked out, obliterating what he had seen with his nihilist soundtrack.

At the gig, Flash was pulling Repo closer to him, closer to the huge

PA bins at the side of the stage. Kim Gordon's bass boosted them both, a funked up rumble. 'Ah, but this is what's like to feel!' Flash shouted into his ear but Repo shook his head. Flash then pulled Repo's head closer and spat the words into his mouth, a beery, smoky kiss. They all kissed at a saliva level, his friends. No one pecked anyone on the cheek nor was there an air kiss to be caught. There was some signal that Repo nearly always missed that told them when to start. Somehow they also knew when to stop.

Even before Flash let go of his mouth, Repo could feel the aggression of some men close to him, who had a wobbly moment taking stock of these tactile times. As always the tall Morte and Ichan and the fearless Violet were the omniscient perimeter guards to the kiss. And there were plenty of others pushing boundaries within those sweaty walls; from Huysmans acolytes smoking Black Russians to speedy young men who flew like acrobats with no safety net. It was the Zeitgeist of the sensitive and it precluded anything more than beery banter from the lads as Flash and Repo disconnected into a group hug that writhed to the rhythm of the music.

In the cellar at 3.00am they were playing tag mixed with hide and seek, with a twist, with several amendments. They'd all taken the acid Ichan had picked up for them. Ichan the broad shouldered provider for them all.

Micro dots. 'Small but mind blowing I was told.'

Flash announced eagerly, 'We hide within the cellar and then when each person is found they have to remove an item of clothing.'

'You'll never see anything of me, I am dressed for winter,' Espers laughed.

'Do glasses count?' Morte asked. No one asked what they would do once they were naked in a dank Victorian cellar that ran the length of the old house.

It was only when they reached the house and made their way down to the cellar, that the acid kicked in. Repo noticed when his body went electric and the stone stairs disappeared from under his feet. While they had tripped plenty of time in clubs and at the Union, this was their first time in the cellar. 'Which,' as Violet summed up approvingly, 'is like one huge Goth's dressing up box.' Flash loved games especially when drugs and nudity were involved and Repo could hear his whoop as he charged into the cavernous cellar, lit only by low wattage and filled with the detritus of the dozen flats above, the remnants of the graduated or dropped out.

Repo usually wanted to say no but didn't. The acid picked up their personalities and accentuated everything – from Flash's outlandishness to Violet's theatrics – and with one swallow Repo knew he had hours of his own neuroses to look forward to. Morte would go quiet too, but his silence was characterised as mysterious whereas for Repo he was being timid. Reticence was hard to share when surrounded by excitement.

It's not that the group was unaware of Repo's holding back, his less than forthcoming nature. It was something they actively involved themselves in. In the middle of one their explorations – Espers hated the word orgy with its organised overtones – they had all given Repo one on one attention, all of them pressed close to his taut body.

'You are beautiful, you are loved.'

It was a mantra that sunk home without a trace. He could not be more loved.

As the cellar walls rippled and turned into crocodile skin, he was tagged and hugged by Violet, who whispered, 'Got you,' into his ear. Repo pulled his coat off. Perhaps it was the setting, maybe it was the kind of acid, but Repo's body vibrated with energy and everything around him buzzed like the unearthed. Cobwebs lit up and the hulks and bulks of battered old chairs and ripped-up mattresses became the pistons and plinths of a cellar machine that groaned and grumped like an old man. Panache would have loved it, the challenge and absurdity of it. Repo liked to think this was his kind of territory when he wasn't lecturing. He could easily see Panache's winkle pickers turning a corner as he announced advertorially to his cellar audience 'Wondering about the mind/body connection? Don't worry about it. Rational thought is a spanner in the works!'

Repo could hear Flash's off key voice and he could picture him waiting to pounce, treating the acid trip as sexualised paintball. He heard laughter from the other end of the cellar, Ichan then Morte's voice, 'Not my trousers!' The tone was comedic and suddenly the menace of the dark cellar was lifted and it was pantomime instead. It was difficult to keep up with the effects of the acid and he was always advised not to. 'Try to leave your rational mind behind. Don't let it hold you back.'

But this was Repo and acid gave him clarity whether he wanted it or not. He caught sight of Espers in her own world, hands holding on with a climber's grip to the cellar wall and he thought she would understand but he didn't want to disturb her. This acid nutshelled everything, it grouped pros and cons, the way forward while looking back and like a surreal seminar on truth it did all of this in a bubble blown from an anus in the wall which grew larger and larger then popped, little pools of the past splashing on the stone floor.

This was all stronger than expected. Previous acid had entertained with fractals and unending giggles.

In a surge of adrenalin, Repo took off all his clothes without being tagged. Was this cheating? Would anyone mind? It didn't matter. He was the prisoner in *Chant d'Amour*, blowing smoke, receiving smoke through a hole in the wall. In the dank atmosphere of the cellar he radiated heat and light. He didn't need to squint in the dimness anymore. He found Flash, hiding beside a mannequin, both smiling, like twins full of life and he took his face and dug into Flash's mouth with his lips. Just when Flash pulled back for air, Repo swaggered towards Espers who had moved away from the wall and was skipping between old wardrobes, a tune ambling out of her mouth. When she saw him, she stopped and smiled and Repo felt as though he was melting, his body suddenly wrapped in furs. 'Can I touch you.'

Espers nodded, 'Of course. Anywhere. Repo.' And he did. He kissed then gently pushed her against the wall, angling his body to fit into hers, legs and arms linked as he vibrated, surge after surge pouring out of him like a wire split open, fizzing. With saliva still glistening on Esper's skin, his staccato thoughts were already on Morte's slender thighs.

'You were like a slick machine.'

'A well oiled machine...'

'Smoothly moving from one to another.'

'So much conversation too...'

'Instructions, directions and even compliments.'

'We've never seen this before from you.'

Violet laid a mug of coffee beside Repo where he lay on floor cushions in front of the fireplace with the tawdry, brown ceramic tiles that everyone used to mock and abhor.

'But we all knew it was in you. It was powerful. Beautiful.'

Repo's head ached and his throat felt so dry. When he squinted up at the others in various states of getting up – Flash eating a huge sandwich, Morte carefully rolling a joint – he felt nauseous, foggy and although he knew what they were talking about, he had no specifics, no details in his head.

Espers was nodding her head, leaning down to stroke Repo's hair, all wild and spikey, like anemone being brushed by ocean currents.

'To actually witness someone letting go of all the shit in their head was amazing to see.'

Flash, cramming a piece of bacon into his mouth, nodded, 'Yeah, I mean people talk about it, say how free they feel, but you were unleashed, man.'

'Acid opened the cage and you escaped.' Morte chimed in sagely as he blew a plume of joint smoke into the gathering.

Ichan nodded, 'I know, that's what I remember. One moment I was in some kind calm safe place and the next there was Repo, clamped, like the vampire he is, to my neck promising to only let go when he had enough blood in his mouth. I mean, wow! I loved it.'

'Here's to a great night.'

Ichan toasted Repo from the dregs of a left over absinthe while joints, herbal tea and strong coffee were also raised. All eyes were on Repo, the gentle cheers of a Sunday morning accompanied of course by their hedonism's eponymous song.

What would Panache say? How would someone with such wealth of experience, such a library of anecdotes and clever conversation gambits, summarise to an eager audience? He wanted to say he didn't remember a thing although each time he felt a bruised twinge in his groin, his memory would quickly, weakly flash, like an old man in the park. Of course it all happened as they described now, as they had been describing since he first woke up. He was the talk of the group rather than the worry of the group. No wonder Flash triumphed:

'Let's celebrate. More nudity, more drugs, more fun.'

The others groaned and laughed but Repo responded like a new convert and with Panache in mind, his exhortations to seize whatever moment suits, Repo pushed himself up from the sofa cushions and stood a little shakily in his tatty boxer shorts, his arms first crossing his bare, narrow chest then opening up to embrace the group. 'What are we waiting for. There is no time like the present.'

David Downing

The Quilt

Mrs Campbell's ample frame bounced against her luggage as the taxi turned from the smooth curves of a road she did not remember onto the lane she could not forget. The route ran to track by a dead-end sign hidden in the verge and they rattled on more slowly over potholes.

The scattering of houses revealed itself only at the last moment, tucked as it was behind hills and high stone dykes, concealed from view of the casual passer-by. The sound of the motor preceded them and the car's appearance was met by a few already-turned heads, permitting her only a cautiously brief half-look at the once familiar street.

From her snatched glimpse she realised nothing much had changed, and the thought occurred again as they pulled up outside the old house.

She stood by her luggage, attempting to reconcile her time-softened memory of the place with the harsh reality that presented itself before her. The paint was grey and flaking; the sills rotten; the heavy tired eyes of the windows edged by the faded backs of curtains she felt she might vaguely recall; a gangrenous brown, green and yellow stain, evidence of long-leaking pipes, leached down a side wall. At her feet, the shattered remains of storm-shifted slates.

Instinctively she lifted the tin bucket, half-filled with rain and slime and puffed drowned snails, which sat on a slant by the steps. Under it, a cold brown key. Unlocked the latch lifted easily and the door edged open onto the flagged floor of her childhood, the solid ramshackle kitchen suddenly familiar as if she had never been away, though smaller, perhaps, than she had expected. There was the smell of stone and hearth and time, stale home baking and an old person's mustiness. In the silence she felt her womanly self shrivel back to the mere girl she had been when she left.

Someone had set a fire in the grate, an aged kindness that still prevailed, and she busied herself with matches. The floor screeched as she pulled out a chair, the wood groaning as she slumped herself heavily onto it and palmed her hands towards the flames' feeble heat. She sat for a while, letting the journey settle in her veins.

As what little was left of the day began to draw itself to a close outside she thought back to the brief exchange with her husband when she had told him of her sister's passing and of the phone call that had brought the news. He had said only, 'Well, I suppose you must go.' And she had said 'Yes, I suppose I must,' as if the idea had only just occurred to her. She had sat and watched him after she had spoken, as if he were somehow to blame for the sadness that did not quite come. However, several days passed before she began to pack suitcases, one of which would have been sufficient to contain the essentials for a few nights away. She would be gone for as long as was necessary, she said, and she wondered to herself at the open-ended possibilities of it all.

Recovered enough to be curious, she took a look around with a display of interest that suggested she could be trying the place for size, contemplating its impracticalities, piecing it together to see how it might fit. A draught cut sharply across her ankles and, in search of its source, she found herself leaning into what had once been the living room. A sheet of blue plastic flapped where it had untacked itself from a window-frame housing only broken panes. Curving down the wall a gap as thick as a rolling-pin ran its jagged path between disjointed bricks and crumbling mortar, and, through it, the branches of unpruned fruit trees were slowly fading into the evening light. She pulled the door to and, with her foot, slid a rug until it rucked to bar the chill invasive breeze.

She thought of unpacking, making herself at home, but the prospect of finding places for her belongings did not immediately interest her. From her cases she took a few night things, settling on the idea that a bath might warm her through. Pipes knocked elsewhere in the house as rust-brown water began to fill the tub, though the absence of reassuring steam showed the fire had failed to heat it beyond tepid. Here were old ways to which she had become unaccustomed and she missed, for a moment, the reliably timed comforts of her own modern home. She watched the water drain away again, splashing a lukewarm handful onto her face: it tasted of iron, as if the house itself was bleeding though the taps. Perhaps an early night would be a better idea: she would be fresher in the morning.

The floorboards' gentle creak-and-give warned of her climb but otherwise the house seemed indifferent. At the top of the stairs three doors faced onto the landing. Her long-empty parents' bedroom, the door left ajar; her sister's room, open too; then her old room, the door shut against her. She entered it with a determined air, as if expecting a scene that would be best dealt with suddenly. Glancing round, acknowledging it as benign, she peeled herself quickly from her clothes, pulled on her warmest nightdress, drew back unaired blankets and slid between worn and bobbled sheets. She felt the sag of the badly sprung mattress and lay blindly waiting for the warmth to hold. As her eyes accustomed themselves to the darkness the ceiling threw back rust-rimmed patches where rain had seeped through, damp-curled edges of wallpaper and the dangling tatters of long-deserted cobwebs. She thought of her husband, the useless bulking mass of him, far away and alone in their warm bed, their high thread-count sheets.

The chill was too much, it had set too deep. She flicked the light back on and tiptoed into her parents' room, rummaging fruitlessly in drawers and cupboards until a sliver of moonlight fell on patches of colour she instantly recognised. Folded thickly on top of the wardrobe lay the quilt they had made, together, the winter before she left: her sister, their mother and her; nights in front of the fire, stitching and sewing, storytelling or silent. She lifted it down, carried it back to her room, felt the rush of cold air pushed aside as she spread it evenly over the bed and its weight as she crawled beneath it. She ran her hand over the jumble of threadbare fabrics, silently acknowledging the changes in texture, and comforted by them.

*

The young minister hoped he had said the right thing. Not too solemn, not too familiar: it was so difficult to judge with people you did not know and, despite his vocation, he had not yet come to terms with the demands placed upon him by the vagaries of death. He apologised and so did she, for not being able to delay the funeral any longer and for not being able to get there sooner. It could not be helped, she said. Nevertheless, she had appeared grateful for the handful of groceries he had pulled from his own cupboard and taken across with him. 'Not at all Mrs Campbell, not at all,' he had insisted, dismissing her reach for her purse.

Mention of her return had prompted hushed comments and knowing nods amongst his parishioners. Memories were long in this place. Knowing and remembering were enough. The details were kept quiet, kept from him, his conspiratorial acquiescence their only requirement. He wondered as to her crime, her daring to have done.

As a passing remark, prompted only by the lengthening silence, he had suddenly mentioned the ceilidh, to which she had instantly shown an obvious delight. Rather than add that he hoped she would not be offended by their heightened spirits at this time of sadness for her, her reaction left him feeling unexpectedly compelled to proffer an invitation. It will be the usual modest affair, he had warned, not at all the occasion to which one must be used in the city. But she had accepted immediately.

In full daylight the house appeared even more decrepit and only the Reverend Mackenzie's early arrival with an invitation had made it all seem slightly less daunting. It had given her new resolve but, later, standing by four generations of graves that shared with her her maiden name, she had faltered again. Everything seemed so vast and impossible, foreign almost. She browsed other headstones, here and there, finding names once familiar to her, only leaving after she had glanced at them all and not found another on which to dwell.

She occupied herself with a small lunch, fed logs onto the fire. She cleared surfaces, slid boxes from shelves, lifted and replaced lids, unable to imbue unfamiliar objects with any significance. She was lost for a sense of purpose.

In the evening she sat by the fire, the wind haunting the chimney breast with hollow whistles and calls, ghosts of long-silent voices. But the warmth began finally to penetrate the cold walls of the house and she felt the fire's burn on her shins and her cheeks. Thoughts played at the periphery of her mind but she brushed them away. Her mind drifted elsewhere, back to the leaving, all those years ago, the unspoken insistence and the dry goodbyes, and to wondering why she had returned, why she sat there now. As if. It was this wondering that kept her company and would not depart. From the hall the grandfather clock still marked out time's passing in soft lazy seconds that seemed longer, more drawn out, than the urgent little ticks that came from the brass timepiece on her own distant sideboard. Here time seemed to pass so slowly it might have stopped altogether.

The fidget of a new loneliness sent her wandering again through the old house. Looking once more into rooms that refused to give up further evidence of times past. It felt so empty, emptier than any place she had ever been. The feeling, she realised, was loss, and the house felt it more than she.

But then a memory, thrown up from nowhere. She almost ran to her old room, knowing the impossibility of it. On her knees in front of her chest of drawers she composed herself, reached for the bottom drawer and pulled it out onto the floor. She turned it over. And there, still, the brown envelope, taped in place so long ago. She lifted it free and held it close before, with nervous hands, reaching inside. And there, with a renewed familiarity, were a small hand-embroidered hankie and an old black and white photograph.

Propelled back through the years, Mrs Campbell wept.

*

Standing at the kitchen window, flecks of light glittered through the silhouetting trees. Her earrings and bracelet glinted weakly back in the reflection in which she was little more than a shadow. The night carried snatches of conversation and footsteps as people headed towards the hall but she felt a growing reluctance. She had done her hair and applied her make-up in the mirror of her sister's dressing table, but it had cast back her image differently, severe, unforgiving. She looked older here, the colours she brushed onto her cheeks harsh and unnatural, her neat russet suit seemed garish. Still, she sucked in a deep breath which stifled her reservations and encouraged her towards the door.

The Reverend Mackenzie sensed a sudden sharpness forming in the air and interrupted his conversation to find its cause. At the far end of the hall he spotted a full-figured woman wearing rather too much makeup. It was a look that might mark out a place for her elsewhere but, for a moment, he failed to recognise her.

Mrs Campbell glanced round, looking for something, someone familiar. The desire to retreat eased when she saw the minister making his way towards her.

'Welcome to our little gathering,' he said in a generalised way. 'How pleased we are that you came.' He felt unsure of his words but hoped they rang true.

'I wasn't sure...' she began, but stopped herself. Instead, she passed him an unlikely bottle of whisky she had found tucked away in one of her sister's cupboards. Taking this as a sign, he led her to the improvised bar round which some of the men had congregated.

She felt happier with a glass in her hand, though the rumblings of oblique interest she provoked amongst the women unnerved her again. She had thought, hoped even, there might have been faces she would recognise, despite time's changes, and she wondered what it must be like to grow old under the scrutiny of those who had watched you grow up. More people arrived, mingling easily, fitting in as if the whole occasion had been carefully rehearsed. Talk was sporadic, sentences grazed over but seemingly undigested. A rising warmth released the smell of damp timber, her own perfume intrusively artificial in comparison.

Launching into practised small talk with the minister she soon felt more composed as she covered the familiar ground of the life she had left behind. It felt a comfortable distant thing, almost the boast of someone she did not know but found both vaguely interesting and slightly ridiculous. He listened with his head turned towards her, his eyes looking away. He nodded and offered an occasional soft guttural murmur, non-committally set somewhere between indifference and disagreement, as if he saw beyond it. Here was a woman of too many words, he thought.

Musicians she had not noticed on the way in briefly tuned up their instruments, prompting the formation of short lines of aging crofters, before feet that would normally trundle with inelegant purpose over clodded ground began to mark out nimble steps that flowed as naturally as the burn that still skirted the village. Each move, practised and precise, had grown to accommodate the subtle peculiarities of its partner's. Old hands clapped in steady time. Mrs Campbell tapped her toe and her whole body wiggled discreetly where she stood. She wondered if the Reverend Mackenzie was a dancer and she looked at him to see if he appeared to be the type of man who might be. But he excused himself and she was alone again. It seemed disorientating. Clutching her drink she was unable to add to the brief ripple of applause that accompanied the end of the first dance, but she gently tapped her spare hand against the glass instead, the chink of her ring a sudden reminder of obligations that waited elsewhere.

The hall continued busy with the music and feet sounding out their reeling and jigging code. Big soft-edged wedges of atmosphere held it all in place. Well-rooted tunes accompanied now by the tiny warblings of two thin women in small-flowered dresses and a grey-haired man, smaller in his skin than he might once have been, whose appearance belied the voice that resonated from him. The songs were those she had heard coming from the hall when she was a child, those to which she too had danced many years ago.

Scattered along the walls, no longer young bachelors lurked in the shadows, ruddy with the routine of outdoor work, awkward in the suits they would remain unmarried in. Their attendance alone appeared insufficient to distract the few remaining girls, shy practical imitations of their mothers, already resigned to the demands of familial duties, just as her sister had been.

During an intermission the grey-haired singer came and stood by her at the bar. Eventually, in a low voice, he spoke.

'You'll be wondering about that lass, I'm imagining.'

She looked at him briefly but he was looking away. It was his words alone that were meant for her. Mrs Campbell was silent for a moment then, uncertainly, 'Yes, I was wondering.'

'She went,' he said. 'Moved away. A long while back,' and inside her something went cold. 'Never married, that one. Not for the marrying they say.' He looked around him 'And they'd know of course!'

Mrs Campbell smiled at him, grateful for his conspiratorial jibe, noticing the insipid glare of his wife as she did so and wondering if it was prompted by the reason she had left or for having dared to return.

'There's been no word,' he added. Then a long silence before, finally, 'Well, I hope I haven't spoken out of turn.'

'No,' she said. 'No, Andrew. Thank you.'

He looked at her then, across the years. His eyes still those of the classmate she had finally recognised.

She watched for a while, trying to enjoy the continuing spectacle, but alone felt unable to enter into it, increasingly aware of the threads of melancholy that wove themselves through the occasion. Needing air, she stepped out the side door. Small groups of men enjoyed a good-humoured argument, shared laughter at a story or a joke, little breaths of mist lingering in the cold night air.

From the outside, looking in, this could have been any group of people at any party; any party from which her absence would not have been as conspicuous as her presence.

Mrs Campbell did not re-enter the hall that evening but wandered quietly back towards the house. She sat on in the darkness until silence returned after the last person had headed away home. She lifted the latch, the shadows gathering in around her, and paused before stealing out again, weaving her way behind the overgrown garden, hauling herself up the steep stony path she had climbed nimbly as a girl. Her legs strained and burned, her heart thumped at the effort: she was glad the night hid such lunacy. Underfoot the ground was soft and forgiving but she had to wave her arms wildly out in front to make a way through the tangle of branches and brambles that caught and tugged at her clothes and her hair. She wound her way alongside the old wood in which the seasons lagged behind, as if winter had been unable to escape completely. Night scents gathered thickly around her.

Finally, above the treetops, she emerged onto the ledge where, when young, she would sit, arms clasped round bent legs, her chin on her knees, the wind freeing her hair. Annie MacGregor had come up here with her too, once or twice, before. Below had been the crofts, pieced haphazardly together, tiny houses, the barely perceptible shift of a herd, hillsides speckled with a grazing flock. Yet, back then, they had been preoccupied not with these details but with the infinitely unimaginable possibilities of all that might exist beyond it. Where the two of them might escape to, if they dared.

Now it was all the monochrome same. A few pallid lights from the manse and from croft house windows. There was subtle movement all around, a vitality at night that she had not remembered, silver backlit clouds across a star-cast sky never permitting total darkness. Water ran invisibly nearby. The distant town's constant amber glow claimed more of the sky, edging the horizon closer than it had once been. The rumblings of vertigo fluttered in her belly, a growing sense of her precariousness, the fragile uncertainty of her age. She felt the chill of the stone on which she sat and the overpowering smell of the earth.

Memories rekindled until she could almost sense her sister, her mother and father, as if running back down the path would find them in front of the fire, pots steaming on the stove, the day's stories in the middle of the telling. The taste of a clandestine good night kiss still on her lips. The soulless rooms of her own distant home suddenly repulsed her, as did the husband she had made do with, glamorising him in her mind so that she might convince others of his worth and her fortune at having seen it before them.

Annie MacGregor, Annie MacGregor, if only you could have waited.

The breeze blew again and, for an instant, it seemed it might take her with it, she suddenly felt so light and insubstantial the lightest dew might have dissolved her. And, in that moment, she knew she would leave again and head back to what she knew, the life she had pieced together for herself. The girl who had sat here almost a lifetime ago had been someone else entirely and now she was simply a foolish old woman sitting on a hillside in the middle of the night, getting cold.

Few people saw Mrs Campbell the following week, though it was reported she had been to the shop for a few groceries. They had exchanged knowing looks and too long silences. They had left her alone, but she was too busy to notice.

She worked feverishly. The scissors sliced purposely through hemlines in search of a particular square of pattern, cut holes in the back of an old worn-out coat, pinking shears left jagged bite marks in shirts and dresses. The wardrobes and drawers upstairs spilled their remaining contents which now fell in floods of fabric from all corners of the room. She had found a sewing machine stashed in a cupboard and it hungrily pecked its way along the materials it bound together, piecing together the remnants. She worked with determination, using skills she had no idea she had retained. She lost track of the days, aware only of their passing as the small stitched swatches grew into one diverse whole. She fastened the backing to the poles, heaved it taught over chairs, and on it lay the batting. She shook the new counterpane out on top but did not permit herself a proper look until her hands, so raw she had had to search out gloves to continue, had finished passing the long fine needle up and down through the layers, binding them tightly together. Not until the last edge was firmly stitched and her work completed did she allow her eyes to linger, to see the patchwork quilt woven together into its final complex design. A small embroidered handkerchief set square in the middle.

*

The taxi the Reverend Mackenzie had called for her arrived on time. The same reluctant driver piled cases back into his car: the things she had brought with her, a couple of small framed photos she felt unable to leave behind. And two quilts: one old, one new. She had explained things briefly to the minister: that she was leaving and would not return. He had listened, hearing no room for discussion, and told her that he understood, though feared he did not entirely.

She had set a fire in the grate before she left, a small thing really but she owed it to the house. However unlikely, she could not deny it the possibility that eventually someone might care for it again.

The latch slid cleanly into its niche, the oversized key rattling in the too-big lock but turning smoothly. Mrs Campbell replaced it under the bucket. And took one last look at the house to which she had always felt she would one day return, the place she had held in reserve, the home that she had thought would always be there. The life she might one day be able to live, to share.

The car clipped the outskirts of the small tight-knit community, headlights briefly illuminating everything with a ghostly light before returning it to darkness once again, then headed up the track towards the road.

Leaving, the first time, she had cast a dry-eyed glance back and been surprised that it had already disappeared completely from view. She recalled that now and knew the futility of turning to look again.

Carol Ann Duffy

The Female Husband
– *Taken from* The Bees, *Picador 2011*

Having been, in my youth, a pirate
with cutlass and parrot, a gobful of bad words
yelled at the salty air to curse a cur to the end
of a plank; having jumped ship

                      in a moonstruck port,
opened an evil bar – a silver coin for a full flask,
a gold coin for don't ask – and boozed and bragged
with losers and hags for a year; having disappeared,

a new lingo's herby zest on my tongue,
to head South on a mule, where a bandit man
took *gringo* me to the heart of his gang; having robbed
the bank, the coach, the train, the saloon, outdrawn

the sheriff, the deputy sheriff, the deputy's deputy, caught
the knife of an enemy chief in my teeth; having crept away
from the camp fire, clipped upstream for a night
and a day on a stolen horse,

                  till I reached the tip
of the century and the lip of the next – it was nix to me
to start again with a new name, a stranger to fame.
Which is how I came to this small farm,

                        the love of my life
on my arm, tattooed on my wrist,
where we have cows and sheep and hens and geese
and keep good bees.

Orta St Giulio

– Taken from The Bees, *Picador 2011*

My beautiful daughter stands by the lake
at Orta St Giulio; the evening arriving, dressed
in its milky, turquoise silks, her fortune foretold;
assonant mountains and clouds all around;
an aptness of bells from here, there, there, there. *Ella.*

I watch her film the little fish
which flop, slap, leap in the water, hear
her hiss *yes, yes,* as she zooms on fresh verbs
and my heart makes its own small flip.
I slip behind her into the future; memory.

A bat swoops, the lake a silence of dark light;
how it will be, must be.

You

– Taken from Rapture, *Picador 2005*

Uninvited, the thought of you stayed too late in my head,
so I went to bed, dreaming you hard, hard, woke with your name,
like tears, soft, salt, on my lips, the sound of its bright syllables
like a charm, like a spell.

                Falling in love
is glamorous hell; the crouched, parched heart
like a tiger ready to kill; a flame's fierce licks under the skin.
Into my life, larger than life, beautiful, you strolled in.

I hid in my ordinary days, in the long grass of routine,
in my camouflage rooms. You sprawled in my gaze,
staring back from anyone's face, from the shape of a cloud,
from the pining, earth-struck moon which gapes at me

as I open the bedroom door. The curtains stir. There you are
on the bed, like a gift, like a touchable dream.

Quickdraw

– *Taken from* Rapture, *Picador 2005*

I wear the two, the mobile and the landline phones,
like guns, slung from the pockets on my hips. I'm all
alone. You ring, quickdraw, your voice a pellet
in my ear, and hear me groan.

                        You've wounded me.
Next time, you speak after the tone. I twirl the phone,
then squeeze the trigger of my tongue, wide of the mark.
You choose your spot, then blast me

                                 through the heart.
And this is love, high noon, calamity, hard liquor
in the Last Chance saloon. I show the mobile
to the Sheriff; in my boot, another one's

concealed. You text them both at once. I reel.
Down on my knees, I fumble for the phone,
read the silver bullets of your kiss. Take this . . .
and this . . . and this . . . and this . . . and this . . .

Jenni Fagan

In the Middle of the Night I Eat Mirrors

The postman knows
I never sleep
jellied eels and champagne
I don't need
I don't need
the soul ache
the fear
stubble
too rough for sunlight
Buddha
miracle stare
hours of feed
the world asleep
stroke
cheek to nose
and cry
you love love
too much
too much
I am a soul
gone to seed
the fictional stories
we tell ourselves
when we want out,
I think of this as the first breath,
the first step
into owning my own two feet.

New Poem

Your mum thought I was a weirdo
something to pity,
she mistrusted
a girl who coveted
neither fruit, loom or two-stripes
straight
as a high-street
which could only be sailed
tolerably
on elless and dee,
every lunch-time
the school bell,
I'd sit on your front step,
your neighbours
tweaking curtains
watching-the-weirdo
watching-it-stare-the-other-way,
a chain-smoking
wolf-cub who slept-in-the-woods
sang that same old
lichened echo
down
the
long
black
well,
while you asked
me
to love you
to dress in your brother's
football top,

instead i wore your mother's spectacles
and you played tic-tac-toe
with tablets
we both knew
would bury
us,
until
one day
we found they'd impaled our heads
on the gates
of the city
so we could smile
at the children
who came there to fly.

Unrequited

In your bed,
(my foot by your foot)
I do not care
if a volcano from Iceland
brings forth a 75,000 year ice-age
or if meteors
rain,
or if the walls are paper
blowing in the wind,
I have no fear,
(my toe touching your toe)
of
even
the last breath.

The Rocks, the Crags, and the Sun-Worm.

There are things
you will never see
in me,
places I have understood
in welly boots,
the bare rock
and its ancestral stare
warriors in woolworths,
fire-bombs
through letterboxes,
debris,
spires of smoke,
rising through rain.

It Would Have Been the Action of an Insane Woman, But I Know the Thought of It, Would Have Amused You

I wanted to break into the morgue
with new pyjamas
champagne
a fat joint,
white maltesers,
intricate as we were
I wanted to hold your hand,
a blackbird
singing
to you in the dead of night,
I wanted lorries to line
the streets
and honk their horns
by way of goodbye,
I wanted
to say sorry,
instead i read
poetry
to a roomful of strangers
went home
to dark
curves in the road
to a fevery baby
I went
to your graveside
on no sleep
watched them lower you
from a distance

and at the wake
I was unwelcome
your mother insisting i was still the weirdo
who never dressed like the other kids
but it was something more
something in me
she could see
but never understand
(you did)
(you were)
(we knew)
and it never sat right,
in the graveyard
you sent
a breeze
to lift my hair.

Ronald Frame

After Ovid
– an extract from a novel in the making

Sometimes a waiter would catch my eye, and I would pretend that I hadn't seen. Or a stranger walking towards me on the street would do a double-take, causing me suddenly to avert my admiring gaze.

The Knotts invited me to mind their house when they went away for half the summer of '49. The gardener one day brought a youth with him, who had a knowing look about him. I preferred to stay indoors, squinnying all the while from the sitting-room window – at how the lad would stand, weight concentrated on one rounded buttock before he shifted it to the other, one hand on his hip and the other hand combing through his floppy fringe of hair. (He didn't reappear. She-Who-Did told me there had been some kind of falling-out between the two, and I hoped against hope that it would be made up.)

An assistant in the University Library, with sleepy eyes and long trailing fingers, had a habit of busying himself at shelves near where I was sitting – until he too vanished. (I spotted him one day, sitting in the passenger seat of a Lagonda coupe parked outside a picture-framers. A customer inside was explaining his requirements with theatrical arm gestures, and I presumed grand old house/high ceilings. The erstwhile librarian didn't notice me, too busy raking through the contents of the car's glove compartment.)

I had supposed that I made myself inconspicuous. But something must have shone through: like a watermark through paper held to the light.

For all that I did cadge on to – narrowing eyes, a sideways glance, the gulp of an adam's apple, slowing footsteps – I probably missed just as much. My natural instincts were still a good way short of aptitude.

I was intrigued, yes. Normal everyday life was threaded by these covert connections, behaviour was coded in all sorts of arcane ways. I had penetrated the surface, certainly, but I hadn't yet trained myself to be as observant as I wished to be.

*

I had gone up to London to record a talk for the Third Programme. The subject was 'Ovid in Exile'.

I went off for an early light supper afterwards with the producer. He had a young family to get home to, and perhaps I drank too much on too little food.

I couldn't decide what to do next. I turned into Shaftesbury Avenue, to study the billboards outside the theatres. The first didn't appeal, nor the second.

On the corner of Rupert Street someone brushed past me.

'Sorry, sir.'

A couple of minutes later, waiting to cross Wardour Street outside the Queen's Theatre, it happened again. The same young man, but travelling in the opposite direction.

'Sorry, sir.'

He stopped and looked over his shoulder. I smiled at his beauty.

'Becoming a habit, isn't it?' he said.

'What is?' I asked through my smile.

'Us crossing tracks.'

'Oh that.' My voice was lighter than usual.

'What habit did you think I was talking about, sir?'

We seemed to be talking, dreamily for my part, from the same prepared script.

When I started walking, he fell into step beside me.

'Just taking air, are you, sir?'

'I thought I'd put off some time.'

'Yes?'

'It's a nice evening.' He had turned and was looking at me as I said it.

We moved between the other pedestrians, coming back together again every time. There was a bump as our hip-bones collided – and then came a second impact.

I was sufficiently aware to feel generous, magnanimous, on this not so ordinary evening. Completing those radio recordings always left me eager for something different to come along and happen.

'You like walking?'

'Yes,' I replied. 'Idling, really.'

'I like that too.'

'Do you?'

'These streets are good for it.'

'Yes, they are.'

'We've got the same tastes, I'd say.'

I realised that there was some special significance in that remark. The words hung in the air – air flavoured by exhaust fumes – and accompanied us as we walked.

I fell a step behind, so that I could study him properly.

Thirty or so. Older than my students, at any rate. Good-looking, short strawberry blond hair starting to recede. Neat and trim, but with some muscles in those shoulders and arms.

A pleasant expression on his face. He didn't have that tightness about the eyes, the primed mouth, nor the coiled-spring posture which frequently served as a sign. I might have thought he was quite the other way, but in my book unavailability only added to a man's attractiveness.

I could feel my breath building in my chest. My heart was beating faster. My mouth was sipping at the warm complicatedly-London evening air. I was aware of two damp patches under my arms, thankfully concealed beneath my jacket.

My legs carried me forward. I didn't want to stop. I had stopped too often in my life.

'*Quod licet ingratum est* – '

Why did those words come into my mind at this instant?

'*Quod non licet acrius urit.*'

Ovid, of course. The *Amores*.

'What we're allowed to do gives little pleasure, compared with that which is forbidden to us.'

Ovid was never very far away, dead as he had been for nearly two thousand years.

A suit and tie. His formality seemed strange. Mostly the men who watched other men in these parts wore casual wear, even if the objects of their attention were in flannel or tweed. Or they stood with their hands sunk into the pockets of a donkey jacket or a raincoat.

A no-nonsense nothing-fancy off-the-peg suit, as hard-wearing as the modest cost would permit. It already looked as if it had taken a soaking or two in its lifetime.

The soft collar of the shirt was frayed, and the tie was creased: but the knot of the tie was neatly done, and tight, and exactly dead centre of the collar.

His shoes were quite heavy. Not a construction worker's. Say, a railwayman's? Shoes which were expected to give hard service, maybe to offer some protection to the toes.

He'd had something of the sun, so I guessed his job must be one that kept him out of doors for a fair bit of time. If indeed (on second thoughts) he had a job? This might well be his sole occupation: picking up male strangers on the street.

I had a rush of panic. What sort of business was I getting myself into? This was off the map of the familiar for me. Far, far off.

But I kept on walking.

It seemed to me that I was participating in a waking dream. Yes, I was quite conscious of what was happening, but it all felt so very unlikely.

He slowed just enough for the two of us to get back into step.

We proceeded like that, along the pavement.

I waited for him to speak again. His accent was ordinary enough, but suburban outer London, not East or Sarf. The timbre had been pleasant on the ear.

The approach of another two men caused us to move closer. The backs of our hands brushed together momentarily.

It was like an electric charge.

Only later, hours later, when I could detach the shock of that contact from all else, I remembered a detail. One of the two men had caught the eye of my companion. A glance which hadn't lasted for longer than a single second. Expressionless, and yet somehow not accidental.

We ended up entering the underworld.

It was a public lavatory on Charing Cross Road.

An attendant sitting in a cubicle found something else to do as we went in.

The reek of disinfectant, water gushing – cascades of water, running down the porcelain urinals and from raised cisterns inside the cubicles.

White-tiles, dim lights, feet visible overhead through glass bricks in the pavement.

I had never dared before.

This seemed to be both the low-point of my life, but also a harbinger of something intensely exciting.

Another kind of relief was waiting for me. The unleashing of tension was giving me heart palpitations.

'No, after you,' I said, as he pushed open the door of one of the cubicles and stood to one side.

'You're nabbed!' he snarled at me, drawing something from behind his back. Before I could understand what he was doing, he had clamped my wrists with handcuffs.

I spent that night in the cells.

First thing in the morning I had a visitor.

'My name's Tindall. I'm a barrister.'

'I haven't asked for anyone.'

'I know you haven't.'

'Then, I don't follow – why are you here, Mr Tindall?'

A young man in the lavatories at the time had seen what was happening. He had left Cambridge a few years before, but he recognised me. He had gone to his uncle, George Tindall, at one of the Inns of Court.

'Have you made any confession to the police?'

'Not yet. I'm seeing them later.'

'Then don't.'

'Don't see them?'

'No, you have to show up. But don't confess anything.'

'Why not?'

'Because they haven't got enough evidence to charge you. The policeman who targeted you, he jumped the gun a bit. So don't say anything without me being there.'

'I can't ask you to – '

'This is me returning a favour to my nephew. It has everything and nothing to with you, Mr Kilpatrick. I shall do the very best I can. But you need to act *only* in consultation with me, if you would.'

I said that I should do so.

'Is that a promise?' he asked me.

'Yes, it is.'

We shook hands on it.

'I trust I shan't fail you, Mr Kilpatrick.'

He was as good as his word.

I paid for his services, which didn't come cheap. But it was worth every penny to me. After all he had managed to get the case dropped before it could go before the Bench. I also made a donation to the Metropolitan Police Service Benevolent Fund ('a handy euphemism', my saviour Tindall told me).

'You have my name and telephone number.' His eyes caught the evasiveness in my own. There was little about human nature he couldn't reckon on. 'But if you're up in London again and genuinely get caught short, I'd advise you to stick to the facilities in hotels and restaurants, or even department stores. The rest – public conveniences, railway stations, pubs – forget them, don't even give them a thought.'

'Very well.'

'End of lecture. Times will change. But until they do, just watch your step.'

I nodded.

'"Gang Warily", as our friends in Scotland say.'

'Oh, did someone tell you – '

I was meaning to own up to being not the archetypal Southern English public school type of Cambridge don. In my case appearances, and vocal delivery, were a sham. I was Scottish, and another archetype: the 'lad o'pairts', common boy made good through his own ambition.

'Certainly I've never gone out of my way to – '

'Keep your own counsel, no confessions necessary,' the lawyer said, jumping to his feet and sweeping up his papers, before – as he imagined, misunderstanding completely – I had a chance to incriminate myself.

I was summoned to his study in the Lodge by the Principal.

'This has been a great personal embarrassment for you, my friend. I wouldn't want to add to your woes.'

He watched me shift in the chair.

'There have been no complaints about how you carry out your duties for either the College or the Faculty. So long as that situation continues, I don't foresee any reason to interfere.'

That final word seemed to trouble him. An unfortunate choice in the circumstances.

'I shan't need to suggest any alteration in the, erm, *modus operandi*.'

'Thank you,' I said, a little drily.

He hadn't asked me to justify myself, to protest my innocence. There, I sensed he was thinking, had gone plenty of others but for the grace of God. He too, perhaps – which might have explained the regularity of his lecturing commitments in more enlightened centres of learning, mostly on the west coast of America or within a shout of the Mediterranean.

'I think that's all I have to say about that, Desmond.'

He turned to the window, and to the prospect of walled college garden, and to delights ahead.

'It looks as if we're going to land a bumper crop of fruit in the orchard this year. I'm so glad we didn't let the Goths have their way about the trees, or the ground would've been turned into a bloody car park by now – '

Word got around.

I noticed the eyes moving off me, and the voices dropping.

It could never have been kept hidden, I appreciated that.

No one directly commented on the matter. There was nobody I might have gone to to discuss it with, either.

That told me about the state of my personal relationships. I wasn't sure that I trusted the truth even to myself.

The thing had happened. Now I had to get over it.

I could determine the behaviour of others by how I myself behaved.

I carried on as little different, on the outside, from how I had shown myself on the morning of the day when I had gone up to Langham Place to record my talk on 'Ovid in Exile'.

There shouldn't seem to be any distinction. No 'before' and 'after'.

I defy you to find the fault-line.

Catch me out, if you can.

The social invitations started to dry up now.

Some of my colleagues – or their wives – persisted, wanting to appear more liberal. I accepted once or twice, but the results were painful, since not all their other guests felt the same and let me see so. It was easier, all things considered, simply (and politely) to say no.

'Kilpatrick's gone back into his shell.'

That and other remarks reached me, transmitted almost gleefully by a network of sources about Cambridge.

'You'll need a very long, very sharp nut pick to winkle *him* out!'

Roy Gill

Generations

'This is for you.'

Ally's father hands him an envelope. On the front is Ally's name, and nothing else. It's been hand delivered.

'Who's it from?' Ally asks.

His father says nothing for a time.

Ally is used to this, and waits.

Eventually, his dad says, 'It's from a lad in my class. Malcolm. A bright boy, but he doesn't try –'

(Ally's father teaches Management, or sometimes Computing at the local college. Or maybe it is 'Managing Computers' or perhaps 'Computing Management' – Ally has no idea really. He has asked, but somehow the answer always slides out his head.)

' – he was reading *Doctor Who Magazine* at his desk the other day, and I said to him, "My son is into that crap too." Ally's father sighs deeply. 'The next day he gave me this.'

'Why's he writing to me?'

'Why don't you open it and see?'

There is a pause while Ally scans the letter.

'Oh my God. He's got "The Ice Warriors". Episodes one, four, five and six.'

'So not the whole thing, then? He missed a couple.'

'No, you don't understand!' says Ally – *he's used to saying this* – 'only four episodes exist. They're like, really rare. They've never been repeated, or put out on VHS. How did he get those? And he's happy to copy them – if I want.'

Ally's father sighs again. 'Do you really need more Doctor Who tapes? You've got a cupboard full of them.'

'Yes,' says Ally. 'Yes, I do.'

You know how to copy a VHS tape, right?

You, reading this on your 21ˢᵗ century Mac, tablet or PC, with your DVDs and your iPlayer, your iTunes, your Personal Video Recorders and your sneaky BitTorrents; used to perfect, instant copies, often for free...

First of all, you need your own VCR.

This is not easy.

They cost at least a hundred and fifty quid.

You will have to sweat and beg for it, because having your own video in your bedroom is medically proven to rot your brain, and prevent studying for your Highers.

Next, you need to get hold of a second video recorder, probably borrowed off your folks. This usually lurks under the big telly in the living room, quietly storing and replaying programmes that are – somehow – less brain-rotting than the adventures you'd personally choose to watch.

It's best to borrow the VCR when your parents are out the house.

Your mum is worried that moving the VCR might disturb it on a subliminal level. Much like a troubled chicken could be put off laying, or an anguished cow might give out soured milk, there is a concern that – after you've touched it, and used it for your own devilish purposes – recordings of Inspector Morse and the PD James Mysteries might come out twisted and wrong. So you bide your time, wait until your parents go out on one of their boring Sunday afternoon drives. You plead homework, revision. Then you pounce.

You lug the VCR's grey battleship-bulk upstairs – making mental notes so you can put everything back exactly as it was.

Now you have to get this video – and your video – to talk nicely to each other...

'Malcolm says there's a monthly fan meeting over in Edinburgh on Tuesday nights... if I wanted to go.'

'Whereabouts?'

'The King's Arms. It's a pub.' Ally hesitates. 'I don't have to drink or anything.'

'I'm not worried about you having a beer, son.'

'Then what?'

There is another of Ally's dad's silences. Ally stares at the clock, at the wall, at the dog. There is no point interrupting these silences. You must simply wait, as long as it takes, for the newspaper page to be turned, the coffee to be drunk, for civilisations to rise and fall...

'You should be aware,' Ally's dad says carefully, 'that young Malcolm is a little sexually ambiguous.'

'*Oh.*'

'That's not a reason for you not to go. Just be aware.'

'That he might – he might fancy me?'

'It is a possibility, yes.'

'Oh.'

This is simultaneously the most terrifying and the most exciting thing Ally has ever heard.

'Well, I'll just say to him, I'm... straight. I'll tell him I like girls. That'll be ok, won't it?'

Ally's father's attention is back on his newspaper, and if he notices the effort Ally has put in to sounding completely calm and utterly normal, he doesn't give any sign at all.

So...

You've got your two VCRs. Now you need a length of aerial cable with a pointy plug on one end, and an insert-y socket on the other.

(These are correctly-termed 'male and female connectors'. Ally's dad will later tell him this, and Ally will find it very funny.)

You next need to tune one video recorder to the other. This probably works ok – but you may get a bit of interference. In the unlikely event you have two really new VCRs, they may both have SCART sockets you can use instead. The plugs for this type of cable are the same at both ends – both male – and this, for some reason, tends to work a lot better.

(Ally also finds this funny.)

Next, once you've got your two VCRs speaking to each other, you put the tape you want copied into one and push play; you put another blank, hardback-sized cassette into the other machine and push play-and-record. And you wait.

You wait the same length as the entire programme you are copying – and no, you can't watch anything else to pass the time.

You can't surf the web, or check your texts, or Facebook, or Twitter or YouTube: because this is 1992, and none of these things have been invented.

After about three or four hours, you have a dub that sort of looks 90% like the original. Pretty good, really, as long as you don't watch the original side by side.

This is called a first generation copy.

Ally imagines Malcolm.

He imagines him in great detail. He will have, perhaps, longish hair in a great sweep, like River Phoenix in My Own Private Idaho, and a challenging, sulky expression. He'll know all about obscure books, and cool music, and strange films.

He will never have told anyone he's gay. (Ally conveniently forgets his dad has somehow already noticed...) But Malcolm might just tell Ally, in a mumbling, awkward, deeply endearing way.

'I think I might be... you know,' he'll say, looking deep into Ally's eyes. 'Are you cool with that?'

'That's ok,' Ally will say. 'I might be too.'

And then...

Malcolm is nothing like this.

Malcolm is funny and loud. He loves Absolutely Fabulous almost as much as he loves Doctor Who.

Ally has never really watched Ab fab. As far as he can tell it's about two awful old women getting drunk and shouting at each other.

'But you must watch it!' Malcolm enthuses. 'It's even camper than Doctor Who!'

'Doctor Who is camp?'

'Oh yes. Screamingly so. You know that bit in "The Green Death" when Jon Pertwee dresses up as a Welsh cleaning lady to sneak into the enemy's base? *That's* camp. And you know the bit when Jo Grant stands up to the Brigadier, and says that she's gonna have her own way, and if the Brig doesn't like it, he's just gonna have to "seize her and fling her into a dungeon?"'

Ally nods, sinking back into the embrace of the British Rail chair on the lurching, shuddering train through to Edinburgh. 'I remember.'

'I'm having that line printed on a t-shirt. Can you imagine? I'm going to wear it to the next convention I go to. "Seize me and *FLING* me into a dungeon!"' Malcolm delivers this at top volume. All round the train, heads turn.

Ally looks at Malcolm, half in horror, half in amazement. 'Everyone's *looking...*'

'So? Let 'em stare. What do I care?' Malcolm grins defiantly. 'Have you ever been to a convention, Ally?'

Ally shakes his head.

'You haven't been to a Local Group fan meet either, have you? My, you have got a lot to learn...'

The thing is, tape-dubbing never stops with just one copy.

All round the country, in bedrooms and pubs, libraries and bookshops, people are meeting to covertly swop VHS tapes. Men – and in those pre-Billie Piper, pre-David Tennant, pre-Russell T Davies days it is nearly always men – are trading tape for tape, like for like, passing the stories on. Whispers of half-forgotten childhood, traded like gold dust. And each time a tape is copied, and finds a new owner, it gains a generation. The next one down the line is 90% like the previous, but it's a copy of a copy, and so on, and so forth...

Rock steady pictures develop twitches, then jumps and rolls, and no amount of telly-tweaking will ever steady them again.

Luridly coloured 1970s planets with pulsating spacecraft and antimatter blobs become, step by step, less garish, until finally the colour gives up altogether.

Gesticulating actors, conquering monsters, screaming faces all gain halos: outlines of analogue black, thickening with every dub.

Sound loses clarity, throws off BBC RP diction, becomes muffled, lispy, hiss-ridden, indistinct.

And still the generations go on, passed from hand to hand, like a secret shared. Binding disparate people together, in reels of analogue tape.

Ally views his Ice Warriors bootleg, back in his bedroom. In the hallucinogenic black and white maelstrom that seethes across his portable telly, he sometimes can't even tell who is speaking. The reptilian Martians are almost indistinguishable from Doctor Who's sidekick Jamie, flashing his hairy legs between kilt and chunky socks as he dodges their sonic deathrays.

But that doesn't matter...

Ally's found a way in – and a way out – a path that leads out from the ordinary humdrum world, just as surely as if a blue police box had materialised fuzzily at the end of his bed, and a charismatic, oddball stranger held out his hand and said, 'Don't be frightened. Come with me. Let's have an adventure...'

And twenty years later, when Doctor Who is on the telly at Christmas, Ally will look across the sofa at his husband, and smile.

'That was a good one, wasn't it?' he'll say.

And Malcolm will agree.

As the titles roll, he'll glance down at the names that pop up on his phone, and his laptop, and be amazed at this strange family he's been drawn in to, some scattered across the globe now, but still bound together; writers and programmers, artists, librarians, academics and engineers: a whole generation of wonderful freaks, geeks and gays, connected forever by the Doctor, and the whir of VHS tape...

Kerry Hudson

Grown on this Beach

We are at the beginning. New and old we lie side by side on the pebbles which have kindly given way to the rise and fall of our bodies. The stones smell of the North Sea, which bellows further down the beach from us. I tell her I think the sky is the colour of washed out school socks and she laughs. We're still at the place where she thinks everything I say is a small miracle, though we've been here enough times separately to know that this feeling is fleeting and that hangs above us, grey tinged in the bright white of our finding each other.

In return for my small miracle she tells me how she likes to think of the echoes our entwined bodies will leave on this beach. How that impression of us will be spirited away by the waves slowly, slowly beating their way up to us. Or no, she rethinks, how the shapes of long-gone us will be smoothed away like the once-sharp edges of these pebbles.

I am absolutely still. Afraid to lose connection from the warmth of her body beside mine, frightened movement might break something. Perhaps she is thinking the same because then her little finger hooks around my forefinger tightly, as though she were anchoring herself for a storm to come.

'Tell me then. You said you would. You promised.'

'What?'

She turns her head slightly, her lips brushing the smooth pale brown surface of a stone as she talks, and I try to dampen a ridiculous flare of jealousy. The urge to pick up the stone, throw it towards the sea and press my lips to hers.

'What we spoke about. I want to know about them all.'

I give a short laugh, feel a small bird of panic flutter in the nest of my ribs. 'It's not a short list you know.'

'Come on, you said so. I need to understand how we got here.'

'Where's that?'

'Right here. Beside each other.' She turns her head fully, looks right at me and the bird starts beating itself against the meat of my torso as though bidding for escape. 'How did we get here and what's next. And to understand that we've got to understand where we were before.'

'Where I was before you mean.' It comes out harder than I wanted but the swell of the sea, the salt in the air dulls some of the harshness. As though they are colluding, these old pals of mine, urging me to not fuck-up. 'Ok. You can't interrupt though. Just let me tell it to the end.'

She turns onto her back, shimmies herself a deeper nook in the beach, the stones click-clacking their approval of our plan. 'Aye, sure. Start at beginnings and work your way through.'

'Ok.'

I sit up, but keep my finger locked in hers. I watch the scattered, feral swoop of seagulls battling against the wind, an escaped white chip paper turning joyful cartwheels along the shore. 'Ok... let's start at the very beginning. There was Jenny–'

'Reenie...'

'Whisht, no interruptions remember? So, Jenny lived on the same estate as me just a few blocks away. Her mouth always tasted like salt or sugar and nothing in between. When we kissed we didn't know what to do so we just pressed out lips together harder and harder the longer we did it. Sore bruises of kisses. Each afternoon one summer we ran out and bought penny sweets and Monster Munch from the ice-cream van and–' I turn, see her eyes are closed, the softness of her eyelashes on her olive skin and resist, just, the urge to stroke a fingertip across them. '– and, then we'd go up to my bedroom, take off our clothes and feed them to each other under my duvet. We called our fannies "fushies" and would say, as we ate our smackery, "I can see your fushie" giggling the whole time.'

My eyes are back on the shore and so, when her laugh comes, it's as though the soft, sweet sounds are climbing up each of my vertebrae.

'Funny, we used to go to a place not far from here before they stole that stretch for a golf course. We'd lie on our bellies in the waves until our thighs turned corned-beef pink with cold, staying away from home as long as we both could, both for our own reasons.' Her pinkie squeezes a little tighter. 'Anyway, she was the beginning. My first love. I would have done anything for her. I watched her all of the time, the way she moved. Once I stood in front of a rabid pitbull for her and I told Tania Sweeney, the hardest girl on the estate, that she was a dog-face and took a kicking for her. I was only six but Jenny gave me innocence and tenderness when there was none to be found at home. She woke me up to exploration, to wanting and protecting.'

We're quiet for a minute as a helicopter goes overhead, probably headed to the oil rigs. I twist expecting her to open her eyes, say something, but she's quiet and so I stretch my legs, pale as an Aberdonian woman's rightly should be, and start laying stones in a line up from my ankles. I'm three stones up before I realise this is what I used to do when I was six too.

'And then... and then there were boys. Boys' hands up my skirt at school discos, boys jack-hammering away on beaches, boys thinking if they kissed my neck before putting their hands in my hair and demanding "a gobble" that they'd been romantic. But it filled a hole in more ways than one and so I kept going. And then there was a man. Just one.'

The lines of pebbles, different colours and sizes, run up both white legs to my bunched up skirt hem. 'The boys took only what they needed in the twenty minutes or half hour they occupied but this man, he took everything.'

I must have moved, though I don't feel it, because the stones topple off and I pull up my knees. Take a breath into my tight as a drum chest. 'For a while. For a while he took everything. When I say "took" I mean he stole it. Because he didn't ask. And he doesn't have a face, though sometimes I think he might have had a moustache. That's the sort of thing your brain invents though, isn't it? A Bad Man, give him a big moustache like a ridiculous seventies porn actor.'

I give a barren laugh. She releases my finger, only to grab my clenched fist, her fingers splayed around it. I feel her tense with energy behind me but she doesn't move, says nothing. And I don't think I can be more grateful for her stillness and silence in that moment. 'No, I don't think I really saw his face. So his face became the bruises on my legs. A baby I didn't want and didn't keep. The abandoned degree, more drinking. No more fucking though, not for a while. I was so black, so hopeless that—'

Like an assault, the rubber bacon rasher flies through the air, and then a shock of black and white fur, a pink tongue lolling wetly too close to my face. The dog, a mongrel, turns its paws in excitable semi-circles then stops, stares – as though it's tasted something in the air. Her hand, long, thin and strong like the rest of her body, reaches over my shoulder to give its ears a pet and it bounds off towards its owner: red jumper, gender undiscernible, waving from far down the deserted beach.

I won't turn around because I'm full of crying. Not actual crying, but the soreness of the holding it in, the ache behind the nose and eyes, the burning pink heat of it on my forehead. And her lips, when they touch the back of my neck, feel tight and cold and of course that small kindness makes it worse.

'Go on, go on. I'm still listening.'

This time I lay down, keep my head turned away, lowering myself on the hinge of my hip, curling slightly away from her. But, as if my body has spoken up and asked for something, I feel her knees in the crook of mine, her arm circling my waist. The bird inside stops panicking, beating wildly and settles somewhere dark and warm, as though it knows rain is coming.

'And then there was Amanda... but you know most of this now.'

'Tell me anyhow, it's your words I want. I love the way you talk.'

Love. Her first mention of it. Though it's been buzzing around us for weeks like static in the air.

'And she rescued me. And I loved her. And we loved each other in passion for six years and then, well, then things became more complicated.'

'That happens.'

'Aye, but she gave me her family and travels. She...' I wonder how I would feel if I was listening to this but go on anyway, this is part of me and I want her to have all of me. '... she made me strong. Steady. She might as well have coated my bones in iron and filled my guts with sand. She made me and saved me and I did the same for her.'

'But...'

'But ten years is a long time. She couldn't understand where I'd come from, not really. You know, you know as well as I do what it's like.' I take her hand and smooth the skin on her ring finger. I don't mean it to be pointed, it's not a reprimand, more like instinct, but she pulls her hand away and places it between my shoulder blades anyway. I wonder if her palm is picking up my insides pulsing at her touch. 'And then there was Danny. A sad-eyed dog of a man. Not a dog as in an arsehole. Dog like he wanted petting and feeding and loving but couldn't really do more than wag his tail and be a breathing warm living thing next to you.'

'The depressed one?'

'Yeah he was that an' all. Not his fault. I honestly believed I could love him better and into being. We rode bicycles through Vietnam. And then there was Rosa the Spanish chef who loved anilingus.'

'Ani...what? Ach, Jesus, Reenie!'

'What? That's what I remember most, it was only a few brief mouth-centred months then she pissed me off by insulting my olive oil but she was good for me. Then... do you want the not-special ones as well as the special ones or not?'

'You've mentioned arse licking, how unspecial are we getting exactly?'

'Well, then Charlie, early transitioning, she had tiny strong arms, we ate pink iced cakes shaped like breasts naked in bed. A saxophonist, Peter, who was thirty when he lost his virginity after he decided he wanted to fuck more than he wanted a space in heaven. Matt, the media-twat, who liked spanking, his safe word was New York. The biter, Dougie. Ach, you know, loads of non-specials, think of them like non-speaking extras picked up from basement bars in East London. Actually, consider them especially non-specials.'

'Like having a piece and marge when you'd wanted fish and chips because you couldn't be arsed going out?'

'Exactly. Just something to remind me I was part of the human species still. There were travelling ones in Vietnam, Russia, Budapest, a French curator in Seoul, a Moroccan with a full-Buddha tattooed down her back in Berlin, a stable boy from New Zealand in Paris who broke my heart by telling me he couldn't really read.'

She's laughing, practically a growl, a 'fag-ash Lil' laugh my Ma might have called it. It wasn't smoking though. That laugh was full of sex, warmth, surrender.

'Ok. Shut-it. I get what you're doing but stop it. I want real stories.'

'They're all true. He wasn't a boy but he worked at some stables. And... ah, Shannon the South African who was always so nervous around me. Then –'

'Always men and women? You never wanted to, you know, pick a side.'

I push myself back into her then, hope my closeness will act as a reassurance to her as hers does to me. 'Aye, and I know, I know it doesn't make sense to you. It's hard for even me to understand, so in the end I stopped trying to really. But, to me, every one was different and at the same time all the same. Mouths, hands, tongues, hot breath, ribs to count by trailing my finger down them. The same wanting and giving. But they were all different too.'

'Delicate wee snowflakes.'

I offer her a single note of laughter even though her sarcasm doesn't hide the glint of something sharper underneath. 'Kind of, yeah. All bodies looking for another body but each one unique, a new story. And none of those differences were ever to do with whether they were men or women. And if I'm picking sides I always pick the side of –'

Her hand arches over my face and covers my mouth leaving the word 'love' still battering behind my teeth.

'What then?'

I kiss her fingers, try to nip at the briny taste of her palm with my teeth. 'Then, then I felt empty and I knew there weren't enough bodies and countries for me. Then I came home. Came home to this shitty city with its beautiful coast. Came home to put the home I never wanted to come back to, that I couldn't get away fast enough from, to peace. Then... then I found you.'

I turn heavily, shifting the stones with my weight so that we're in our own small cove. I take my hand to the curve of her jaw, wait until she looks at me with those same fierce-wary eyes she always had. Her short hair the colour of wet sand, her pale blue eyes with a scatter of brown freckles in one iris. She looks like she was grown here on the beach, like she came from the sea. I kiss her. Not a big one, not a slow, tender one. A hard, dry bruising kiss as though we're just learning how to do it for the first time. She puts her hand just under the hem of my t-shirt, dips her middle-finger into my belly-button.

'And what am I, then?'

'You? You, Jenny are my beginning, and this? I want this to be the ending.'

Jackie Kay

Grace and Rose
– Taken from Reality, Reality, *Picador 2012*

Rose

Our wedding is drawing nearer and in three peerie days' time I will have married her, after twenty years of saying *I do* and *I love you* in as many ways: in the Shoormal restaurant on the ferry coming back and going away; walking the coast curves along the southern shore of the voe, round the wave-battered Braga Ness; by the great Standing Stone of Bordastubble; in the Wind Dog Café over a bowl of soup in Yell. *Dem at waits, guid befides.*

I wouldn't have believed that we'd ever get a chance to say it in front of other people. I'm already nervous about it; we've been so private for years, so secretive. We started off pretending to be *colleagues* – for goodness' sake! Then we progressed to *chums*. Then it was *best pals* and then we said 'we're like sisters' though of course we were nothing like sisters at all. And then – when would it have been maybe six years ago? – we both told our parents. It was a silly thing because we were women in our late and middle forties, still feart o' telling oor mammies the truth!

When you love somebody, you want your family to love them just as much as you do and of course they hardly ever do, not in the way you want, because nobody measures up. Because the family is its own wee measurement; it doesn't think anybody else fits. But once I saw my mother notice the way that Grace threw back her head when she laughed and my mother smiled alongside her, and I couldn't ask for more than that.

But in three days' time I am to marry Grace, the woman I love. When I first met Grace I felt I had known her for ever and a day. I felt like all my life I'd missed her and now here she was come to be with me at last. I've never felt any differently. Our love is delicate like these islands, a fretwork of rock and heather and water.

At night, I can hardly sleep. We decided we would be apart for this last week. It seems a silly thing to have decided on because we've hardly been separated the whole twenty years. I can't sleep now without Grace. The day of our wedding I'll likely have big bags under my eyes! Oh, well. It's not me that's the beauty. It's Grace. *A bonnie bride is shun buskit*, they say here. But Grace was never interested in marrying a man; once, she said to me she liked the idea of men but not their apparatus! Grace, as well as being beautiful – her grandfather was Italian and she has lovely olive skin and dark black hair and a pretty mouth – has quite a turn of phrase. It's her that has planned our wedding, detail by glorious detail. At first it was great fun planning everything, and then it got stressful and we'd find ourselves waking up in the night worrying about scallops and oysters and flowers and rings. And whether or not we had remembered to invite the local councillor. We'd go for a drink in the Queens and watch the winter sea heave and lash at the old building and count for the umpteenth time our list of one hundred and fifty guests. It was like counting the waves themselves. Old people would be forgotten, new people would be remembered. The list shifted and reshaped itself until we had everybody we wanted.

Goodness me, I said to Grace, knocking back my pint one night, how on earth have the heterosexuals managed all this wedding stuff for years? It could give you a heart attack. It could leave you bankrupt! Grace decided we had a big advantage because both sets of parents would have to pay seeing as we are both daughters, so we can afford to go to town, she said. So – doesn't she want to turn up at Lerwick Town Hall in a vintage Rolls-Royce? (The Rolls-Royce had to be brought from Aberdeen across on the ferry.) Doesn't she want her brother in a kilt and her father in a kilt, and me in a kilt too! She bought me beautiful cufflinks for my shirt, made with opals, my birth stones. And doesn't she want the most beautiful dress, in gold and green silk, handmade for the occasion? Oh, doesn't she want pipers and fiddlers! And why not, my love, I said, perspiring and shaking with fear and anticipation, why not, why shouldn't you have anything you like after all the years we have waited?

'Is it any wonder I've not been sleeping?' I said to Grace. 'Well, if we have all that, we'll have to forgo the honeymoon?' 'Forgo the honeymoon!' she said to me. 'You can't be serious. We'll need a holiday. We'll be exhausted. I'm only getting married so that we can have a honeymoon and so that people can throw confetti as we get driven away.'

'I thought we were getting married so that our relationship can be acknowledged to the world.'

'To the world?' Grace laughed. 'This is Shetland, darling.'

'Yes, well.'

'I'm teasing you,' Grace said, patting my leg and rubbing my inner thigh. She knows if she does that I can't concentrate on anything. Grace knows me through and through. But funnily enough, planning our wedding has shown us both a new side to each other, a more vulnerable, tender side. I don't know how to say it exactly. I tried a few nights ago, I said to Grace, I never knew you were so soft, but that wasn't exactly what I meant. I suppose I never knew that things mattered in the way they matter until we decided to get married. We went out for a walk the last night we had together, a week before our wedding, under the swooning moon, under the sharpest of stars. Do you love me? Grace said. I knew it wasn't a question. It was because she was in love with the words. I do. I do, I said. I stopped and kissed her lips in the cold night air.

Grace

People are talking. People are talking. Our wedding is the talk of the islands. Those that didn't get invited wanted to be up among da rhubarb. I can't wait to tell you all aboot it. It's a story, our love. We'll tell ourselves the story when we have surprised ourselves by taking up knitting and are sitting watching the tides in Bressay and the fulmar, the puffins, the black guillemots arrive to make their homes in the summer on the east cliffs of Noss. I said, Rose, I never knew you were so romantic. Isn't romance a wonderful thing? Romance is like a wee cove that nobody found but you. Rose makes me feel like the first woman on the moon. We're no that far away from being that, actually: being the first women to marry in Shetland is not so different from being the first women to land on the moon.

I remember the first time I came to Shetland, twenty odd years ago, how strange the peat bogs looked after Glasgow, like something my imagination dreamt up, how astonishing it was never to be further than three miles from the sea.

Let me tell you aboot our day. Both sets of parents were there, all dressed up to the nines. My father in his kilt and long socks and sporran. Oh a man looks handsome in a kilt. Rose wore a kilt too, and I told her to promise me not to wear anything underneath; that was our secret too, the whole wedding day long. Rose looked as if she could die of desire. Was I glad I had insisted on oysters! What an aphrodisiac!

I arrived at Lerwick Town Hall in the Rolls-Royce, a beautiful cream-coloured car. Rose went on ahead with her father so that she would be there before me. My father walked me down the aisle. He had tears in his een. He was proud of me, he said. Prouder than he could be and he never thought he'd see the day, he said, when he would be giving me away. 'I've waited a long time for this, Grace,' he said. Tears sprung to my eyes with gratitude. To think of all the years I worried what he'd think of me!

My father walked me down the aisle and we had lovely fiddle music playing. Aly Bain played a slow fiddle version of *John Anderson my Jo*. Then we said our vows to each other. Rose said to me: Grace, I love you. I loved you from the minute I met you. I think I even loved you before I met you. I want to walk with you to the end of time.

My mother's eyes filled with tears and Rose's mother's eyes narrowed and sharpened a bit.

I said to Rose: I never thought I would know this in my life, what it is to be loved by you. I want to be loved by you always, for ever, always.

Then Rose put on my ring and I put on hers. Then we kissed; it seemed the whole island cheered. I imagined we even made the puffins and the whales and the seals happy that day.

Rose and I had the best time planning our wedding feast. We'll all be paying for it until we look like auld fish wives, Rose said, laughing. But it didn't matter. I wanted to have a feast for the whole island to feast their eyes on.

Our feast: five tables, each laid for thirty people, long trestle tables with red crepe covers over each one. To begin with, a soup: smoked haddock, potato and sliced onion soup. Then oysters steamed in almond milk – hand-reared Pacific rock oysters, fresh, plump, very juicy and very clear. Rose and I sucked the flesh out of an oyster in the same pearly minute of time.

Angus, big with a bold stomach, said, 'Do you know there is no way of telling a male oyster from a female by examining their shell?' Nobody really answered him. A few lassies giggled. Then Angus said, 'While oysters have separate sexes, they may change sex one or more times during their life span.' Jessie, Angus's wife, shifted uncomfortably. 'Whit are you saying, Angus?' Angus knocked back his dry Spanish sherry. We were serving small tall glasses of dry sherry with the oysters. Perfect. Then Angus said, 'A pearl is just an irritation for an oyster.' Then the fiddlers started again and the music drowned Angus out. I smiled at Rose and she smiled back at me, raising her eyebrows and shaking her head a little towards Angus.

There was bread flavoured with ale. There were plenty bannocks, gilded peacocks and festooned boar's head, tarts filled with veal and dates, Shetland lamb cooked with fresh coriander, seared salmon with walnuts and thyme, stuffed roast suckling pig, goose cooked in a sauce of grapes and garlic, stewed cabbage flavoured with cinnamon and cloves and grilled asparagus.

For dessert there was fruited custard in huge friendly-faced, born-again pies. We asked our guests to bring small cakes and pile them in the centre of a table. When everyone has finished eating, but not yet finished drinking, Rose stands up and takes my hand and leads me to the table with cakes. She stands around one side of it, fine and sturdy in her kilt, and I stand over the other. We lean towards each other and we kiss, a long, soft, melt of a kiss, and after a minute's lovely silence, everyone cheers. Someone shouts, 'Hurra fir da bride and da bridegroom.' The fiddlers start playing faster and faster and people get up and dance in the middle of the hall. Choocking and whooping and spinning. Hooch! Da whisky wis flowin oot da door.

By the time our wedding feast wis over everybody wis jist pleepin. 'There are days and there are days,' Rose says to me when we drive off for our honeymoon at the Buness House in Unst where we will walk and talk and go over and over our day, telling it in the present tense, in the past. 'Oh, Rose,' I say. 'What if we still hadn't had it yet and we still had our wedding day to look forward to?' Rose groans and shudders, reeling. 'Oh, I'd do it all over again, again and again and again!' she laughs, helplessly. 'I swear the stars look happy for us,' I say to Rose. 'Grace,' she says. 'Oh my dear Grace.'

David Kinloch

Felix, June 5, 1994
– after a photograph by A.A. Bronson

You thread a sea with your eye;
each time the needle enters your flank
the pain composes you;

trees that hung your voice
among these patterns
wrap your quilt in foliage;

a dog barks through the branches;
a girl's arm passes like an oar
across the sunlit patches;

now your song kneels
at the river's edge
and will not flow;

your passport head is pinned in silk.

I am in Washington and it is January, 2011. I am wandering around an exhibition of portraits of and by gay, lesbian and transgender artists. They range from a magnificent and touching photo of Walt Whitman taken the year before he died to a series of postmodern exhibits that playfully interrogate the issue of sexual identity.

This poem comes into my mind as I stand before Al Bronson's photographic 'memento mori' for his late partner, the artist Felix Part: the dead man lies wide-eyed, staring out at us, mouth open as if in astonishment; but the quilts and rugs and pillows that surround and wrap him vie equally for our attention. They remind the viewer of the great AIDS quilt begun in 1985 which now comprises some 50,000 woven panels, each one commemorating an individual who has died, and it is this aspect that has brought my poem to mind. It was first published in 1994, the very year Bronson made his photograph, and formed one of the final pieces in a long sequence called *Dustie-Fute*. This mixed original elegies with adaptations, fragments of newspaper reports that first documented the outbreak of a strange new disease, as well as snippets from a medieval herbal. The aim was to create a text that was as patchwork as the commemorative quilt and suggest also the complex network of conditions that combined fatally to suppress the immune system of those they attacked. The sequence is now almost twenty years old and the events it chronicles – the early years of the AIDS pandemic – nearly thirty. It is a time of anniversaries. In a moment I'll explain why I reprint it rather than try to write a new poem in response to Bronson's image. It is also a fact that I cannot get beyond this image in my overall response to the series of portraits I have been viewing and the issues they raise. I was going to say: 'personal issues' but there is a sense in which they are not 'personal' but 'general' and akin in this respect to Bronson's own form of art practice summed up by the name he gave to his collaborative work with Partz and Jorge Zontal, *General Idea*.

But first, 'Felix' himself commands more attention. The visual image itself is quite large and takes up a good part of the wall of any gallery where it is hung. I haven't made an exact calculation but it is probably about the same size as the individual patches that make up the AIDS quilt, which are three by six feet, roughly the size of a human grave. To this extent, therefore, it is the most extreme interpretation of the quilt's function. Assuming Bronson made the image partly with the AIDS quilt in mind – and this is far from certain – I wonder whether his aim was not slightly satiric: while it can be overwhelming to experience the quilt in person its mission can strike the viewer as softly commemorative, particularly when panels are viewed in isolation. Pathos is the emotion most readily induced. But Bronson's art here is more visceral. He does not deal in metaphor and symbol as the makers of the quilt inevitably do. He more or less gives us the body of the deceased itself, pinning it to the wall of the gallery. What's more, the 'itself' is still, uncannily, a 'himself'. This is because the image is not complete without the explanatory description, provided by Bronson himself, which accompanies the photograph. The whole work is a mixture of image and text. There we discover that the photograph was taken in the hours immediately after Partz's death, that in the final stages of his various illnesses Partz suffered from extreme wasting of flesh and muscle and that it was impossible to close his eyes after he had died. In the years since then Bronson has given various interviews about his work and it has become clear that Partz was to some extent 'dressed' for this photograph and that it was a final act of collaborative art making by the two men. He has also spoken about Erwin Panofsky's work on tomb sculpture which he discovered after the photograph was taken and, although it could not have influenced the work itself, Bronson wishes to set it in the art historical context Panofsky evokes. In particular, Bronson mentions the late medieval phenomenon of the 'transi,' or cadaver tombs, in which an image of the deceased is presented as if in the process of decomposition.

Nevertheless, I believe that Panofsky's opening essay on Egyptian funerary art is at least as relevant and fits better with comments Bronson has made about the way Partz's life force seems to have drained off into the brilliantly coloured fabrics on the bed around him. Indeed, Felix becomes an Egyptian in this photo. As Panofsky points out, the ancient Egyptians did the exact opposite from what seems natural after someone's death. They opened the eyes and the mouth so that the dead might see, speak, enjoy whatever type of afterlife was available to them. And they tried to make the dead happy by providing the necessities of food, drink, locomotion, service, all placed within the shelter of tombs that were often constructed as if they were houses. So, if you look closely at the photograph, you see that Felix lies just within reach of some of his favourite gadgets and personal items: his cigarettes, his tape-recorder, the remote control for the TV, all objects that will come in handy in the millennia ahead. Bronson closes his explanatory description with the following invocation: 'Dear Felix, by the act of exhibiting this image I declare that we are no longer of one mind, one body. I return you to General Idea's world of mass media, there to function without me.'; General Idea, in this context, perhaps bearing some relation to Egyptian Chū or, as Panofsky expresses it, 'general world-soul'. So Bronson's photo is not so much commemorative as what Panofsky calls 'prospective' or 'projective'. Like the ancient Egyptians, Bronson knows that Felix still has work to do in the afterlife.

Bronson and his partners were brave men, saddened but heroic in the way they made use of their bodies in their art right up to the last possible moment and beyond. They are defiant and upbeat, certain that their art is of central political importance to the age they are living and dying in. They live with the daily spectacle of death and don't accord it too much respect. When something is as commonplace as that, you don't. It becomes a kind of tool of the trade.

For those of us that survive to contemplate this image twenty years later, however, some of the immediate political impetus that the photo itself attempted to galvanize and which formed its conditions of reception, has dissolved. 'Felix's' return to the General Idea allows other associations to cluster around it, many of them existential.

For this image remains a 'portrait' and in any portrait it is the eyes of the sitter that give life, that focus attention. Felix's eyes are dead *and* open; and it is in this conjunction that the uncanny force of this piece of visual art resides. Indeed there is something puppet-like about his general demeanour and it was to Hoffman's doll, Olympia, that Ernst Jentsch turned in his initial attempts to theorise the uncanny, that unsettling mixture of strange and familiar. A little later, the French philosopher of excess, Georges Bataille, would remind his readers of Robert Louis Stevenson's 'exquisite' definition of the eye as 'a cannibal delicacy', 'the object of such anxiety that we will never bite into it'.

Bataille goes on to evoke the final illustrations of J.J. Grandville made shortly before his death. These depict the figures of a nightmare in which a disembodied eye observes a criminal who strikes a tree in a dark wood believing it to be a human being and from which human blood certainly flows. Again perhaps, a vision of Felix as a broken and dismembered Dustie-fute and a tortured echo of the Rilkean tree that 'surges' in the listener's ear floats to the surface.

Above all, though, it is the embodied nature of Bronson's 'Felix' that most disturbs, a body that is dead and yet in which the traces of life remain visible. It fascinates precisely because it presents us with a view of that which we most dread and most desire to see: to describe this as 'an image of our own death' is not quite right. Nor is it an image of passage or transition, despite Bronson's evocation of the 'transi'. It is rather the way in which the photo *makes death present to us* as it can never be in life. One thinks of Dr Donne having himself painted in his shroud, although there Donne 'plays' at death while Felix multitasks in a much more profound manner. Only art can do this for us, although humanity's continual prosecution of war and torture also stems, in part, from this impossible desire to view, to observe our own dead body. Felix seems to offer the viewer an image of a human body whose constituent parts somehow seem able to witness their own – not *death* – but 'deadness'. This touches on the still controversial Freudian idea of the death drive whose existence helps to explain the repetitive actions and dreams of the trauma victim. When we catch Felix's gaze in this photograph, what we see, then, are the bars of a prison that has held humanity captive from the moment it understood that it was mortal and desired a literal view of that mortality.

However, this still does not account for the full power of this visual image. And it seems to me that we cannot fully appreciate it without placing it within a specific historical moment which is the earlier catastrophic phase of the auto immune deficiency syndrome.

The uncanny nature of Felix's gaze stems also from our knowledge that his deathbed was also the bed of love. I realise that this kind of remark could take us into a world of morally threadbare and intellectually puerile sociological commentary in which obscene equations were once made – and in some countries of the world continue to be made – between plague and homosexuality. My purpose in saying this, however, is simply to suggest the way in which this photograph both feeds and feeds off a century of Freudian speculation about the connection between eros and thanatos. In this respect the photograph delivers a shock of recognition: our lives and our deaths are made simultaneously present to us and held out to us, offered by Felix's gaze.

Shock and an image of prison bars were also present in my mind and that of many of my contemporaries in the early 1980s as we read the first reports of what would become known as AIDS, and gradually took stock of what this meant for our love-lives and for our lives. At that time, I spent quite a few years living in Paris researching the life of an eighteenth-century oddball called Joseph Joubert. My days were mostly spent in the old Bibliothèque Nationale in the rue de Richelieu, occasionally noticing the bald pate of Michel Foucault who often sat in an area of the library called the 'hemicycle' which was reserved for the study of rare books. I was a much more timid figure than Foucault and this timidity may have saved my life at the time. Gradually, I became more politicised and towards the end of the eighties left the shelter of my libraries to take part in activist protests. I won't ever forget the one organised by ACT-UP when a whole crowd of us sat down in neat rows, one behind the other, on the Boulevard de Sebastopol. We were carted off, surprisingly gently, by the CRS, the French riot police, and taken to the local nick where I was let go after a couple of hours. No-one spoke harshly or insulted us but I did notice that the police never took off their gloves.

Another image that remains from those days is a visit – several visits if truth be told – to a notorious bar just off the rue de Rivoli. I must have been all of nineteen at the time but the definite chronology of these years is blurred for me now. Downstairs, it was just a noisy, crowded bar. After I had managed to buy my 'demi' and been smiled at ironically by the handsome barman, I stood right at the back just watching what was going on. Eventually I spotted what I hoped I would see: now and again men would nonchalantly stroll up some stairs at the back and disappear behind a curtain. More men went up than came down and it took me several visits to pluck up the courage to follow them. I found myself in quite a large space divided up into different rooms by partitions and curtains. It was pretty dark, though my eyes adjusted eventually to all but one of the rooms which was pitch black. I remember standing on the threshold of this room and trying to make out what was going on inside. At first I thought it was empty but after a while I realised that something was breathing or sighing. I became aware of sound first of all, and then, now and again, I made out the glimmer of an arm or a leg rising or falling. The room was filled to bursting with a mass of heaving, undulating human flesh. Looking again at 'Felix' lying on his quilts, I can't help wondering if that glimmering darkroom could not be seen as a kind of reverse image of Bronson's photograph: moving limbs – this time – caught up in acts of ecstasy that morphed suddenly into immediate stillness. Again, I know that saying such things takes us into the forum where homosexual 'promiscuity' is 'punished' with death. But such thoughts and statements belong to a different order of commentary. What we are dealing with here is not 'promiscuity' but an uncanny 'proximity' that characterizes ontology itself. In that room, as in this photograph, life and death commingle as intimately and as naturally as light and shadow.

But that decade of discovery was also a moment of imprisonment: the realisation that we would spend a lifetime – those of us that were lucky – of living at one remove (the remove of latex) from the most immediate and intimate expression of our love for other human beings. Unless, of course, we were willing to take continual, and for very many years, immeasurable risks. Not that I was as 'marked' or held as those contemporaries who did not survive of course. I have enjoyed a much longer lifetime than they. But this is why I cannot honestly get far beyond the art of Wojnarowicz, of Mapplethorpe, of Haring or Bronson, cannot respond with poems to all those playful, postmodern, sometimes joyful sheddings of identity that characterize the final images of the exhibition. I do not say any of this in a pessimistic frame of mind. My accent here is not intended to be calculatingly tragic. I am simply trying to understand and articulate the nature of an existential experience: the fact is that I was caught by that era; I would say 'branded' almost, in all senses of that word. And there is a sense in which everything since the early 1980s has been a strange kind of 'afterlife'. Is it right or sensible to make so much of that basic, sexual act? From every rational perspective, from every emotional perspective – in terms of what we owe to our families, friends and existing partners – no. But to write a new poem based on Bronson's image would involve a form of repetition of something that cannot be repeated, cannot be copied because it always accompanies you at some level of your being and because that 'original' poem is always happening, always being said. I was going to admit to a kind of artistic impotence here but I have come to believe that there are some essential experiences – among them this experience of the prison – that you carry with you, that you constantly although not always consciously inhabit, and that rather than attempting to 'transcend' them and 'move on' – to use the threadbare vocabulary of the agony aunt – it is better simply to remember them and, if poetry is at issue, to recite them. Recitation is not the same as repetition. Bronson's photograph shows us something very primitive. Felix's astonished face admits to both horror and joy. He is Egyptian and he is extinction. He is the prison gate, one side of which is opening, just as the other side is closing.

You thread a sea with your eye;
each time the needle enters your flank
the pain composes you;

trees that hung your voice
among these patterns
wrap your quilt in foliage;

a dog barks through the branches;
a girl's arm passes like an oar
across the sunlit patches;

now your song kneels
at the river's edge
and will not flow;

your passport head is pinned in silk.

Kirsty Logan

Dog-Bait

Doll-eyes

Daddy is my birthday present. I know it from the very nanosecond I come downstairs for breakfast and see him beside my cake, leaning on the kitchen counter with his elbow cocked and his thumb flicking the wheel of his Zippo. *Hey princess*, he says, and lights my candles one by one. I lean in and blow them out slow, so he can see the way the candlelight glows off my skin. No wrinkles on me, not like Momma. She's got bird's feet at the corners of her mouth, and dark places under her eyes that won't ever go away.

He's the right sort of man, my Daddy – clefted chin, skin tanned like wood, arms I can hang off like a monkey, all that stuff. Not that I do the arm-hanging thing, not now I got enough candles on my cake to set your hair on fire.

I thought I'd get him all to myself for the day, like maybe we'd go out for a soda or down to the pier, throw stones out past where the water goes white and frothy like shampoo. But then Momma starts on about the party, and oh-my-stars all the things she has to do, and will Daddy go get this, will Daddy go get that. I know she only did it to get him away from me.

I did think for a little while about all my candles and how Momma's bleached blonde hair would flame up in seconds, but before I know what's what, Momma's at me about the party list. *It's me and the girls,* I say, *just us, like always.*

We're together all the time, me and the dolls, like as if we're girls from television. My girls might not be ladies but they know what they've got. Doll-mouth puts Vaseline on her teeth so her smile is wide-wide-wide, and Doll-legs wears dresses so tight she's breathless. She used to look so damn stupid in the flowered cotton her momma made her wear, but she just tosses it in a dumpster the second she's out of the front yard. We can do things like that now we're grown. I'm smiling at the thought of seeing my girls but then Momma's all *Now, little doll, don't forget about going next door for Dawnie.*

And then I know for sure whose hair I'll be setting on fire. I'll call her Dawnie in front of Momma but I know she's really Dog-bait. Ugh, she makes my cuticles crawl. She acts like butter wouldn't melt but I know her mouth is dirty. It's okay though, it's okay, because I might have to let her come into my house but I'm sure as hell not letting her anywhere near Daddy.

So off I go next door, my cheeks still warm from my candles, practising in my head all the ways to make my party sound like the least fun thing ever so that Dog-bait won't come. That girl will refuse me quick-smart, if she knows what's good for her.

Dog-bait

There are lots of things in this world that I do not like, and Eve's party will, I know, wind up being at the top of that list. But what can I do? My mom says I have to be nice to her, so I'm nice to her, even though it makes my teeth scrape together to do it.

She comes around in her gooey lipstick and with her bra strap showing. Is that supposed to be sexy? Well, if that's sexy then I should just hole up in my bedroom until high school's over, because there's no way on this earth you'll catch me flashing my underwear.

It's my birthday, Eve sighs through the screen door at me. Her lipstick makes the words soggy.

Many happy returns, I say back, not sure whether I should invite her in. I'm holding a book with my finger trapped inside to hold my place, and the longer I stand there the more the edges of the pages dig lines into my skin. Eve glares at the book like it's a nuclear weapon and scuffs her toes on the porch steps, her chipped toenail polish red as meat. I do not want to invite her in.

And then she tells me about the party, not in a way like she's asking me to come, but like a threat. The threat of her and her little gang of friends – the dolls, they call one another, and just for a second I'm struck with horror and desire that maybe she'll make me a doll too.

I'm having a party, she says with her eyes, and you'll be sorry.

I'm already sorry, I say with mine, because I have to be friends with you.

It would be an honour, I say. *I'll get my mom to make snacks. S'mores or something.*

Eve rolls her eyes like the earth just flipped on its axis, then stomps back to her house. She seems to remember herself halfway and turns the stomp into a sway, her barely-hips tilting up and down with each step. Before she's even through the door she's calling out *Dad-eeee,* the vowels stretched out like elastic.

I do try and convince my mom not to make me go, I really do. But before I even finish my sentence it's out with the clip-on earrings and the hairspray and the homemade cookies – even though she doesn't really make them, she just takes them out of the packet and heats them in the microwave and wraps them in a clean dishrag and puts them in Tupperware. She doesn't actually say out loud that she made them, but the lie is still told. That's why lies are so bad, I think – because they sneak.

I buy as much time as I can with homework, but then my mom is swiping lipgloss across my mouth and then there's nothing more to do but cross the lawn to Eve's house. Well, hey, I think to myself: at least I'll get some funny stories to tell everyone when I'm at college or a world-famous surgeon or buying and selling stocks or whatever. I tuck my shirt into my jeans, take off my earrings, and knock on Eve's door.

Doll-mouth

Doll-eyes' party started out fun, you know? I mean, she had the chips and dips and balloons and that shit, and the three of us were all matching in our little black dresses and red mary-janes. We like to do themes sometimes. You know, like candyfloss day or mown-lawn day, and then we all have to try and match the colours of our outfits. My black dress used to be my mom's about a thousand years ago, and she was going to toss it so I stole it from the thrift-store pile and ripped it up sexy-like so I could wear it. No point having a body like mine if you're gonna waste it. I was thinking when I'm older I could maybe strip for a few years, but only if the guys are okay and I get lots of money and gifts. My cousin Jenna says it's great, a guy gave her a car once and it was almost new. That's what I want.

But the thing about the party wasn't the dolls in our black dresses or the balloons or even that gutterslut Dog-bait. It was Doll-eyes' poppa. He thinks he's goddamned Rhett Butler or some shit, that phony Southern drawl so thick you'd get your heels caught up in it. He was probably cute when he was young, because he's got dark hair and big hands, but now he's getting a belly and I don't think he ever shaves because he's always rubbing his fingers across his jaw and it makes this rasping noise, like when you open a bottle of pop.

Marya, Lisa, he says as Doll-legs and me are coming up the sidewalk, and his voice is solemn as a preacher's. He brings his hand up to his forehead as if he's tipping the cap he isn't wearing. *Pull up a pew,* he says, and he pats the cushion beside him on the swing. We walk up to the door and I wink at Doll-legs so she'll go inside, and she rolls her eyes at me before tugging open the screen door.

He's got a beer in his hand so I say *Can I have one?* He tosses his empty into the yard and lifts a beer from the stack by his feet, then pops the top and hands it to me – but before I can touch it he pulls it back and takes a long sip, and I see his throat working as he swallows. *Now miss,* he says, *I think there's a while to go before you're twenty-one. Go on inside now. You don't wanna miss the party.*

And I know I should say something cool but I can't think fast enough so I just pout at him and go inside. In the living room the dolls are there, and so is Dog-bait – gross – and Doll-eyes' mom must have started cocktail hour early because her lipstick has started to smear and as we're playing CDs and having snacks she's dropping kisses on the tops of our heads way too heavy, like she's using us to lean on, and she's wearing this big heart locket – ginormous it is, big as my fist, and it sits right between her tits. Or, I mean, where her tits *should* be, but you know, she's old so they've fallen. It might be having kids that does that, I don't know. I'll have mine early so I'll be a hot mom. Or maybe I won't have them at all. I haven't decided yet.

Anyways, I wasn't really paying attention because I was thinking about Doll-eyes' poppa out there on the porch, and the way he patted the seat beside him. I felt like maybe, if I really tried, I could have gotten him to give me a car.

Doll-heart

Oh my girl, and oh her girls. They're all such dolls, and I do love them so. They gleam and they're glossed and they're so small, like they could fit in the palm of your hand. Every bit of their flesh is so tight, and I do remember how that felt. It wasn't so long ago.

There's Dawnie always thinking too much and Marya with her big bright smile and Lisa in her cute short dresses. And my doll, my Eve, the girl with the most cake. She knows nothing but it's right for her to be that way, for her to stay a doll. Someday she'll know what it is to ache.

So I wisp around my home, pressing kisses to my girls, and I think of nothing but their happiness. That's what a mother should do. But the more I kiss them the more they curl inwards like mushrooms, grow shells like snails, and I can't get close to them any more.

I go outside, porch-side, and I'm not alone. My man used to be a man, but now he's nothing more than a shadow. For years now we've just circled around one another in this old house like we're dancing. But we'll be okay, because we've got our little Eve there at the centre. We're a family, and that's what family is.

The cushion by my man is warmed by his skin, and so soft. I could close my eyes and I could sleep. I could sleep forever and not even wake with a kiss.

But I want to show the girls – and my own girl, my special one – that we are a family. That we're real. I cough up that sleep and hock it out between the boards of the porch. I tug on my man's hand until he stands up from the swing-seat.

Love me, I say. *Love me, goddamn you.*

He looks at me and his eyes are glitter-shot, and it might be the beer but I think it's love.

I want to, he says. *I really do.*

So I tuck my body into his, and he lays his arm out along my shoulder and I slide my hand into the back pocket of his jeans – and just like that we're both seventeen again. I'm tall and skinny enough to touch the sun, and not even pregnant yet. Just then, before I've had time to blink, I love him.

He leads me back into our home. Everything I see – the couch, the stereo, the kitchen door – is ringed in gold. Everything is beautiful, and Eve is the most beautiful of all. The girls are partway through some game, so it takes a few breaths for them to look up. Eve looks at us for a long time, and then she closes her eyes, and I can't even dream what she's thinking.

Then something snaps in her. It breaks, my little doll's little heart. She stands up, slow as a queen, and walks upstairs. She does not look at us.

Doll-legs

So the party was mostly lame, with the balloons and crap, and obviously we couldn't eat the snacks because we're all trying to drop ten pounds, except for Doll-mouth who is a total cheat and thinks it's okay to be fat because then you get big tits. Not true, I've tried to tell her. Your tits look bigger the skinnier you are because you're smaller in comparison. That's what my sister says, and she's always got a boyfriend so she should know. Mostly we were just trying to ignore Dog-bait, or trick her into doing something dumb, but then Doll-eyes' mom and daddy came in all kissy-kissy – it was pretty gross, don't get me wrong, but it wasn't reason enough for Doll-eyes to stomp up the stairs like she did.

I don't know, she must have thought we'd left or something because she was up in her room for forever. We would have gone, but her mom was fussing around, rearranging the snack bowls and changing the TV stations so that we couldn't leave. It seemed like ages had passed and I don't know how long Doll-eyes had been standing there at the top of the stairs but it seemed like all at the same moment we heard her humming. We all looked up in one movement, like we'd practised it as a dance routine.

And oh my god, you just wouldn't believe it. She's standing on the top step in white cotton underwear with this raggedy baby-doll cradled in her arms. Then she looks right at her daddy and she stops humming and she opens her mouth wide as it will go.

I'm the doll, she's screaming, *I'm the doll, I'm the mom, I'm the doll,* and then it all just blurs together because she's screaming or crying or something and it's not even words any more. All of us just stand there, thinking oh my god, because what are we supposed to do?

She runs down the stairs so fast it's like she's falling and she's on her daddy, pressed right up against him like she wants to tip him over, and she reaches her arms up around his neck so the baby-doll is trapped between them. He must be in shock or something because he just stands there as she paws him and coos little nothings and gazes up at him. I feel this pressure inside my ear and I realise it's because my mouth has dropped open and it's been just hanging there ever since I saw Doll-eyes on the stairs.

Her daddy is still standing there like a brick wall, but her mom steps forward and whisks that baby-doll out from between them and tosses it on the floor. It feels like the whole entire world is holding its breath, and I know I sure am. I feel like anything – literally any damn thing – could happen next.

But Doll-eyes just takes one step, one tiny step, and then she's right by her mom. She wraps her arms around her mom's waist and rests her head right on that big heart pendant. The whole world exhales, and so do I. And I guess that means we can all leave. Except for Doll-eyes. I don't think she'll ever leave here.

Dog-bait

Eve's dad says he'll walk me home, but I think it's just an excuse for him to get out of that madhouse. I don't know whether I should feel more sorry for him, or for Eve, or for Eve's mom.

Dawnie, he says, when we're safely off his lawn and onto mine. *Dawnie, I don't know what –*

Dawn, I say. *You can call me Dawn. Names like Dawnie are for little kids, and I'm not a little kid.*

I guess not, he says.

And I'm sure not a doll, I say, and I think maybe that's going too far because I didn't mean Eve's performance there, I just meant the way her friends call each other dolls. Our steps across the lawn seem unnaturally slow, like in those dreams where you're trying to run but you don't go anywhere.

No, he says, and from the corner of my eye I think I see him glance back at his house. Right then, I feel a kick of sadness that in the end I will win and Eve will lose, and that one day she'll figure that out.

We get to my house and I stand in the open doorway, the outside air hot on one side of me and the inside air cool on the other. I take Eve's dad's hand and tug it so that he has to bend a little. I stretch up and I kiss him, hard, right on his lips. It's beer and minty gum and sliding saliva. His stubble scratches. Inside his mouth it's warm, then it's hot.

He pulls away and stands there on my porch, his empty hands stretched out in the space between us. I go inside and close the door behind me. I don't want him to hear me laugh.

Marcas Mac an Tuairneir

Iùnnrais

Iùnnrais os cionn Sràid Sheòrais
Is mi a ruith às a dhèidh.
Mo sgamhan acaideach le ànaich
Is stoirm a' bhùitich nam chluais.

Doras dìomhair a' fosgladh,
Tro bhalla eadar na bùithtean.
Bu shin acarsaid bhon uisge,
Nach faighinn idir na asgall.

Suas na staidhre linne, ro
Spreadh putain mo lèine
'S a chrudhan ri ubhal mo sgòrnain
'S mo ghuth fo mhùchadh na làmhan.

San dorchadas dongaidh a sheòmair,
Ob-obagail fhuar nam chridhe.
Cha tug mi aire do phuinnsean
Measgaicht' lem spèis as ìsle.

Nam laighe mar sgeoldair na leabaidh,
Dh'fhairich mi fallas air m' òdain
Is teannachadh teàrmann an t-solais,
An aghaidh sgaoileadh mo fhradharcan.

Le buille a dh'ionnsaigh nam fhànas,
Chaidh e a thionndadh caoin air ascaoin
Is nochd e mar bhogha 'n chlann Uis,
Thairis ionaol an t-siomail.

Tro sgeilceil sgrìobach m' fhaillein,
Thàinig fuaim guth cagar-adhair
Ri ghlaodh gach buaidh thruail;
Faclan prìseal an dòchais:

Chan EIL...

          mo SHÙIL...

Chan EIL...

          mo SHÙIL...

Chan EIL...

          mo SHÙIL...

                    air CALbharaigh...

Chan EIL...

          mo SHÙIL...

                    air CALbharaigh...

Chan EIL...	mo SHÙIL...	air CALbharaigh
no air BET...	leHEM...	an ÀIGH
ach air CÙIL...	GHROD...	an GLASchu
far a BHEIL...	an LOBH...	adh FÀS
agus air SEÒ...	mar AN...	Dùn ÈIDeann,

seòmar BOCHDainn 's CRÀIDH

far a BHEIL...   an NAOIDH...   ean CREUCHdach

ri AO...   naGRAICH...   gu BHÀS.

..   ..

..   ..

..   ..

..   ..

..   ..

Iùnnrais os cionn Sràid Sheòrais
Is mi a' ruith às mo dhèidh,
A' siubhail tro mo thuisleadh
'S mo chasan ri chamacag lag.

Brag mo ghlùine air na leacan,
'S mi laighe bog bàite sa ghuitear.
M' inntinn ri shàmh nan sgòthan;
Samhlaidhean aislignean sgapte.

'Calbharaigh' originally written by Somhairle MacGill-Eain.
Translation by Marcas Mac an Tuairneir.

Tempest

Tempest above George Street
And I chase after myself.
My lungs wheeze with anger
And tinnitus rings in my ear.

Clandestine doorway opens,
Through a wall between the shops.
The haven from the rainfall
I would not find in his embrace.

Up the stairs we go, before
The burst of shirt buttons
And his fist to my larynx;
My voice mute in his hands.

In the languid gloom of the bedroom,
The chilly palpitations.
I caught not on to poison
Mixed in with no esteem.

Languid, like a jellyfish on the bed,
I felt the sweat on my thumbs
And shrinking light's asylum,
Against mydriasis of my pupils.

With a blow to my void
I was turned inside out
And the milky way displayed itself
Across the whitewash of the ceiling.

Through the scratch in the eardrum
Came the sound of wireless voice
Against the howl of every foul blow;
The precious words of hope:

My EYE...

        is NOT ...

My EYE...

        is NOT ...

My EYE...

        is NOT ...

                on CALvary...

My EYE...

        is NOT ...

                on CALvary...

My EYE...	is NOT ...	on CALvary...
or on BET...	leHEM...	the BLESSED
but on PUT...	rid ALLEY...	in GLASgow
where EVERY...	thing ROTS...	as it GROWS
and ON...	a ROOM...	in EDINburgh,

a ROOM of POVERty and PAIN

Where a SCAB... by SOILED...   wee INfant

WALlows...   unTIL its...   DEATH.

..   ..

..   ..

..   ..

..   ..

..   ..

Tempest above George Street
And I chase after myself.
Travelling through each stumble,
As my legs trip, thin.

The crack of knee on pavement
And I lie sodden in the gutter.
My mind at swim with nimbus;
Symbol of splintered fantasy.

Leòmhann

Ath-dhealbhte mar leòmhann.
Allaidh;
Sgrios mi do sheiche,
Le mo chrògan is mo spògan
Is laigh thu air làr na cidsin,
Lag is deòrail.

Lion

I became a lion.
Savage;
I ravaged your skin
With my claws and my paws
And you lay on the kitchen floor,
Feeble and weeping.

Bogha Chlann Uis

Fosgail, a m' uinneig don ʃpeuran.
Briʃt ioma-chrith nan tìm is talmhainn
Is seall dhomh an saineas
Eadar comasachd is miann.

'S thu clàr suilean is colainn; gach
Ceathramh ar domhain.
Geàrraidh mi sgrìob thuca,
Gun ach òdan air putan.

Abair, gur mi tha pòsta
Aig gach gin àraid aca.
Ann an cruinn-cè co-shìnte,
A' sireadh cothroman eadar-dhealaichte.

Ach san roinn seo,
Suidhidh mi air an t-sòfa,
No anns an taigh-seinnse,
A' feitheamh ri freagairt,
Bho bheul an aineòlais.

Agus fhad 's a ʃtrìochdas
Gach coltas don dorchadas is
Gealladh nas danarra;
Saoil...

A bheil fleasgach ri ʃporadh
Na h-iarmailt,
Son boillsgeadh m' aire-sa,
Làn dòchais is follais,
Ri ʃpeuradaireachd

The Milky Way

Open, my window to the stars.
Break earthquake in time and territory
And show me the diversity
Between possibility and fancy.

You grid of eyes and chests; all
Quadrants of our universe.
I'll cut a route through to them,
With mere fingertip on button.

They say I am married
To each one in their exclusivity.
In each universe laid parallel,
Dogging different chances.

But on this plane,
I sit on the setée,
Or in a hostelry,
Suspended on response
From the mouth of ignorance.

And as each likeness succumbs
To the darkness
And a bolder promise;
I wonder...

If there's a fellow fumbling
Through the firmament,
For the glimmer of my devoir,
Full of hope and openness
In his stargazing.

John Maley

A Guid Cause

When smashing a window it is most important to choose the correct stones. Weigh the stones not with scales but with the hand. I would hold the stone loosely in my palm and feel its pressure. Too heavy and it could strain in the act of throwing. Too heavy and it could maim or kill. The dilemma is in the weight. Too light a stone and it would barely crack a window, perhaps bounce off with no ill effect to the glass whatsoever. This would be a waste of time and resources. If fortune and circumstance are against you, do something by half. But do not fail to do it at all. One of my dear companions would proceed by trial and error. Gradually she would build up the weight and size of stones until they were sufficient to the task. The carrying of stones was another art, or perhaps I should say a science. A large rock in your bag might be tolerable over a short distance but if you were to walk half way across a town or city, you might as well carry a cross upon your back. No, there must be some correlation between weight and magnitude of stone and length of journey. I think we women of this world carry burdens enough. Strategy is all. A short distance, a street perhaps, you may carry a boulder if you must. A long journey by tram, carriage or foot, a smaller stone would be advisable.

I noted a lady of considerable standing used a fine handkerchief in which to enfold a stone, as if it were something delicate and exotic. She said she was trying to protect her hands. I liked to feel the stone in my palm, its rough texture, or smooth surfaces. The best shot I had was with a smooth large stone which must have weighed nearly a half pound in my hand. I stood facing the mannequins in the shop window, like well-groomed animals in a zoo. I have to say, the blank faces were nothing novel to me. I have seen real, living women, their faces frozen by ignorance or shame, or simply years of silence. Years of being invisible and irrelevant. Vital women who have had all life and independent thought drained away. Women's sweet little mouths pursed against unsayable things. Unthinkable things. Mannequins in drawing rooms and factories, hospitals and kitchens, walking in the street as if they were asleep. I have known some personally. I knew a mannequin who came to life whenever her husband left the room and then slowed to a stop like an automaton when he came back in.

Sometimes women have to be out of earshot of men. So that we can say the things that are in our hearts and minds. So that we can be ourselves. I once asked a woman her opinion on a certain matter, a matter of no great significance, and she told me she mustn't offer an opinion. She said her husband would have her over his knee. We were in a tearoom at the time. I called her a naughty child and asked the waiting girl to fetch a bib. Perhaps some women like being mannequins, china dolls perched on a window ledge, fearful always of falling.

As we advanced towards the windows, illuminated as they were by lamplight, it was not the mannequins that drew my eyes but my own reflection, my bearing, my purposefulness. I lifted the first stone from my pocket and dashed it towards the window. There was a sound of smashing and a cheer rang out. I had cast the first stone. None of us are without sin in this world but my friends and I had a cause. More stones rained towards the window, the broken glass flying around the mannequins. One delicately dressed demoiselle toppled and fell as a rock bounced off her chest. Down like a skittle to a louder cheer. Soon the police were upon us and one tried to take me by the arm as if he were my beau. I shrugged him off like a bothersome dog. He then grabbed me from behind in an indecent manner and I had no option but to kick like a horse. He was a big heifer of a man and, as men often do, used brute strength to overpower me. I went limp in his arms to make it all the more enervating for him to apprehend me. I can honestly say I was dragged into custody with both cheers and jeers ringing in my ears. Vandal, I heard a cry. I was no vandal. A vandal destroys and degrades, my mission was to raise up, to ennoble. What is it about men that they forget they have mothers who bore them, sisters and aunts and grannies who have shown them manifold gentleness? These men must have amnesia, who suckle at their mother's breast and then whistle or scowl at women in the street as if they had never set eyes on one before. I suppose they are reared that way, with law and tradition at either side, egging them on. It was ever thus, they say. Most women are happy with their place. But this is our common place, all God's creatures. Yes, there are dolls who seem content to blink at their men and crave only their affection. Strategies.

I was hauled and frogmarched and generally manhandled all the way to the station. I cannot say I was mistreated upon arrival. I was clearly a woman of good breeding. I raised my head and spoke to them as if I were the Queen. I said an injury to me will be an injury to the whole of Edinburgh. I explained that I was a physician and a woman from a highly respectable background. They all but bowed and the young fellow that locked me in the cells looked as if he were about to cry. Later, I heard a dear young friend cry. She later told me she was spat on by a ruffian as she was paraded through the streets like an outlaw. When I heard that woman weeping I wanted to reach out to her. 'There is comfort in our cause', I cried out, 'There is comfort in our cause.'

I was in service and had a nice uniform and the master and ma'am were kind. Then sometimes they would dismiss me and I would feel ashamed that I had lingered too long in a room, listened longer than I should have. They never beat me. I had a friend I went to school with who was in service too. Her mammy died and she never had anybody who could help her. She once showed me marks on her bare back where she had been thrashed. She said there were marks on her arse as well but I asked her not to show me those. She said not even her ain father had belted her so ferociously. Not even Miss Turner at our school, who had a moustache and a bad leg and was always beating lassies, was ever as vicious as this master. One time the lady of the house cried and begged him to stop and he never hit her again. But sometimes he looked at her and she couldn't understand what was on his mind. She pulled me closer in the park one day and whispered in my ear that he had pressed himself against her in the scullery and smelled of sherry. I said watch out for those ones, they'll give you a baby and throw you in the gutter.

I slept in an attic room in their big house near the park. The mistress had a wee silver bell she would ring. Sometimes their wee boy would ring the bell out of play or mischief. Once I was lying down on top of my bed on a warm summer evening, an awful clammy evening where everything sticks to you. My head was sore. Then I heard the bell ringing and it wouldn't stop. As it was just a wee bell they couldn't do anything but keep shaking it. I wasn't being disobedient, I just couldn't lift my head off the pillow. The master must have got angry because the bell ringing stopped and he said in a loud voice, 'Woman!' I supposed he meant me and I went downstairs. It was to clean up something the wee boy had smashed in the kitchen. He could have kicked it into a corner. But they were kind to me really. Later I looked in the wee dressing table mirror in my poky wee room and smiled at the thought of being called 'Woman'. I was eighteen years old by then, of course I was a woman. Aye, a woman who had exasperated a man so much he cried out. But why didn't he say my name? It was as if he was calling out to all of us, us women, who wouldn't do what they're told, who wouldn't stand to attention.

It was the next day, coincidentally a day off, that I went to Glasgow Green. My ain time so I had no need to explain myself. My head was clear then, oh aye it was clear that day. The Women's Freedom League were there as bold as brass and keen to turn every girl's head. They carried themselves like a victorious army. Each speech was like a song to me, each rallying cry lifted me like a lovely hymn. At first I wasn't sure whether to stay or whether to go. I felt like I was hearing something I shouldn't be listening to, like a dirty joke. Something a boy would say in the school shed to scare the girls. I had read about these women in the newspapers. The mistress thought I was reading the cartoons and the recipes. I'm not ignorant. I learned to read and write. My mammy made sure of it, as she couldn't. But hearing these things aloud in broad daylight. In a public place. It wasn't long before I had elbowed my way to the front so I could hear properly, aye and see properly too. I wanted to hear everything, how great a cause, how women must have the vote and how women had minds to match any man's. The struggle had begun and would not cease till the vote was won. My skirts were caked in muck, somebody stood on my toe, I lost a clasp from my hair. But I didn't care. I left there with my heart beating wildly. I was like a bairn running home from school for the start of the summer holidays. Or maybe like running to school, to a lesson you longed to learn. These were my thoughts put into words, stated boldly. I had an auntie stayed in the Saltmarket so I took some refuge there. She shook her head as I sat at the scullery table reading the pamphlet one of the women had given me. My auntie was a funny woman, she indulged me, vowed to keep my secret. I got the train home the next morning back to work and felt like my ain person. A strange feeling. That I wasn't a bairn in this house. When they rang the bell sure I still answered it, but my hands never shook and my voice never wavered. The thought occurred to me, they're no better than I am. No better, with their big house and their drawing room and their piano and the nanny and the cook and I. In my wee room I stood and looked me up and down in the mirror. This young thing. Foolish young thing. It was as if I had met someone new, for the first time. Someone I liked. I put my shoulders back like a daft auld teacher at school told us, my chin raised a wee bit like I was lady of the manor. Deportment she called it. 'Woman', I said, a loud whisper, echoing the master.

Comfort in our cause. In Holloway Prison I was held down and force-fed until I contracted double pneumonia. These, the scars of battle. But I have no yearning to suffer. I never hankered for martyrdom. But anything that could shine a light where hithertofore there was darkness, this was to be cherished. Women must always endeavour to wrestle attention away from men. Men and their important affairs of state. Men and the economy. Men and the challenges of Empire. Men in the debating chamber. Men making important decisions. I likened it to putting a foot in the door. The occupier refuses admittance to you and closes the door on your foot. So you wear a sturdier shoe, move boldly forward, getting your whole body in the door, push against the door, enter. Enter this world and make your stand in it. If you know nothing of the economy, study it. If you know nothing of the colonies, leap to the library. I've been reading newspapers since I was seven. If matters of law baffle you, then subscribe to the relevant periodical. Do you think men know of these things by nature? Knowledge is acquired. Make the acquisition of knowledge your primary goal.

I refused food as part of our strategy of resistance. Because I had an appetite for equality. I hungered for justice. I had no idea they would stoop to such cruelty. As I gagged and choked on the tube being thrust into me I vowed never to leave this Earth of ours until I was free to choose the government of the land. The pain and distress of those ensuing days and weeks were a test of endurance. But endure I did. Mercifully I was able to recover and was released to a safe house. I was pledged to return to prison but had no intention of so doing. Like a captive bird released to the wild, I flew. Even being confined for such a short time made me ponder my mortality. To be at large in the world again felt such a precious reward. The creatures I saw there, in the prison, you would not believe. Girls who had seemingly never encountered soap or human kindness. One girl told me she had been hunted by a gang of men like a bitch cornered by a pack of dogs in heat. Some of those poor unfortunates were serving time for the crimes of men, others had been driven there by poverty or madness. One creature said she had eaten regular meals for the first time in her whole life.

I was spirited on my release to a safe house in London. The house was owned by a bellowing fool of a woman whose every utterance would have silenced a town-crier, such was her volume. I would have been safer at large, or, as I had intended, returning to Edinburgh. However, my hostess had a heart as big as her mouth and her house was warm and capacious, albeit covered in dust, dirt and clutter of every kind. She told me her maid had run away with a coalman and she had refused to hire another. She declared she wouldn't bother herself with tedious domestic chores. My conscience is clean, she boomed one evening by her crackling fireside, and that is all that matters. My release was temporary as I had been allowed to recuperate from the hunger strike and coerced feeding. On the day I was due to be returned she hid me in an attic room and shouted at a policeman till he fled in despair. That evening I sat by her fire and my hostess regaled me with tales of her two husbands, rich fools, one she had adored, another despised, both now dead. She said she would have liked children but had never carried one. They were never on me often enough, she laughed, referring to her late husbands. Although she was completely without shame or discretion in many matters, she had shielded and protected me like the proverbial mother hen.

I returned to Scotland and spoke to those who would listen and those who wouldn't. I began to sound like my foghorn hostess and at times grew hoarse and no amount of whisky or honey would help. Plain rest guided me back to rude voice. I was told I was a disgrace to my sex, a threat to public order and a walking breach of the peace. I was manhandled, pushed, pinched, skelped, shirriked. I was subjected to catcalls, wolfwhistles, harangued by Holy Willies, booed by boisterous boys. But I was also hailed like a new found land, welcomed like a hero home from battle in this divided land. In the hushed village halls, the packed town halls, the besieged church where I was given sanctuary and stage, I shot truth out like an arrow and it pierced many hearts. Truth has a way of overcoming many obstacles in its path. Sometimes hurtful truth, truth which shames and humiliates, is the most commanding truth. Gentle truths that illuminate injustice, prejudice, can struggle to be heard above the din. But all one can do is speak the truth and ask that God grant the silence to hear it. They heard, old women who had nursed boys and men from cradle to grave, young girls knocking on the doors of our learned institutions, men too, heard the truth and met it with rowdy cheers. I spoke of women who nurture the young, tend the sick, stitch and sew and cook and clean, who create homes and build fires and make and mend. Glorious women who should no longer be excluded from public life. At night I would sleep in rooming houses, blanketed against the cold, reading, with my gloved hands gripping a newspaper or book. Each day travelling to a new town, another nook or cranny, like a missionary. Sometimes the word is all we have and the word is enough. The truthful word of a good cause.

A handsome young boy once sent me a letter full of feelings I didn't understand. I threw it in the fire and cried. I was angry he had not simply spoken to me, face to face. I think sometimes all you need is a face to tell you something. The day my mammy died I saw it in my daddy's face, something terrible had happened and she wasn't in the room. I put my hand across his mouth, no words were necessary. Only tears and then a shared silence. But sometimes words are all, they're everything. So I read their words, heard their words. I was all ears. The Women's Freedom League. The Women's Social and Political Union. Words that told me, not that I was weak or immoral or dangerous, but that I was entitled. Entitled to equality, to take an interest in matters of politics, of government. For my voice to count just as a man's does. At first I was incredulous, wary even, embarrassed by the boldness of these women. But their message was so obvious, so plain and unvarnished, that it couldn't be anything but the truth.

In the beginning I felt like a silly girl eavesdropping on adults. Some of these women were so educated and high-minded, they reminded me of our school headmistress with her monocle and her sarcasm and her sweeping great dresses. I would ask myself, Are these my sisters? Is this my struggle? But I heard little I could quarrel with and soon I wanted to participate, to play my part. I invested in good sturdy shoes – the master asked what I was doing with what he called 'navvy's shoes'. I was walking, that's what I was doing. Marching. It was during a march in Edinburgh that I was asked if I would be willing to carry out acts for which I might find myself languishing in the jailhouse. I was younger then and already felt like a prisoner. I said yes for the cause. The guid cause.

I walked some distance to find suitable post boxes for the campaign. Pillar boxes by their very nature tended to be in plain view so the stakes were high. I was given a corrosive substance by a tall woman with a nose the size of a bicycle horn. She warned me to handle it with extreme care and to pour it as soon as possible in a post box. I was to feign posting a letter and pour the entire contents of the vial into the mouth of the pillar box. I was so terrified I didn't even take the vial home but carried it about me for the better part of two hours. Finally I walked swiftly to a post box and under the shield of a bogus letter poured the entire contents into the letter-mouth. I walked purposefully away and when I looked back I saw smoke billowing from the post-box. When I got back to the master's house the nanny was just leaving. It was my task to bathe the two children and put them to bed. I washed my hands thoroughly in case I would somehow injure or contaminate the children, although I had worn an ugly gardening glove when handling the vial of incendiary liquid. That night, in the confines of my attic bedroom, I gently wept with the shame of my crime and felt sure the next burning would be of my foolish soul in hellfire. Three days later I had collected a further supply of combustible material and was again bringing carnage to the Royal Mail. My hands shook and I stammered when spoken to. I was sick in an alleyway. I was a pathetic criminal but when I read of our antics in the newspapers I had a terrible fit of giggles.

Soon I grew bored of the commands of my household. It was not that the master and lady were growing any less kind or any more cruel. I had simply outgrown them like a child outgrows a doll. One day she has to set the doll aside and move onto other things. I was offered the chance to work in a semi-official capacity for the cause and this was a gradual process from being nothing much more than a lady-in-waiting to a speaker in my own right. I was told I had the common touch and would broaden the support base. I left the master's house with a heavy heart, missing the children and the security the position had afforded me. But I was soon embedded in a mission behind enemy lines, so to speak. The enemy was ignorance. In its truest form. Women were being ignored, their thoughts, goals, ambitions, voices, sidelined.

Years pass and alliances are forged and broken. Burning letters became burning buildings. There were times I barely recognised myself. I was boarding in a house in Edinburgh when I met a woman through an acquaintance of mine. She was a doctor and had worked in children's hospitals. She was an independent spirit, forty, and with no children or dependants. She told me she was unmarried and by the tone of her voice I felt she did not consider this to be a calamity. She offered me some port from a crystal decanter and began trying to pick fights with me. It was useless, I agreed with everything she said. I told her I had gained a position in an academy for girls and was taking a teaching qualification at a ladies' night school. She told me she loved working with children, especially young children, boys and girls who cried the same and played the same, before adults bullied their differences into them. Later, she came to my room and put her fingers in my hair. She said it was the colour of honey. She asked me to come and live with her. She said she wanted to take care of me for the rest of my life. I think in the end it was I who took care of her. Sometimes I think I talk like her, even look like her. I became her.

What is love after all but finding common cause with one other? So this unpolished girl, who had an innate wisdom, who had learned on the hoof, became my companion. My years of lonely struggle were at an end. I had met her at a house of a friend. This honey-haired girl had stood in the doorway of her room and said yes, a word I had heard so little of in my life. We lived in my home and worked at the hospital and school and walked arm in arm in Princes Street Gardens. I loved to cook and clean for her, although she declared I was hopeless at both. We would read to each other, like tender mothers to infants in a nursery.

Years later I developed a disease of the nerves. I began to falter in my stride. My feet rebelled and stuck to the floor. I lost the threads of conversations or stuttered like a bashful child. I sought the advice of a colleague who examined me thoroughly, tested my reflexes, studied my posture, and made me share my private, despairing thoughts. He respected me enough to tell me the whole truth. At first I protected my companion from this truth. I suppose in all honesty I was frightened that she would flee. She stayed. More attentive than ever, more loving than ever. If I dropped something, she dashed to pick it up. If I cried, she placed her shoulder under my head and petted me.

Yesterday was her birthday. She joined the ranks of mature ladies allowed the vote. We shared happy memories of our struggles and she bade me dance with her, guiding me around the parlour like a mannequin. When I was quite exhausted she had helped me undress and sat me on the end of the bed. She took off her clothes and left them in a heap on the floor. She stood in front of the mirrored door of our wardrobe, this gregarious girl. 'Woman!' she exclaimed, in a gruff voice like a small boy pretending to be a man. She laughed and danced and laughed and danced and landed in my lap.

Val McDermid

The Road and the Miles to Dundee

I hate this dress. It's lemon yellow with blue roses and it makes my skin look like semolina pudding, my cheeks like dauds of strawberry jam in the middle of the plate. This dress, it's Bri - Nylon and it cuts in under my arms and it makes me sweat. I hate the crackly white petticoat that's sewn in. It's like plastic, scratchy and rustly. You can hear me coming half way across the town. Mostly, though, I hate it because it's a hand-me-down. It belonged to my cousin Morag who I'm supposed to like because she's my cousin and she's only a year older than me, but I hate her too. She's a clipe, always telling tales. She's a Moaning Minnie. And she's boring. And I get the horrible clothes Auntie Betty makes for her after she's outgrown them. And they never fit because she's a beanpole and I'm not. But I have to wear them. According to my mum, they're too good to throw away. Me, I'd build a bonfire and set light to the lot of them.

It's my big cousin Senga's twenty-first, which is why I'm wearing the party dress. We're all crammed into my Auntie Jean's living room, and the adults are all red in the face and cheery with the drink. This is my first grown-up party, and I'm supposed to be pleased that I've been allowed to come and stay up past my bedtime. But there's nothing to do and nobody to talk to. I can't even torment Morag because she's not here. Auntie Betty made her stay at home because it's too late for a big jessie like Morag to be up, even though she's eleven and I'm only ten. Next time I see her, I'll tell her how great it was. She willnae know it's a lie.

I'm that fed up I've made myself a den. I'm sitting under the table with a tumbler of lemonade and a bowl of crisps I sneaked away when nobody was looking. I've never had crisps like this before. They're sort of square and very yellow and if you look at them really close up, they've got lots of tiny wee bubbles under the surface. They don't even taste like crisps. When I suck them, they sort of burst on my tongue and taste of cheese and salt, not potatoes. The bag they came in said, 'Marks &

Spencer Savoury Crisps', so I thought they'd be all right. I'm not really sure if I like them or not. But I'm bored, so I'm eating them just the same.

Somebody turns off the record player and now it's time for people to do their party pieces. Auntie Jean first, just as soon as she's finished telling off Uncle Tom for not refilling her rum and coke quick enough. She's always telling Uncle Tom off for something. I feel sorry for him. I thought it was only bairns that got picked on like she picks on him. I thought when you were a grown-up, folk stopped bothering you.

Anyway, Auntie Jean's got her rum and coke and she's away. Eyes shut, swaying a wee bit with the emotion. She always used to sing *Grannie's Hielan' Hame*, but lately she's taken to that Julie Rogers song, *The Wedding*. Maybe she's trying to tell Senga something. Her voice is rusty with fags, but she belts it out all the same. 'And I can hear sweet voices singing, Ave Mar-ee-hee-haa.' Dad says when God was handing out voices, Auntie Jean was in the lavvy. When she finishes, everybody whoops and cheers. I don't know why, unless it's relief because it's over.

Then it's my dad. I squirm around under the table so I can see him better. He plants his feet a wee bit apart and squares his shoulders in his good grey suit. I know what's coming. *The Road and the Miles to Dundee* is his song. Nobody else would dare sing it. Apart from anything else, it would just make them look stupid, because my dad's got a great voice. He's as good as Kenneth McKellar. Everybody says so. He clears his throat and out comes that sweet voice that makes me feel like I'm snuggled up someplace safe and warm.

> *Cauld winter was howlin' o'er moor and o'er mountain*
> *And wild was the surge of the dark rolling sea,*
> *When I met about daybreak a bonnie young lassie,*
> *Wha asked me the road and the miles to Dundee.*

He's on the last verse when everything goes wrong. Without thinking about it, I've eased out from under the table to hear better. And that's when that evil witch Auntie Betty spots me. My dad's just coming to the end of the song when she bellows like a bullock. 'My God, have you ett that whole bowl of crisps yoursel'? Nae wonder you've got all that puppy fat on you.'

I want to die. Instead of looking at my dad, everybody's looking at me. The last note dies away, and though a few folk are clapping, mostly they're eyeing up the yellow lemon dress straining at the seams. I can see them thinking 'Greedy wee shite' as clearly as if they had cartoon thought bubbles over their heads. I want to shout out and tell them I just look fat because it's not my dress.

There's a horrible moment of hush. Then suddenly my dad's feet appear in front of my face. 'Leave the bairn alone, Betty,' he says in a different voice from the one we've all been listening to. This one's hard and quiet, the one I know never to argue with.

But Auntie Betty's stupid as well as evil. 'Jim, I'm only speaking for her own good,' she says, and I can hear exactly where Morag gets her slimy ways fi'.

'Betty,' my dad says, 'You've always been an interfering bitch. Now leave my bairn alone.'

Auntie Betty flushes scarlet and retreats, muttering something nobody's listening to. There's a flurry of movement and Uncle Don launches into *The Mucking o' Geordie's Byre*. My dad drops to the floor beside me, says nothing, puts his hand over mine.

My hero.

Says I, 'My young lassie, I canna' weel tell ye
The road and the distance I canna' weel gie.
But if you'll permit me tae gang a wee bittie,
I'll show ye the road and the miles to Dundee'.

At once she consented and gave me her arm,
Ne'er a word did I speir wha the lassie micht be,
She appeared like an angel in feature and form,
As she walked by my side on the road to Dundee.

I'm off to university in a couple of days. I'm really excited, but I'm a bit scared too. I'm off to England. I've only ever been there twice before – the first time, a holiday in Blackpool when I was eleven, the second, my university interview. Both times, I felt like I'd been transported to another planet. Now my life as an alien is about to begin, and I can't wait to get away and dive into this new world. I can be anybody I want to be. I can make myself up from scratch.

But for now, I'm still trapped in who I've always been. This time next week, I'll be in the shadow of Oxford's dreaming spires, drinking coffee with intellectuals, talking about politics and ideas and literature. Tonight, though, I'm at Dysart Miners' Welfare for my cousin Senga's spree. She's marrying an Englishman. 'I don't suppose they have sprees in England,' I say to him.

'No,' he says. There's something about the way he says it that makes me think he's another one who's feeling like his life as an alien is only just beginning.

The show of presents is at the far end of the hall, a row of trestle tables covered in white paper, groaning under the weight of china, linen, glassware and the strange assortment of things people think newlyweds need for a proper start in life. There's a whole subsection entirely devoted to Pyrex casseroles. My cousin Derry whispers to me that Hutt's department store had a special offer on Pyrex last month, that's why there are 23 of them on display. 'Do you think they'll be able to swap them?' I ask.

'Christ, I hope so,' he says. 'Otherwise we'll all be getting Pyrex for Christmas.'

The demarcation lines are clearly drawn. The women sit at tables round the perimeter of the hall, leaving a space in the middle for the dancing. The men congregate round the long bar that occupies most of one side of the room. I'm already getting the hard stare from Auntie Betty and her cronies for standing with the men at the bar, drinking underage pints and smoking. Morag is staring wistfully across at me, like she wishes she had the nerve to come and join me and Derry and Senga's fiancé. But she won't budge. She hasn't got a rebellious molecule in her body.

The band's been playing a wee while now, and a few folk have been dancing, but nothing much is happening. 'Is it no' time for a wee song, Jim?' one of the other men asks my dad.

'Aye, you're probably right. I'll away up and have a word with the bandleader.' It's a grandiose term for the leader of the trio of accordion, drums and guitar that have been serenading us with a competent if uninspired selection of Scottish standards and pop songs from the previous decade. But my dad walks up to the stage anyway and leans over the accordionist, his mouth close to the wee bald man's ear.

When they finish their rendition of *The Bluebell Polka*, my dad steps up to the microphone. 'Ladies and gentlemen, the band has kindly agreed that they'll accompany anybody who wants to give us a song. So if you don't mind, I'll start off the proceedings.' And he's off. The familiar words float above the band and he treats us to his usual graceful rendition.

But tonight, I'm not in the mood. I'm not daddy's wee lassie any more. I'm a young woman on the threshold of her life, and I don't want to acquiesce quietly to anything. He finishes the song and, by popular demand, gives us an encore of *Ae Fond Kiss*.

By the time he gets back to the bar, Auntie Jean is up there, belting out *The Wedding* with all the smug complacency of a woman who has got the difficult daughter boxed off on the road to the aisle. My dad takes a welcome swallow of his lager and smiles at me.

I scowl in return. 'Does it not strike you as a wee bit hypocritical, you singing that song?' I say.

He looks baffled. 'What?'

'It's all about a man who takes pity on a lassie who's trying to get to Dundee. Right? He helps her. With no thought of anything in return. Right?' I demand.

'Aye,' he says cautiously. The last year or two have taught him caution is a good policy when it comes to crossing verbal swords with me. I've learned a lot from the school debating society, and even more from the students in Edinburgh I hang out with at weekends.

'And you don't find anything hypocritical in that?'

'No,' he says. 'He does the right thing, the fellow in the song.'

'So how come you won't pick up hitchhikers, then?' I say.

Game, set and match.

At length wi' the Howe o' Strathmartine behind us,
The spires o' the toon in full view we could see,
She said 'Gentle Sir, I can never forget ye
For showing me far on the road to Dundee'.

I took the gowd pin from the scarf on my bosom
And said 'Keep ye this in remembrance o' me
Then bravely I kissed the sweet lips o' the lassie,
E'er I parted wi' her on the road to Dundee.

I'm staying with my friend Antonia and her husband, who have a house on the shores of Lake Champlain, a long finger of water that forms part of the border between Vermont and New York State. Antonia and I became friends at Oxford, in spite of the difference in our backgrounds. She was a diplomat's daughter, educated at public school, born to privilege and position. And it didn't matter a damn because we were equals in the things that mattered.

We're having a good time. This feels like the life I've always wanted. My first book is due to be published in a week's time, I'm travelling the world, young free and single and I have appropriated Antonia's sense of entitlement with not a premonition of what might change that. I'm swimming in the chilly dark waters of Lake Champlain when it happens, though I'm oblivious to it the time. We come out of the water and run up to the house, our only thought how soon we can get dried off and settle in front of the log fire with a glass of good malt whisky.

It's the middle of the night when I find out my life has changed irrevocably. I drift out of sleep, woken by a distant phone ringing. I turn over and set my compass for unconsciousness when Antonia is suddenly standing in front of me, her face crumpled and distressed. 'The phone... it's for you.' I can't make sense of this but I roll out of bed and go downstairs anyway. Her husband is standing mute, the receiver held out to me.

The voice on the other end is familiar. 'I'm awful sorry, lassie,' says Uncle Tom. 'It's your dad. He was playing bowls. He walked out on the green to play the final of the tournament. And he just dropped down dead.' His voice keeps going, but I can't make out the words.

Later that day, I'm walking in the rain in Central Park. Antonia has organised everything; a flight from Burlington to New York, then a night flight back to Scotland via Paris. I've packed my bags, but I've still got four hours to kill. So I buy my first packet of cigarettes in years and walk. Smoke and rain, good excuses for a wet face and red eyes. The dye in my passport runs as I get soaked to the skin; for years, I can't escape remembrance of this day every time I travel abroad.

It's taken them a couple of days to track me down, so I don't get back till the day of the funeral. The crematorium is packed, standing room only for a man so many people loved. The minister's doing a good job – he knew my dad, so he understands the need to celebrate a life as well as mourn a death. He actually makes us laugh, and I think of my dad watching all this from somewhere else and maybe realising how much his life meant.

Back at the house, after the formal funeral purvey, it's family only.

I'm in the kitchen with our Senga making potted meat sandwiches. I feel dazed. I'm not sure whether it's grief or jetlag or what. I'm taking the bread knife to a tall stack of sandwiches, cutting them into neat triangles, when Auntie Betty barges into the kitchen. She puts a hand on my shoulder and says, 'Are you awful upset about your dad, then?'

It's a question so crass I can't believe she's uttered it. I feel Senga's hand gently easing the bread knife from mine. Just as well, really. I stare mutely at Auntie Betty, wishing with my whole heart that it was her burned to ash instead of my dad.

Senga says, 'If you don't mind, Auntie Betty, there's not really room for three people in here and we need to get the sandwiches done.'

Auntie Betty edges backwards. 'Right enough,' she says. 'I just thought I'd come and tell you Simon's going to give us a wee song.'

Simon is the late baby, born when Morag was twelve. There has never been a child more beautiful, more intelligent, more gifted. Well, that's what Auntie Betty thinks. Personally, I prefer another set of adjectives – spoilt, arrogant, average. His thin, reedy tenor makes me yearn for Auntie Jean singing *The Wedding*.

'Aye,' Betty continues. 'He's going to give us *The Road and The Miles to Dundee*.'

I feel the blood draining from my face and the room loses focus. I push her out of the way and head for the front door, grabbing my jacket as I run. I tear from the house and jump into the car, not caring that I've had more whisky than the law allows drivers. At first, I'm not thinking about where I'm going, but my heart knows what it needs, and it's not my cousin Simon murdering my father's favourite song. I drive out of town and up into the hills. These days, you can drive almost all the way up Falkland Hill. But it didn't use to be like that. The first time I climbed it was the night before my sixth birthday. My mum wanted me out of the way so she could ice the cake, and my dad took me up the hill. It felt like a mountain to my child's legs; it felt like achievement. We stood on the top, looking down at Fife, my world, spread beneath our feet like a magic carpet.

Now, twenty-six years later, I'm here again. I want music. I finger the tape of my dad singing that one of his friends from the Bowhill People's Burns Club's concert party pressed into my hand as I left the crematorium. 'I made a wee compilation for you,' he said, his eyes damp with sorrow.

But I'm not ready for this. Instead, I slam the Mozart Requiem into the tape player, roll down the windows, turn the volume up full and stand on the hillside, staring out at the blurry view. I know the world is still at my feet.

The difference is that today, I don't want it.

So here's to the lassie, I ne'er can forget her,
And ilka young laddie that's listening to me,
O never be sweer to convoy a young lassie
Though it's only to show her the road to Dundee.

I'm thirty thousand feet above somewhere. I don't much care where. I'm flying to a festival to read from my work in a country I can't point to on a map. I'm flying away from the ending of the relationship I never expected to die. My life feels ragged and wrecked, my heart torn and trampled. It's as if the last dozen years have been folded up tight like tissue paper, turning into a hard lump that could stick in my throat and choke me.

I take out the book I've brought as a bulwark against the strangling gyre of my thoughts. Ali Smith's *The Whole Story and Other Stories*. I chose it deliberately in preference to a novel because I can't actually concentrate for long enough to manage more than bite-sized chunks.

A few stories in, I start reading one called *Scottish Love Songs*. It's magical and strange, tragic and funny, but most of all, it's an affirmation of the power and endurance of love. A bitter irony that I'm far from immune to. I'm bearing up well until the pipers in the story start playing *The Road and the Miles to Dundee*. Then I become that person that nobody wants to sit next to on the plane, the one with the fat tears rolling down her cheeks and the trumpeting nose-blowing that shocks even the screaming toddler in the next row into silence.

Two nights later, I'm lying in a bed in a city in the middle of Europe, limbs entangled with a virtual stranger. We're in that charmed place between satisfactory sex and the recognition that we probably don't have much to say to each other. I don't know why, but I start to tell her about the incident on the plane, and all the other memories associated with *The Road and the Miles to Dundee*. I don't expect much response; I recall once writing that casual lovers are like domestic pets – you can almost believe they understand every word you say.

But I'm pleasantly surprised. She shifts her long legs so she can more readily face me, pushes her tawny hair out of her eyes and frowns in concentration. At one point, when I pause, searching for the next point in the narrative, her hand moves to my hip and she says, 'Go on. This is interesting.'

I come to the end of what I have to say and she traces my mouth with a fingertip. 'Sad,' she says. Then shakes her head. 'No, strike that. Sad's too small a word. Too simple.'

But simplification is what I need. I suddenly understand that I want to strip away every association from this damn song except the sweetness of my father's voice. I don't know how to express this, but somehow, this woman grasps the essence without being told. 'It's a love song,' she says. 'You need to remember that. You need to replace the bad connections with good ones.'

'Easier said than done,' I sigh. I want to change the subject, so I choose something else to occupy our mouths. It's sweet, this encounter. It doesn't touch the core of my pain, but it reminds me that sooner or later, there will be mitigation.

Three days later, we detach from each other in the departure lounge, heading for different provincial airports. We've made no plans to meet again, mostly because I've headed her off at the pass every time.

I'm only home an hour when there's a ring at the doorbell. I'm not expecting anyone, but of all the people I'm not expecting, the florist would come high on the list. But she's there, presenting me with a dozen yellow roses. Puzzled, I check they're really for me and not the woman next door. The florist smiles at my distrust. 'No, they're really for you,' she says. 'There's a card. I hope I got the spelling right.'

I close the door and walk slowly through to the kitchen. I wriggle the card free from the cellophane wrapping and tear open the envelope. I read the words, and I can't keep the big silly smile from my face. '*O never be sweer to convoy a young lassie, Though it's only to show her the road to Dundee.*'

The phone's ringing, and I have a funny feeling it's going to be a voice asking for directions.

Katherine McMahon

Origami

We crumple bedwards,
like grateful paper, corners
coming in to touch;

deft and cosy sheets –
mountain fold and valley fold;
shoulders, elbows, knees;

our bellies curve a
complex rise – softened creases
folded and unfolded;

hands and necks become
reverse folds, pleats, which we build
from the familiar

starting furrows into
varied lovely things – roses,
frogs, waterbombs, stars.

Cartography

Sometimes when I'm in the car
people forget how to get where they're going
she tells me, brows furrowed like horizon lines
and roads that end sooner than you realise.
I don't want to be that person –
someone who makes people forget to be sure
of themselves,
like when you get sat-nav
and can't read maps any more
in case you're wrong, or even
just a little less direct.

I sigh.
Me, I've already spent too much time praying
to the unheeding saints of green lights
to get me somewhere in time,

and right now her eyes glow darkly in candles
like thick forest with the sun behind
and I can only imagine different gods –
the kind who deal in earth instead of tarmac,
rivers instead of roads,
and I want to say that maybe it's just because
she makes people feel safe to wander –
but somehow I don't.

Instead I stay quiet
and try to communicate it by tracing
all the parts of her face with my gaze,
treading new paths in my synapses,
roaming across her bones,

our eyes lighting each other
like beacons
saying someone's coming home.

Pride

I am proud of my belly button.
I am proud of my strong legs for marching
and the soft skin of my arms,
I am proud of the hairs on my chest.

I am proud that my body spells out
us as well as *me*,
that my skin sparkles nerves to feel
and elasticity to keep my organs in.

I am proud that we touch
across all the broken things.

I am proud that we build ourselves umbilicals
when our originals are cut;
I am proud that we have worked
out how to raise our bodies
into barricades, to link
our skins in salt defiance.

I am proud of what we share,
inherited from all those seasons of resistance –
there is a reason
that I look so queer:
I am proud of the creases in my loose boy's shirt
and the waistband of my boxers, sewn
with strength inside
like coins hidden for adventures.

I am proud that this is mine.
It was passed to me through fences
made of cruel barbed wire, by people
who I've never met, who died before,
who called me
sister.

I am proud that we write our visible
with ink from scavenged terms,
mix it into colours that had no names 'til now,
tattoo them into places
we didn't know we even owned.

I am proud that we build homes
of reinvented meanings,
bricks baked in fires of needing
each other, with saws
of every snide remark
and hammers of their fists,
reversed to serve us,
and gardens of our newly grafted
family trees, our orchard fingers
blushing green.

Our pride is here.
We hold it like lions
hold their cubs –
with gentle teeth
and fierce paws.

Paul McQuade

Per Aspera Ad Astra

There is something unreal about the night. Something not quite there about it. As if the world is painted on; the sky too blue, the moon too bright. He thinks, for a moment, he can see brushstrokes on the sky, as he and Tom walk up the mountain trail, toes numbing in the chill pack of earth.

'It must be a big change for you,' Tom says.

'Yes,' Willard says, and immediately regrets it. Too formal. 'I mean, yeah. It's not Baltimore, I'll tell you that. It's nice, though. I don't think I've ever seen this many stars before.'

'It's not normal here either. Tonight's special. Some sort of meteor shower.'

'Why so many stars if it's a meteor shower?'

'They're going to fall.'

'All of them?'

Tom clears his throat and speaks in a different voice. Will attempts to translate.

'Letting white bouquets of perfumed stars snow through his half-closed hands?'

'Something like that. With a bit more poetry. It's Mallarmé.'

Willard has no poetry in him. He can arrange the words, grammatically, place them in cases, let each element discover its order: gendered, plural, in agreement. But he has no poetry. Every time he translates an assignment, his lecturers write the same comment: 'Technically accurate but lacking in poetry.'

Tom, on the other hand.

Tom has poetry in him. Willard sees it course in each vein, night-blue, on his forearms where the sleeves of his sweatshirt are rolled up despite the bite of the October air. Willard likes to think that one day their professors would see the same thing in him: that same sharp spark of life that seemed to constitute Tom at the core.

To Willard, Tom is poetry. Something untouchable, utterly ungraspable, something lost in the gesture toward it.

Seeing something in Willard's expression, Tom says, 'Relax, Will. It'll come.'

Willard shrugs, embarrassed, pleased. When Tom calls him 'Will' he feels as though a better version of himself has been given back to him.

'I hope so,' Will says. 'But I doubt it. It's okay. Europe needs translators for the boring things right now, as it rebuilds. It doesn't need poetry. It needs bureaucrats. And I may be a terrible poet but I think I can manage to be a passable bureaucrat.'

'That's an awful thing to say,' Tom says. 'Times like this, people need poetry more than reason. Reason is never enough. And you're no bureaucrat, Will. You're destined for great things. I can feel it.'

Will wishes the night were darker. The heat in his cheeks meets with the cold air. His skin feels alive with electric jolts.

'Not much longer to go now,' Tom says. 'When we get to the top, there's a flat area, all laid out, almost deliberate. We'll have a great view of things. Then we can bust out the hooch.'

The air is getting thinner the higher they climb. Will is finding it harder and harder to breathe the closer they get to the stars.

*

He is moon-crazy, moon-sick, positively lunar. Voices scream in his ear. They shout flight plans, turn back, arrest, arrest. But he is not in full possession of himself. Something else moves his arms. He flies the jet over the black water of back country, over the living islands of cities, live with electric light, and still he flies, out from their constellations, out to the star-dots, the little hamlets, the places in the mountains. He flies over the mountains. The voices in his ears tell him to stop. But another voice commands him, it says: *fly, soar, be weightless.* The voice comes from the hole in the sky where the moonlight pours in. And beneath it, another voice whispers, echoing not in the delicate cocchlea but in the thick columns of spine and tibula, through rib-cage and carapace and organ. It says: *velocity, violence, descent.*

The pilot maintains the course he must not: he flies north, toward the border. There are more stars tonight than usual. They watch, nonplussed, pulsing, as he communes with their fat mother. The moon speaks and he listens.

*

The world appears in a circle. Appears and disappears. All that matters remains in the glass, while the dross, the detritus, the deadening world, is sliced off with a clean crescent. The only thing left is the stars, the moon. This is all that matters to Edward.

He knows that this is not the case with other people. But Edward does not care for other people. They are too temperamental, too transient. He has learned, in his sixty-five years, not to take notice. They are on the other side of the circle, these impermanents. He has better company.

Cassiopeia and Orion glow. Edward does not look at the stars beneath Orion's belt, out of politeness. Two dogs assume their positions: major, minor. A swan streaks across the vast blackness of sky.

And others. Other stars. New ones. New friends. They are blue-white. They burn fiercely, that much closer to the earth. The telescope feels warm on Edward's cheek.

These other stars are not good enough for Edward. They are too volatile. In such a rush. They are not immortal as the stars he knows are.

But they are beautiful all the same, these other stars.

He waits for them to fall.

*

The starlight brings the headstones to life. She notes the cruel shapes time has worn in them, where the rain has taken the names.

As she walks the path, she wonders if they remember him, his friends. She supposes they must. But not the same way. They were younger. It is easier to bury things then. There is so much to come;

one loss can be suffered. She supposes they have new friends, don't talk about him any more, let him be dead. At her age, each loss is final. There is no replenishment, no recovery. No time left to heal the wounds.

She doesn't blame them, not really. He was their friend. He was her son. It is different.

When she reaches the grave, she puts her hand on it. A part of her always touches the headstone when she talks to him. She imagines her voice travelling through the marble. Down into the earth. And not to a coffin, or a corpse, but to a cavern, where Robbie is secure in a secret hideaway filled with books and candles and a radio. The cavern is perfectly spherical; her voice fills it like air in a balloon. He has not aged, there. Twelve years and he is still the same age, down there, in that place where only she sees him.

'Hi, honey,' she says. 'I know it's late but there's a meteor shower tonight. I thought it'd be nice for us to watch it together. I'll describe it to you. We'll make a night of it.'

She sits herself down on the night-damp ground and presses her back against the stone. She feels the gaps, the letters of his name, against her back, and feels comforted that, for tonight, at least, someone remembers him.

*

The stars are closer up here. They blare blue-bright. The words seem closer, too, as if with just the faintest extension, a finger in the right direction, he could touch what he wants to say. But the Jameson is an amber flare. And the more he pushes to touch them, the further the words slip from his fingers.

He drums his legs against the log beneath him. The sound echoes through it. He imagines beetles in the hollow, crawling. Starless and cold. He shivers.

'You all right there, buddy?' Tom asks. Tom rubs Will's arm to warm it.

The sky is ablaze with blue points. Will wants to trace lines through them. New ones. Not the old constellations, not the archer in the sky, arrow destined to never land, but an octopus, a beehive, a snowflake. New constellations. New words.

Tom is talking about his first time up on the hill.

'It was the fourth of July,' he says. 'And a bunch of us, all first years, came up here to watch the fireworks. We had three six-packs of the same local beer, same kind and everything, each of us thinking we were so original, doing the exact same thing.' He laughs. 'But it was great, you know. Really great. I've lived in this town my whole life and I didn't know about this place.'

He gestures around him to the grassy shelf, and behind, to where the plateau meets the cliff face at a right angle, as if a great axe had cleft the mountain, takes in the few tough weeds managing to grow here and there. Purple wildflowers undaunted by the altitude.

'We call it the auditorium,' Tom says. 'And these are the best seats in the house.'

He slaps the log. It makes a hollow sound. Will shivers.

'What was it like growing up somewhere so small?' Will asks.

'I don't know. It was normal. You grew up in a city so you can't imagine what it was like; I grew up here, so it's all I know. It was normal. I didn't know there was anything else.'

'And now?'

'Now what?'

'Would you leave?'

'Well,' Tom says. 'I have left. I lived in France for two years, one after high school and one for research when I got into the programme.'

'And?'

'And it's not so bad here, you know. Sure there's not a lot to do. But you learn to tap into it.'

'Tap into what?'

'I don't know. Something about it. An energy. That's wrong. It's right but it's wrong. *Désolé, j'ai la tête à l'envers.*'

Tom translates in his head: Sorry, I have my head on backwards. He is missing something, he is sure. The poetry of it. He can't think of the right words to say. And the more he talks the more he circles round it, round something he wants to say but can't put into words. His head in a whirlpool; he wants to touch the words at the gap round which everything spins.

There is something dangerous about the words. He cannot quite get at them, but each time he comes close he gets the flash of an image: a rock; a skull; a push from the hillside; sharp snapping bone; saliva. And yet he pushes for them, strives towards them. The words will change everything. He knows that much.

Perhaps it is not words, but death he wants. He has read enough books by suicidal Europeans. Out windows, in bathtubs. They all chose to die. But what Willard desires is is not choosing, not dying, but something like a dive, like a push over the edge. And this, he feels, is something completely different.

He wonders if the stars feel it too.

He looks down, out over the town below, where lights blur and shimmer at a distance. There are not so many this night. The stars are too bright; the night too blue. It is to this sleepy little town that the stars will hurtle. Will is beginning to think he understands why.

*

Casey is looking at the frog. The frog looks back. She moves her head to the left, putting her hand on her desk, leaning back in her pink spinny-chair. The frog's eyes seem to follow her as she moves. It lies there, body unfolded like the mouth of a lily, viscera pulsing in the light. Its face is expressionless. It waits, without feeling, for Casey to look inside it.

Lung, liver, pancreas, stomach, gall bladder, oesophagus, small intestine. Large intestine, urinary bladder, cloaca, anus. Viscera. These are the words she has to remember.

She doesn't want to go to school tomorrow.

It isn't the frog. It's Christine. Christine Madison. That bitch.

It's always something. It's her hair, it's her skin, it's the clothes she wears. Everything comes under Christine's scalpel-tongue: lung, liver, pancreas; zit-face, split ends, lesbian shoes.

Christine is an ugly person. Christine is beautiful.

Casey wants to hate her. But she doesn't. She wants something from Christine, something she can't quite say. Acceptance, maybe. But that isn't quite right. Something else she doesn't know how to get. Something that makes strange muscles in her stomach levitate.

Casey doesn't want to go to school tomorrow.

The frog's eyes follow her around her room.

*

The plane can't go any faster. But it must. He is almost there. Things are almost at the right velocity. Wind and stars and mountains are a jumble. The world moves along strange planes. All of it. At once. *Now.*

*

Tom keeps talking. He is afraid if he stops, he might actually say something.

He switches into French, here and there, *le et la, ce et ça.*

It is easier when he switches. He feels himself pulled toward it, the thing inside him being pulled up by it, like a tree in a gale, hauled up by the roots.

But why Will? He likes him, sure. But they haven't known each other that long. And yet. And yet he feels strangely close, strangely intimate, strange. And the whiskey is as bright as the stars. It burns in him. And his head feels loose. Everything a bit untangled. And it is in the way. It is in the way of a deeper closeness: like a rock blocking a wellspring. And he knows. He knows he has to find the words, has to bring them out. The truth, not poetry. Which is something much harder to accomplish.

'I'm really glad we came up here tonight,' Tom says.

'I wonder when they're going to start falling,' says Will.

*

They are in the way, these other stars. Bright young things. They are in his way.

He is sure that tonight is the night he does it. When he finds one without a name, a little piece of gold stuck to the black fabric of space. One that will last. One that will persist, even when he is gone. One that will bear a name he chooses.

But the sky is full of these bright blue things. The air is too blue. Day-blue. How is he meant to find a new star in all that light?

He stares through the lens. His friends are background; the blue dots take up all the space. They look at him sullenly, ask him to name them. And he could. He could name each and every one of them, and in the naming, know them. But they will fall. Soon. And Edward has had enough of impermanent things. He is sixty five years of age, after all. He is retired. He no longer has to deal with it. He wants only the great celestial spheres. The ones that burn without burning out. He wants a new star to name. A new galaxy of infinite beings of infinite duration. Aglow. Forever.

For the first time, he understands why people wish on falling stars. *Fall*, he wishes.

The blue stars are excited. It seems they have listened to him. They begin to jostle, jiggle, begin to glide. Edward watches through the telescope: fifteen of them — one, two, three, yes, fifteen — in the circle. They begin to swerve. They seem dangerously close to crashing into one another. Two glide by, the space of a thin breath between then. They are almost touching. Almost. Then they stop.

And begin to fall.

*

The gravestone is cool against her back. She has wrapped warm for the weather, a thick wool jumper under a cable-knit cardigan, an old red parka in case it rained, you could never tell with the weather up here. And the night seemed odd to her as she had left the house. As if, at any moment, it could change. Surge down a different path.

'It's beautiful, honey,' she says. 'All the stars. They're so blue. It's as bright as day out here, but all silvery. And the air's crisp and lovely. Has a bite to it. Clean as teeth through an apple.'

She unscrews the thermos of hot cider she has brought with her and fills the lid. Vapour uncoils into the night air. She imagines him down there, in his glowing little cavern of smooth walls, her voice gliding down them, around them, amplified by the shape of it. She wishes she could lower some cider down for him. Tonight is so special. Once in a lifetime. She wishes he could see it.

'Not long now,' she says.

But he can't see it. Not really. She knows this and she doesn't. She knows it and refuses it, buries it deeper than graves. This is how she has lived these years since his death. She tries to think of it as a death, but it wasn't. She knows this, she doesn't know it, she refuses it. He was taken. Not by god but by man, men, boys. Just boys. Just boys, just monsters. That's what they were. She does not know their faces. They are faceless to her, though she has tried, when the police would not, to find the people who killed Robbie. Just some boyishness, some boisterousness gone wrong.

They figured there was a fight. About what, they didn't know. Veiled references to the way Robbie was, not quite man enough for the policemen, who acted as if this whole thing had been inevitable. There had been a fight. They had beaten Robbie up. One of them had kicked him so hard in the side that his spleen had burst – *ruptured*, said the medical examiner. *Rupture*.

She had looked it up later, to know exactly what had happened. The dictionary in the house – from somewhere she didn't know where, just the kind of book that appears, one day, on a shelf – had said: *To break or burst suddenly; to cause to break or burst suddenly; to suffer a bursting; to breach or disturb. An instance of breaking or bursting. A breach of harmonious relationships.*

*

What does it mean to be drawn to something that hurts?

Did the frog long for the scalpel?

Why does she want to be closer to Christine?

Casey spins in her spinny-chair. The frog lies open on her desk.

*

'I,' Will begins.

'Can I tell you something?' Tom asks. The words fall back down Will's throat. He nods his assent.

Tom clears his throat.

'I killed someone,' he says. 'When I was younger. I didn't mean to. We were just picking on this kid. And. I don't know. I kicked him too hard. He just stopped breathing. I didn't mean to. But I did. I did.'

Will is silent. He looks at the ground, studies the shape of their feet. The white toe of Tom's sneakers glows blue in the starlight.

'Did you go to jail?'

'No. Our parents – it was a bunch of us – took care of it. They said they came to some sort of understanding with the boy's mom. That she and the police agreed that it shouldn't ruin our lives.'

Out across the auditorium, stars continue their glittering drift.

'Why are you telling me this?' Will asks.

'I don't know,' Tom says. 'I don't. It just... I feel like I had to. Like I had to tell you before we could move forward.'

'Forward to what?'

Tom laughs.

'I don't know,' he says. '*Per aspera ad astra.*'

Will cannot translate it. And he cannot find a response. He stretches for the words and they are not there.

*

The stars plummet. He soars among them, through white trails of light. The plane seems to drift. The dial on the accelerometer still trembles in the red range, but speed has lost its meaning now. There is only this slowing down, this light, this moment.

He hits the button. The glass sheath opens.

Out, out among the stars.

*

The stars stream down like party favours. Bright strips of crêpe-paper, slowly unfurling, rolling down to earth. They make a cracking sound, like someone unwrapping a present.

She leans her head back on the gravestone and looks up.

'Oh honey,' she says. 'You should see it. It's like the fourth of July.'

*

Casey tries the new words out loud. They feel different when she speaks them. They seem to linger in the air.

'Aorta,' she says. 'Pancreas.'

Then she says: 'I hate Christine Madison.'

Then she tries: 'I love Christine Madison.'

As she hears herself speak these sentences, she realises that both of them are true.

A bright light pours through the window; the words are caught up in it, for one bright moment, for one brief flash. Then the light takes everything.

She goes to the window. There is an aeroplane in the back garden, half stuck in a tree, half burning a hole in the ground. The trees at the edge of the garden are ablaze. The fire crackles and roars, but it seems like such a little thing next to the light of all the stars. She looks up into them. For a second she thinks she sees a darker patch of air, almost human-shaped, falling through the blue light.

The starlight is a painful, bug-zapper blue.

The light consumes love and hate and viscera.

*

'Do you hate me?' Tom asks.

The stars fall. Some peel down, others spark out in seconds. On and on, until the last of them streamer down to signal the end of the party. Willard and Tom watch the new stars plummet. When they are done, only the old ones remain; their familiar faces, tails, bows, and amphorae; their dull, brassy sheen.

Will tries to find the words but they are not there – what would he say? That in the face of all these stars, all this talk, all this intimacy on the mountain, one death seems meaningless? That as much as he is disgusted, another emotion inhabits the same space, separated, barely, by something thin as a page?

The words he wants will not come so he makes do with the ones he has. These other words aren't a proper fit, but they don't seem quite improper either. Will thinks he understands, then, something about the nature of poetry.

'It really was a beautiful night,' he says, and places a hand on Tom's thigh.

Alison Napier

In Stitches

'There it is again. Of course you can hear it.' Rebecca's voice rose steadily with the constant repetition of an unwanted truth.

'I can't hear anything.' Matthew sighed and stared straight ahead, endless sweeps of rain and spray slewed across the windscreen.

'The rattle. Listen, you do hear it, you're just saying you don't so you don't have to do anything about it. It could be a wheel. Or the exhaust.'

'I don't hear it because there isn't a rattle. Not that kind anyway.'

'How can you not... did you see what that bus did? I thought they had speed limits. Why are you slowing down? You've heard it, haven't you? Why are we stopping? You can't stop here, most accidents happen on the hard shoulder.'

'Please Becca. I'm stopping because you want me to fix the rattle. The rattle that is being caused by the plates, the mugs and the bloody cutlery that you shoved into a Tesco's carrier bag and rammed in the cupboard above the fridge. I need to pack them away properly'.

Matthew slowed to a halt on the hard shoulder. He sat for several seconds, his hands still gripping the wheel, feeling the jolt of every vehicle that hurtled past, watching lorries and buses racing towards him in the rain-spattered wing mirror. His head was pounding. He was waiting for the gap in the traffic that never came. Rebecca was staring through glass that was smeary from a faulty wiper. Neither spoke, the grey motorway drizzle obliterated the road ahead and the windows steamed up inside.

'I'll go,' she said eventually. 'I'll wrap them in tea-towels and wedge them under the seat.'

'OK,' said Matthew. He felt exhausted. He tried to picture the next ten days but couldn't. Rebecca opened the passenger door and the noise of a thousand combustion engines rushed in; she left the door open and Matthew leant across to close it but was held firm by his seat belt.

He started to fumble with it but stopped. He couldn't be bothered. And the back door was open now anyway and an additional layer of roaring traffic filled the little campervan. He wound down his window and stretched out to wipe the mirror with his index finger. A fine mist settled on his sweater and the juggernauts thundered past, uncaring.

The campervan was not new and was certainly not a Motor Home. No espresso machine, no swivelling seats. It looked like a flatbed Fiat van carrying the wrong half of a caravan on its back. Matthew's colleague Faye had lent it to them. Faye was experimenting with decluttering. Her former husband had moved to Spain, a criminal in Faye's eyes, though there was little hope of extradition. His new partner was called Marcus and Faye was dealing with this by writing a radio play – as yet uncommissioned – about a woman with an AWOL husband. The first scene was set in a tapas bar in Barcelona and featured much throwing of patatas bravas. She had assured all her friends that they would feature prominently.

'That should stop it. Oh, and the yoghurt's tipped over in the fridge and dripped onto the bacon. Why is everything so bloody small? I'm bringing it inside to keep it upright.'

Rebecca was still talking as she closed the back door and returned to the passenger seat. She placed the yoghurt on the floor, balancing it between her feet

'I really hate this road,' she said. 'Where have you put the map?'

'Back seat. But, hang on, I don't know, let's stick to the route we decided.'

But Rebecca was opening her door again.

'Christ!' she yelled. A large dollop of creamy yoghurt covered one of her navy canvas shoes and spread unhurriedly across the worn carpet and under the seat.

'Jesus bloody wept.'

Matthew started the engine as the door slammed. He signalled, pulled out into the traffic, not speaking, while Rebecca jabbed angrily at the floor with a handful of tissues.

Twenty minutes later he glanced across, and as he moved into the slip road for the motorway exit he could hear the crockery starting to rattle again.

*

Anna rolled another cigarette. She was sitting on a battered wooden chair outside her caravan. Dried yellow lichen and peeling silvery bark decorated the log that served as a table, on which balanced an open bottle of Californian wine, a tumbler, and a commemorative tobacco tin, dated Christmas 1914, rescued from a garage sale. Anna cherished it as if she herself had prised it from the mud and blood of the Somme.

She loved this time of year; days getting shorter but still mild enough to sit out in the evenings, gentle autumn light catching the dying leaves, black branches braced for the westerly gales that inevitably raced in from the Atlantic, stripping the trees and sending the last of the holiday makers retreating back to their homes in the towns and cities, homes that did not need tethering with ropes and concrete blocks.

The caravan was old and built in an age with lesser ambitions but more imagination, a time that was happy with curves and skylights, pre-dating the lines over which the winds streamed, the apartments on wheels with no jolts or tremors, no rocking and rolling in the night. Anna believed that a home should creak and sway with the seasons. The elements and the draughts and the drips were welcome to slip through the cracks; the sealed tomb would come soon enough. She shivered, pulling her cardigan tighter round her shoulders.

Anna was a professional hat maker. She did not use 'milliner' in case she was mistaken for a supplier of fascinators for weddings. Her hats appeared in galleries, on picket lines and on front pages. They were rarely to be found on anyone's head for a prolonged period of time.

It was almost dark. She stubbed out her cigarette and glanced across the field to the gate. An odd-looking campervan had stopped in front of the cattle grid and a woman was climbing out to stare at the notice stapled to the post. The newcomers seemed annoyed and raised voices drifted incongruously across the sleepy no-man's-land of the near-deserted campsite. And while the woman looked around, trying perhaps to summon a fully-staffed reception area with supermarket, bar and restaurant, the campervan was driven across the rattling cattle grid more quickly than was advisable.

It paused, dithered, then crept across the damp grass and came to rest a few hundred yards from Anna's caravan, between the toilets and the water-tap. Meanwhile the woman was picking her way across the cattle grid as if over red-hot coals, shaking her head unbelievingly.

Anna watched them, aware that they would not have seen her caravan at the edge of the woodland. She smiled into the darkness and went inside.

The next morning Matthew woke at seven o'clock. His head pounded and his bladder ached but these were rare moments of solitude and privacy so he ignored the discomfort. Last night they had gone to the nearby Mare and Foal for a late meal and had drunk too much of the cloudy local cider as they tried to make themselves heard above the cowboy-clad Country and Western singer and the shouts of laughter from the men swaying at the bar.

An hour later Rebecca awoke to an engine-roar and a bang as someone thumped on the curtained window. She sat up, glaring at Matthew.

'Why didn't you wake me for heaven's sake.'

'I thought you'd want to sleep. Sorry.'

He twisted round awkwardly and pushed the van door open. A bored-looking man in denim was standing beside a quad bike writing in a notebook. It was the singer from the Mare and Foal. Matthew handed out a ten-pound note, and was about to say something when

Rebecca leant forward, explaining that they might move on sooner than planned. The man said, 'Whatever,' passed in a receipt and kicked the door shut. The quad bike roared into life and rattled back across the cattle grid.

Matthew groped for his clothes and manoeuvred his way out of the van, picking up a teatowel and failing to locate his flip-flops. He made his escape across the dew-damp grass to the concrete toilet block.

Alone, Rebecca dressed, brewed coffee and took it outside. She could see a woman dressed in black carrying large shiny boxes out of the wood and stacking them into a khaki-coloured jeep. She watched her until the jeep shot past the campervan, and she raised her mug of coffee in salute. The woman replied with a mock military salute, and a brief grin as she clattered out of the field.

By mid-morning Rebecca and Matthew were drifting aimlessly round the local weekly market. Stallholders in woolly hats and fingerless gloves were offering sardines peeping out of slush-filled plastic tubs, muddy carrots with limp green fronds, multitudinous pig products, rabbit pies and poultry, timid watercolours, and precarious towers of chutneys and preserves. The market café was buzzing and the air was thick with the hot smell of fried onions. Free-range children in rainbow-striped sweaters and chunky leather boots were running around clutching hotdogs. Rebecca shuddered.

'I could get us some pork and make that casserole you like,' said Matthew.

'In that kitchen? You're kidding.'

Matthew ignored her and was about to head for the Gloucester Spot counter when Rebecca caught his sleeve.

'Look, that's her, the woman I told you about. Bloody hell.'

For Anna stood in the middle of a black, eight-foot high, top hat. The front had been cut away and inside, behind, in front, and on either side were shelves, each covered in rippling pale green silk. Her hats were arranged on every available space.

Rebecca experienced a wave of pure delight, immediately followed by irritation and an inexplicable envy. She wanted to attract Anna's attention but didn't know how to, or why. She hung back, then inched forward. Matthew hovered at her shoulder.

The hats were works of art, they were sculptures and statues, architecture and animation, they were newsreels and fairy tales. Anna herself was humbly clad in black jeans and a black roll neck sweater and a muted tapestry waistcoat. But on her head she wore a vast feather bed, a dozen layers of quilted mattresses in billowing milky white and butter cream with a tiny, tousled, but regally dressed figure, in gowns and flounces, dangling over the edge of the bed but determined not to fall off; and protruding from the side of the bottom layer of bedding was a small leaf-green sphere. The whole hat was eighteen inches high and wider than Anna's shoulders. She was playing a game with the children at the front of her stall.

'No, I don't think that's Jack, not in a ball gown, well not today, but yes, that might be a bean. But not a chicken nugget. Another guess.'

'It's the princess! With her frozen peas!' squealed a small child, jumping up and down.

'Can you imagine anything more pointless Matt,' whispered Rebecca, feeling guilty and treasonous, 'spending your life making three-D pictures for a Z-list celebrity to wear on her head for five minutes.'

But Matthew wasn't listening. He was staring, astounded and mystified, at the display. Anna's hats were stories; they were miniature slices of life. There was the inside of a McDonald's, complete with tiny servers in caps and polo shirts, and trays with red and white bun-shaped packages and cartons of fries. Each chip was hand-sewn, stuffed and stitched by the hatter. There was a tree-top protest in the redwoods of the Sierra Nevada, a miniscule wooden platform swaying high in the sequoias, cross-legged figures eating fruit, with a guitar and a megaphone and cards from well-wishers surrounding them, and rope bridges linking the tree trunks, intricately woven from green garden twine, and a Lilliputian TV crew on the ground.

There were hats of famous landmarks, from Stonehenge to the Golden Mosque with its shimmering minarets. Only the call to prayer was missing. There were glimpses of unsung street life; terraced houses near a railway siding in Darlington, fisher's cottages built side-on to the fierce lashing seas of the north Buchan coast. There were rolling wheat plains and mid-American prairies, and an oilrig dwarfing a Norwegian fjord. And then there was the World Trade Centre.

Matthew leant forward for a better look. Could you do that? Make a pointless frivolous hat about a crime scene? One tower seemed intact but was swaying slightly (or was that his imagination?) and the other had a plane, no, half a plane, that plane, meticulously stitched to the side. Tiny firemen in stiff yellow hats were frozen, sewn to the ground, looking up, turning towards, away, hands over faces, other little featureless faces were at the windows, the ground was rubble and litter and limbs.

He turned to Rebecca.

'She's sick. No one would buy these.'

'Oh but they do', she answered. 'Read the leaflet. She's famous. Anna Willowtree. Willowtree! Isn't that wonderful? Don't you love that name? The Mad Hatter!'

'She doesn't really call herself...'

'Don't be stupid. She's had exhibitions and commissions all over the world, she has a studio up in Edinburgh and a caravan on our campsite. That was her this morning. I saw her.'

Matthew watched Rebecca. Behind her earlier sneer about the woman, she had an alertness that he had not seen for many months, maybe longer. He was pleased. He didn't have to understand, and he suddenly felt positive about their holiday.

The market had got busier again and they turned away from the hats. A Morris Minor had driven into the square. Every available piece of paintwork was covered in colourful fridge magnets and children were sliding them around, making pictures.

'And what's the point of a fridge magnet,' he said hopefully, fumbling for a point of connection.

'I think they're cute. Don't be such a misery. Look, there's a TV crew at her stall now, I'm going to watch.'

She turned and headed back to the Hatter's stall. A woman in a tight leather skirt clutching a fluffy candyfloss microphone was interviewing Anna Willowtree. They could not hear what was being said but Anna was evidently enjoying herself, holding forth and gesticulating. She was wearing a hat depicting a toppling statue of Saddam Hussein, and around the wide brim lounged soldiers in desert fatigues and mirror shades. A child in dungarees with long curly blonde hair was wearing the Pea hat. It came down right over his, or her, eyes and was a prop for an impromptu game of blind man's bluff.

'I need a drink, a proper drink. Come on, before it rains again,' said Matthew,

But Rebecca didn't move. She could see that the interview was over and on impulse, waved to Anna. Anna saw her and waved back. The holiday had begun.

*

Later, as Anna packed her hats away, she frowned. She had recognised the woman from the campsite and watched her in the space of half an hour turn from an angry cynic to a mesmerised convert. It normally took longer than that. She had also noticed that despite the man's intense scrutiny of her hats he had not been captivated. Afraid and troubled maybe, but choosing to look away. Ah well.

Anna had tumbled into hats like Alice down the rabbit hole, by accident, in pursuit of a quite different adventure. She had fallen in love with a quilt maker, an American woman twenty years her senior, a seemingly solitary pioneer with a deep cigarette-scarred voice that scored its way huskily under Anna's skin. Bethany Harper MacColl. Anna had followed her to the ends of the earth, from coast to coast and pole to pole. Bethany Harper MacColl was the magnetic North which tugged Anna like a fish on a line and Anna veered towards her love, hypnotised, drugged, globetrotting in her wake, migrating with the swallows and the wild geese from the farthest faraway to the deepest south, supporting, admiring, rescuing, hovering, fetching and carrying and make-do and mending, stitching and folding and simply threading needles as her beloved's eyesight failed through age and whisky. They needed each other. They fought and bickered and found each other and held each other and vowed eternal devotion, time and time again.

Bethany made quilts and wrote erudite essays and articles which appeared in the New York Times and the Journal of American Folklore, and Anna watched and learned, the sorcerer's apprentice. She had never been happier. They were nomads sewing their way around the world in a Land Rover, the roof rack covered, like one of Anna's future hats, with aluminium boxes of materials and threads and cottons and papers; Anna climbed up the ladder and stacked them high, installation art, and bound them tight with the ropes that Bethany tossed her, both of them blinking into the sun.

The travels were for inspiration and for lecturing. Home was a cabin in Yosemite National Park. And so for years they continued, Anna learning her trade and hoarding ideas, designing hats when no one was looking and then showing them to Bethany Harper MacColl whose approval and astonishment Anna soaked up like water in a drought. But Bethany's husky voice became a hoarse whisper and her cough became unignorably bad and so she sought medical attention, but it was many months too late for meaningful intervention and so Bethany Harper MacColl died, aged fifty-nine. The Studio Art Quilt Associates commissioned a memorial piece which featured their hero, plus Anna, a log cabin and a pale blue Land Rover. It was exhibited at the Crooked Tree Arts Centre in Petoskey, Michigan for six months, then was donated to Anna along with a generous annual bursary.

Anna looked across her caravan at the hanging on the wall. It was fading where the sun caught it in the summer mornings, and the front wheels of the landrover were fraying. There was a cigarette burn on the roof of the cabin where Anna, drunk and crying, had fallen against it. It was the only item in her life that she would rescue in a fire. She raised her glass to the quilt, whispered, 'Still here,' and went outside to sit on her chair, roll a cigarette and watch the unstitching of the relationship in the campervan across the field.

*

It was day three of the holiday. Matthew had cooked dinner the night before and there had been a rare convergence of opinions over the pork steaks, resulting in a decision to stay in the area for a few more days. Anything less would suggest cowardice, that they hadn't given it a chance. They both had a horror of featuring unflatteringly in Faye's radio play.

Matthew had another hangover. He had purchased Calvados to add to his cream and cider sauce. After the meal he had finished the bottle and fallen asleep on the seating bench so that Rebecca had to wake him so she could make the bed up. He hadn't slept well, and had dreamt that he was wearing a glittering bowler hat covered in policemen who were abseiling down golden skeins of rope and hitting him on his temples with their tiny truncheons. His head hurt.

Rebecca on the other hand was uncharacteristically cheerful. She had made them bacon rolls and coffee.

'I saw that woman again. Hattie Willowherb or whatever she calls herself. She invited us over for a drink later on. I might go.'

Matthew glimpsed an opportunity for some uninterrupted sleep, and said,

'Yes, you go. I might listen to the football.'

That afternoon it rained again and Rebecca flicked through a novel. Matthew pretended to listen to the radio through headphones with his eyes closed. Rebecca switched the radio off and his expression did not change. At four o'clock, just as the rain stopped and the sky brightened, she removed a bottle of wine from the miniature fridge, crept out of the campervan and headed across the field.

Anna's caravan was awash with golden sunlight and the first fallen leaves of autumn were stuck to the walls, the windows and the roof like luxurious drops of amber. The sound of a solo flute drifted through the open door and a wisp of silver smoke floated from the stovepipe chimney. Far above the trees an earnest ragged arrow of wild geese, hoarse with instructions to the stragglers, hurried on south.

Rebecca was enchanted. She stood, bewitched, a child in a magic forest. She tiptoed forward towards the wooden chairs while the music meandered on. Was it Japanese? She pictured apple blossom and felt fleetingly tearful. She could see beautifully positioned clouds below the peak of a conical snow-tipped mountain. A perfect hat. She would say this to Anna Willowtree. Could that really be her name? 'Anna,' she would say, 'Anna Willowtree, will you make me a Mount Fuji hat, I saw it in a vision.'

The last note faded away and Anna appeared in the doorway.

'I like to practice when the light's like this,' she said.

Rebecca nodded, not understanding but wanting to.

'Do you play?'

'A bit of piano, but we've only got a keyboard now, its not the same,' said Rebecca .

'Music must only come from living things. Here. Feel the heat, imagine the tree, and how the air leaves my body and vibrates and whispers along its hollow branch.'

Rebecca thought there might be more to it than that but did as she was told. She felt mildly alarmed but the sensation was not unpleasant. Perhaps she ought not to have come. Mystical flute-playing milliners were outwith her social milieu.

Anna climbed back into her caravan as Rebecca placed her fingers over holes and blew across the lip as she had done over Coke bottles as a child. A note, breathy but still a note, emerged. She became aware of Anna again, standing again in the doorway, still watching her. Was she casting a spell?

Matthew didn't cast spells. He cast shadows ands aspersions. Soon he would be cast out, an exorcised demon, a moneylender from a temple, and cast off like yesterday's used skin, or the last ferry from the pier, or the final stitch of a scarf. While she, Rebecca, would triumphantly stride out of the wings and into her life. She had been miscast for too long.

'You've done this before, I think.'

Rebecca jumped, and opened her eyes. Anna was handing her a glass and reaching with her other hand for the flute. They exchanged these gifts, unsmiling.

*

Later, Matthew would break the spell. He would knock loudly on the old caravan door and call out, 'Hey!' in a forced jolly voice, and call out, 'Anybody there!' in a false cheerful voice and they would hear him leaping up and trying to see in the window; they would see the outline of the top of his head through the bamboo blinds. Rebecca would sit up, push guilty fingers through dishevelled hair where her head had lain on Anna's lap, where Anna's fingertips had soothed her forehead, and Anna's lips had touched her forehead, for then Anna's mouth had kissed her fingertips, one by one, light as a pianissimo, and Anna's tongue had licked as gently as ripples in a rock pool the ragged wild arrows between her fingers and her hands had hovered, crackling with lightning, untouching and healing over her stomach.

'Come in Matthew. It's not locked.'

Not locked? Dear God in heaven. Matthew.

But of course it was locked.

Anna waited for a whole minute and unlocked then opened the door and looked down on Matthew.

'We were listening to music. Come in and have a nightcap. Rebecca's in the toilet I think.'

And indeed she was, staring at herself in a small mirror framed in shattered slate, still tugging her fingers through her hair. She could hear Matthew laughing too loudly and Anna's confident voice, part Swedish, Dutch, American, who knew, asking him questions, reassuring him, 'Have a drink, Matthew,' and 'No, I've never had Calvados,' and 'No, I'll stay with the red I think', and 'Oh, here she is, Matthew tells me you're leaving in a couple of days.'

'I'm leaving? No. Yes.'

'You should stay a bit longer. I say I'm a hermit but it's a lie. Stay for a few more days. I'll show you the studio. Rebecca? Can we tempt you?'

Rebecca was looking at the quilt on the wall. She imagined climbing into the dusty Land Rover, her whole life in three crates on the roof, pushing the outsize gear stick up into first and roaring away. Everything could rattle and she would not care. She started to laugh, tried to stop but couldn't. Anna was showing Matthew the wooden flute but Rebecca simply laughed and laughed, leaning now against the Land Rover, with tears streaming down her face. She coughed and choked and laughed again. She was in stitches and she knew that she was going to be in Faye's radio play after all.

Allan Radcliffe

Outing

There's a queue six-deep at the coffee kiosk. Robert winces and shuffles into line, dipping into his jacket pocket for his wallet. I walk the length of the platform and sit down under the departures screen. A boy is standing a few feet away from me talking into his mobile in a language I don't understand. Spanish, maybe, or Italian. He's tall and dark with a slight bulge that hangs over his waistband, and he's beautiful. Head shaved down to the wood, pushed-out lips and high, sculpted eyebrows. An emerald scarf wound several times around his neck. Silver bangles that hiss up and down his arm as he chops the air with his free hand.

As I sit there, trying not to stare, he's joined by another boy who is less festively dressed but still stylish in a thigh-length navy coat with fair tousled hair and ginger stubble. He hands over a takeaway coffee and stands sipping from his own cardboard cup as shaven head completes his call. After glancing around for a moment to see who's watching, the tousled boy leans in and, quick as a wink, plants a kiss on his friend's shoulder. Still muttering into his phone, shaven head grins and they edge closer, letting their fingers touch.

A voice comes over the tannoy: our train is running ten minutes late. People are pacing around the platform, craning their necks in the direction of Edinburgh, too warm in their winter coats. I hitch myself back against the bench. There's a feel of spring in the air. The sky is turning white: it will be raining by the time we get to Perth. If the train doesn't arrive soon we'll have to take a taxi to the nursing home.

Robert is almost at the front of the queue. He keeps sorting through the coins in his hand, checking he has the right change. Every now and then he eases his weight from one foot to the other, blinking at the effort. You wouldn't notice if you weren't looking for it. I should have insisted on queuing for the coffees myself. The pain in his back kept him awake last night. I heard him creak out of bed at four in the morning, groping for his dressing gown, trying not to wake me.

Please stand well clear of the platform edge. Fast train approaching.

Shaven head has finished his phone conversation and now he and the tousled boy are facing each other, smiling and murmuring back and forth. As I watch, tousled reaches across and takes hold of the tasselled end of his friend's scarf and, without breaking eye contact, brings it up to touch the stubbly lower part of his face.

I look down at myself. I'm wearing a dark suit and a plain white shirt. My tie is grey: I'm a shade away from mourning. I sit there, imagining what I would look like with a glittering scarf against my best suit and I bark out a laugh that causes the two boys to frown over at me.

A couple of months ago, while clearing out Robert's mother's house in Perth, I came across an old photo stuck inside a Catherine Cookson novel: it showed Robert and me propped up against a poster-festooned wall at a party. Pale faces, flushed cheeks, both of us impossibly young. A splash of white across my forehead. Wilting eyes and a dopey half-smile. Even in the strong camera light you could see how beautiful Robert's eyes were: blue-green and wide to the world in an expression that was half surprise and half delight. One of his arms was strapped tight around my waist. The fingers of his right hand were curled around a pint glass, the purple liquid sloshing sideways.

Robert wore a Chinese peasant's hat over his sea anemone hair. I had on a t-shirt the colour of a New York taxi underneath my black jacket. We looked like kids who had stumbled across a fancy-dress box and just couldn't stop accessorising.

Standing in that half-emptied house I found myself wondering for the umpteenth time how Robert's mother rationalised her son's relationship. Over the years she has been in our house numerous times. She has seen with her own eyes the bed in the spare room with its creaseless bedspread. Yet, every Saturday afternoon, when we visit her in the nursing home, she makes the same introduction to whichever dour, gum-chewing adolescent shows us into her room: 'This is my son,

Robert, and this is his friend, Michael.' When Robert's father passed away she insisted on both of us sitting in the front pew at the funeral, one at either flank like a couple of bookends. But even now there are things she doesn't like talking about in front of me so I always end the weekly visitation in the reception area drinking hot chocolate from a plastic cup while she takes Robert through the indignities of her bathroom routine.

How long had she been using that photo as a bookmark? It must have been at least thirty-five years old. A friend of mine from work, I remember, was giving the party. Ruth? Yes, her name was Ruth. The picture was taken in her bedroom, I think, or it might have been her living room. Whenever I think back to those daft days when we were first together and still uncertain of one another, Robert and I are always in rooms. You could say all the romantic, exciting events of our life together have taken place indoors, never on beaches or by lakes or on the tops of mountains.

We met in a bar, one of those hole-and-corner places, a door in a blank wall down a close in the New Town. Robert had a bottle of lager in one hand, which he waved in the air as he talked to his friends. With every glass of vodka and coke I shifted closer until I found myself absorbed into Robert's group. His eyes contained a mix of bright blue and green that blazed through an uneven fringe of black hair. His way of standing – anchoring his legs with his knees slightly bent – allowed his upper body to move easily back and forward and side to side while he spoke. His energy seemed to flow up through his body from his feet as though he was being powered from an outlet in the floor. As the friends melted away Robert and I carried on chatting at a vacant table. If I sat my head in my hands and lifted my fingers up around my eyes I could blinker out the rest of the pub, pretend we were alone.

At chucking out time we walked up the road together. He asked me back to his flat in Bruntsfield for a drink and gave me a shy smile that told me he wanted to kiss me. I agreed, making my voice as casual as I could, and we quickened our pace, impatient to be out of the cold. We kept a manly distance on that interminable walk through the Meadows, striding with our hands stuck in our pockets. There was no way either of us would have stolen a kiss, not in the open air. To this day we have preferred to remain furtive. All our most intimate moments, the voiced fears, the planning, the arguments and the making up, have taken place behind closed doors. In the dark, we can spend hours on each other, engrossed in each other's nooks and crannies.

Robert is making his way down the platform, holding the coffees out in front of him as though they're flaming torches lighting his path. There's hesitation in all his movements now. Where age has made me pinched and bony he has filled out a little in the past couple of years.

We are a pair. These days, the colleagues and acquaintances that once referred to Robert with wary hesitancy keep asking when we're going to get married. The two of us laugh and bat away their questions or respond with quips about drag bridesmaids and the length of time it would take Robert's mother to walk him down the aisle. Later, in the quiet of our bedroom, we talk about venues and argue about which song we'd have for our first dance, but in an abstract way, knowing full well that we're unlikely to lift the phone and make arrangements. Who knows, perhaps one day we'll find ourselves at the registry office with a couple of witnesses, tourists collared from the Royal Mile. We'll email our nearest and dearest with the pictures: *There. Finally did it.*

I notice the appreciative sidelong glance Robert gives the young couple, who are standing silently side-by-side now, watching for the train. I move up the bench to give him room.

'Hope this train shows up soon,' he says. 'Mum'll be frantic.'

'She'll be okay.' I lift my face to the sun. 'It's turned out nice.'

He hands me a cardboard cup. 'They didn't have decaf.'

I set the cup down beside me on the bench. Robert lifts the lid off his coffee and wets his face in the escaping cloud of steam.

Shaven head has turned and is watching Robert and I over his boyfriend's shoulder. I wonder what he sees. Sometimes I catch myself in the mirror and don't recognise the skull staring back at me. Shaving without my lenses in I think I'm a spit for Lou Reed on the cover of *Transformer*: wavy hair in a Caesar cut and smudged eyes. A monochrome face, you might say. The close-up is less forgiving. The hair is still reasonably thick and curling at the edges, but the sideburns are creeping grey, and no matter how loose I let my face hang the lines seem deeper, more resolute than ever.

'Rob, put your coffee down.'

'What's that?'

'Humour me a moment, would you?'

He sets his cup on the ground, glancing around as he does so. The platform is full of people, standing or sitting, waiting for the train. I lean in and peck him on the lips. He pulls his head back, a smile perking up his face. The colour in his eyes is still so bright it almost hurts to look up.

'Right,' he murmurs. Then, when he sees I haven't finished: 'Oh, *right*.'

We shuffle into an embrace. He curls an arm around my neck while I take his free hand in mine. Our lips come together, and as I push deeper I feel him stiffen so I lift a hand and place it on his cheek. His hunched shoulders slowly relax. I go under, pulling him down with me. I feel his skin against me, still oddly soft, the breath whistling through his nose. I loosen my jaw and Robert does the same. I feel the shape of his lips as our heads move back and forth to a steady rhythm.

Above our heads the disembodied voice tells us our train will be the next to arrive on this platform. I have a hand in Robert's hair. I can feel the weight of the train under my feet as it rolls into the station, and as the two of us come up together I picture all the Saturday travellers moving to the edge of the platform, bracing themselves for the snap of the train doors, indifferent to the sight of two old men kissing in the open air.

Elizabeth Reeder

Wind Through Branches

Her dad hadn't been happy she was coming back, and the house wasn't hers for the asking, not after he'd contested her mom's will all those years ago, and won. But she'd asked, and he got rid of his brother George when she told him she'd nowhere else to go. Never a truer word spoken. It was a short fast road down, the way she traveled.

A clean light fell on the footpath, which snaked a way up from the narrow road. The car she parked wasn't hers and she hoped it wouldn't be missed before she could tuck it back into the long line of cars in some rich man's garage in the city.

No more than some stones thrown on mud, the path became dry dirt in the summer and then mud again this time of year, and the grimy stones barely gave her purchase on the steep hill. Behind her the occasional car slowed for the curve and passengers looked up at the houses on the hill that used to be fancy.

The white of the house was a decade old but just clean enough to stop the place looking decrepit. Only a year or two old, the freshly painted trim was the color an oak downed for a few seasons and then cut. The rip in the screen-door had been fixed and it looked like George had started to feel some pride in the place.

This small house – just two bedrooms, a kitchen and living room, and never big enough for the people who'd lived there – sat in a cluster of four similar houses. Even though the neighbors had been near and she used to be able to hear the start of lawnmowers, shouts, the clanking of pots and pans and the ring of forks on plates, she felt they never saw or heard her. The windows of the other houses were empty and black, the shutters closed; the summer season had come to an abrupt end with the first frost at the start of the week and it had scared off any stragglers. Woods, unmanaged and tangled, stood to the west and the sky beyond the trees held snow.

The porch stairs didn't creak when she walked up them and the paint hid, and almost seemed to have cured, the buckling extremes the seasons had created in the planks. Maybe George had even replaced a few of the steps, although it seemed unlikely and awfully hardy for the beerbellied asshole she knew.

Even with the new paint, she could see the place where her grandpa's watch had cracked the sill when the stroke took him. She'd been twelve and just fast enough to outrun him. When she touched the rent, she imagined it was warmer than the wood around it, still holding the sting of his fingers. The stroke killed him, although not right away, not fast enough. Her mom had died out back only a few months later, while pulling up her potatoes for a salad, in a thin vegetable plot which had long since been overrun by wildflowers. She'd been buried where she'd been struck down and the house had long lost any sense she'd ever lived there.

She took her time. The roughed up, damp cardboard box her dad had left beside the front door held the sum total of what he'd given her: candles and an axe for pilfering from the woods out back. He knew that without the axe she'd take to breaking and burning the furniture. She knew that the thick cluster of pines, poplar and aspens had become a park recently and if she was caught felling any trees, she'd do more time.

Inside there'd be no tv, nothing in the kitchen to eat, and so she sat for a long time on the porch listening to the cars pass on the road, listening out for a rogue neighbor to arrive. Her bag sitting at her feet was light: far too empty for a woman her age to be comfortable with, much less proud of. She didn't know how she was going to heat or light the place. She just knew she needed a roof for a little while and even her dad's roof would do.

The November night dropped fast and early and she sat waiting for the moon. She'd not been alone for years and she could barely breathe with the punch of it in her lungs, sharp on each intake, absent on the exhale.

She took a thick candle, pulled out her black lighter from the pocket of her jeans, and lit the wick. The unlocked door made no protest and the candle threw long predictable shadows over the same tacky furniture that had never been anything but cheap. Her dad used to make a good whack renting the house to incomers in a time and in a neighborhood where stand-alone houses were at a premium, houses of a certain age. Renters always hoped he'd sell; she always hoped he'd die. She still had her mom's will which said the house was hers, and she knew she could find a way to make it play, in the event of his untimely death. Eventually, people started to buy houses with inbuilt garages, and this row of houses with a 300 yard walk uphill from any car, became inconvenient. Her dad now lived in a new four-bedroom ranch house ten miles closer to the city with his less timid, money grabbing second wife, and his daughter had a feeling he kept the existence of this old place a secret.

To the left, over the hook inside the front door, hung a knitted hat and scarf, candy-striped, but wool and warm. And a pair of snow boots, many sizes too small for her, sat on the dirty, worn rug. Maybe he'd tried, maybe.

Between the living room and the kitchen a floorboard creaked when she stepped on it. She bent down, one board cracked, the other loose. A bit of hair there, the color of the dog they used to have. But longer, like a woman's.

On the kitchen table was a note from George, held down by a bottle of homebrew liquor. 'Make your stay brief, medicated.' She took the bottle by the neck, unscrewed it with an open palm and loosened her throat to take the burn. Behind her, across the cutting board sitting on the counter, lay a knife with the tip broken off, and a glass-fronted cabinet with chipped ceramic mugs in it.

She'd forgotten many things in her life, but this house was not one of them: the familiarity of the furniture, the creaking of the woods, and always an insistent whisper running through this place like blood through arteries, sap through trees. Her mom and grandpa had hated this place and that hate made her mom submissive, but just made her grandpa mean. Her dad and her kept close to the shadows and were protected. What she saw from there, she didn't share, and she gained the ability to see in the dark – to hear the dark, so clear and so pure.

She considered starting a fire but it felt so late she didn't want to waste the fuel. The chill would come in the middle of the night, the snow too, and she'd be tucked up and asleep. The grate was full of ashes and held a big singed pine log – signs of an untended or rapidly extinguished hearth. Her dad would never have abided such waste, he burned each fire down to its last and would sit, poking at it with a stubby stick held in his wide ashen hands. From the dark of the room, in his bourbon twisted voice, he'd tell her a story.

'A long time ago, at the turn of the last century, a man built this house. Since he was made out of mighty redwood himself and his beard was moss, he built it out of materials he knew well.' Her dad rubbed his chin that was, without fail, clean cut. 'He built this house so that one day he could be surrounded by his servants, the smaller, thinner trees. Then he went out into the wild with his sharp-clawed branches in which he harnessed the power of the wind, but one day he'll return and reclaim this house.'

'But we live here,' she'd said, 'we can't just give it to him.'

'You're right, we won't give it to him. He'll take it.'

The fire was embers, the room bristled too cold and her mom was three months dead. With his tall-tale, the forest was in the house now: they sat on the damp forest floor of lichen among snags and her dad leaned back against the trunk of a felled tree, closed his eyes and waited. Her dad used to hunt in these woods, never shooting to kill, but to injure fatally, and he'd track the animal right to the place it had chosen to die. Sometimes he'd wait for hours, late into the night, just to watch death arrive.

When she walked to bed that night, on ground cushioned by pine needles and decay, the house wasn't hers any more, this house belonged to a man who would one day come back and possess it.

By the back door sat an unfamiliar suitcase with a change of clothes and everything valuable that could be snatched with little warning. There was no wallet, although a jury summons jammed into a shoe, when flattened out on the table, gave her a name: Audrey Bellow. Bellow. Bellow Below: underworld Mob king, and his beautiful, gone-missing daughter. Maybe she'd come here to lie low and was found by thugs. Maybe she escaped, without the suitcase. Maybe she didn't make it. Maybe that was her hair on the floorboard, maybe the tip of the knife found a home in a bone of her rib, or the temple of her skull.

The bed in her old room was made with sheets that felt stiff. No pots or pans in the kitchen but starched cotton sheets on the bed, fit for a princess. That was her dad right down the middle. She left the curtains pulled back, the shade snapped snug at the top of the window, which she left open, just a crack, to keep the air of the place fresh.

The comforter was winter weight and heavy, like water, on her feet. The moon flickered as it battled with the shadows of tree branches and it's this that she first thought accounted for the impression she had of the wall. As she lay, she focused on the indented surface and yet even when the trees moved in the wind, when the moonlight escaped and returned, the damaged wall did not change.

The floorboards were cold and heavily varnished beneath her bare feet. She touched the place where violence had been done and painted over, it was a broad indentation, broad as a back or shoulder, or a head. When she pulled the curtain past the pane to expose the frame, the wood was chipped, like something had been smashed into the wall and been pulled out the window. She looked out towards the woods. The trees stood tall, rarely fell, and a path wound itself towards and then through them.

The clouds covered over the moon and in the dark, nothing moved. The old house sounded out around her, the east windows settling, the chipmunks crying out as they dug through into the basement walls. Nothing that wasn't familiar. Her toes felt blue, goosebumps flared on her arms, and she pulled the duvet off the bed and wrapped it around herself.

She used to climb those trees and watch her mom garden and she couldn't remember a time when her mom's face wasn't thin and pulled taut over her bones, her hands shaking as she weeded and dug. If she saw her daughter dangling in the trees, she'd shout her out in her astringent voice. She'd been a cower of a woman, never at home in this house, maybe in the world, definitely not in the trees, and she'd been incapable of protecting the smallest thing from anything. That year all her plants were killed by a hard frost through which nothing fragile could survive. Her mom wept into boney hands, at the place this god had brought her, and in which this man had forced her to remain. His love, her hate, violent stasis. But the girl had never felt threatened here, even when she became a woman and left. She felt this place pulse with a darkness that suited the woods, suited her. Outside fog crystallized the air, making the branches of the trees brittle.

These sheets smelled faintly of another woman's breath and she realized that the note from George was not addressed to her in particular, but to anyone lost enough to try and survive in this house.

Sleep came softly and the house held no new noise.

She must wake, he demanded it of her. When she opened her eyes, he was above her and the high moon cast light upon the bed, but he remained in shadow. She didn't need light to know his hands right round her neck, thumbs perfectly placed over her windpipe.

Ah, it's him. She should have known. Thick dead hands.

And her breath was sharp on the inhale and then held there, suspended, round and round, in descending, decreasing circles. Wind through branches can sound like wheezing, like a breath stopped. There's a crack as he broke something in her. He tried to get her to struggle, to cry out even now that there'd be no sound.

He preferred resistance. She could prevent that pleasure. She wouldn't struggle and the house would never be hers, except here, as he claimed it from her. He'd have killed a man by shooting him in the stomach, painful, slow. But with women he'd not mastered bloodless or long and the marks of frenzy were upon the house. His house. She knew this and appreciated the art of it.

He carried her into the woods, his feet barely marking the floor until he found the spot he was after and then they grew roots, gnarled and intricate. Snow fell thick and fast and the mark of her departure was held briefly, only for a few hours, in the indentation on her pillow where she'd slept soundly for one night, a few hours only, near the window she'd kept open despite the chill.

Helen Sedgwick

Duality

I'm trying to explain, even though I know it doesn't work like that. Imagine snowballs melting at the edges; a swirl of air that pricks your skin, sharp as hailstones. Can you see a buoy freed of its anchor, carried from one continent to the next? And I reach out – yes, maybe that – but just as I think I've got it, it slips through the gaps between the atoms of my outstretched fingertips.

I can hear them in the kitchen. They are talking – laughing together, sometimes – and so I think about how voices move through the walls of our flat, each molecule vibrating, passing the sound wave on. Only I don't understand what they're saying, so I give up and think about other things to use as comparisons: a stream of sand blown through a twirly straw, droplets of blue oil in flowing water – that game Zoë has on her desk, with the plastic cogs that spin when you turn it upside down. It's like a miniature explosion that never starts and never stops, it's like energy you can hold in your palm but not grasp, it's like an orbit; but I also know the deep-down truth is that it's like nothing that can ever be imagined. Nothing. And everything, in a million small invisible ways.

June Solstice

It's Zoë and Christy and Luke on the Downs, watching the sun turn everything inside out, one of those stifling afternoons that make just standing up seem impossible so we don't even try. We lounge and lie and prop ourselves up on our elbows, rolling cans of beer and cider between us then opening them with a cringe, our mouths already wide to catch the spraying foam. Let's not ever go home. Let's live out here forever. Let's be of the land and grass and sun and tell that security guard to go fuck himself next time he comes around here, right, yeah? But I'm watching the sun move down through the evening aware that we are turning away, not it. The sinking dusk and the chill in the air even on the longest day of the year is because we are turning our backs on the sun. I am on my back, too, looking up and just watching it disappear and imagining the waves of light – waves like wiggly lines from the sun to the earth, through the atmosphere and to us, bathing in it all, in Bristol, on the Downs, with Zoë and Christy and Luke on the June solstice.

My glasses are lifted off my face, a lightness over the bridge of my nose and a gentle tug behind my ears from where the arms catch before they are free of my head. And the way Luke pulls his leg away when we touch, a reflex, quick and sharp, although the rest of him stays where he is between Christy and me. There is music, and light, and the tang of unfamiliar taste and oh, Zoë has blue nail polish on the June solstice on the Downs in Bristol and the sun sinks even that day and rises again the next and we are all changed because of it.

Apoapsis

The earth at aphelion, the furthest away from the sun it ever gets, 152 million kilometers and yet, here we are, in summer, in Weston-super-Mare. Our axis is leaning us as close to the sun as it can. At least it's trying. On the beach as soon as we wake, with the sea lapping our bare feet and Zoë's hair glittering like gold thread, we are in a line, in the cold sea that is glinting so bright I have to shield my eyes. Stand back a bit and watch the waves. Waves of water and light, they are the same, sometimes, in the way they move and clash and the way they are needed – yes, that too.

In the night there was the smallest gap between our beds but it made something happen, again, when I crawled out of my duvet and into hers and she let me but said sshhhh. And when I stand back on the beach they are still in a line, still where they were but without me in the middle. I can see the sea in the space between their bodies and imagine what would happen if the waves came pushing forwards, were stopped in their tracks by the people standing there, only allowed through the gaps, becoming semi-circular, spreading out from between Zoë and Christy and from between Christy and Luke, making a cross hatch of wave over wave as they flow out and towards me and beyond.

And of course in the morning it was different, the others had things to say that I wasn't supposed to hear – they had to interfere – and now we will swap rooms for tonight. But not until after we buy ice cream and I get some on my nose to make them laugh, and they will because they always do, and this change is not what I want but the sun is high in July and I can see the interference patterns spreading out from the waves of light as they move through the gaps between the people I know and need, for now, in the sun.

September Equinox

There are billiard balls through the other side of a closed door, I can hear them knocking and rolling and disappearing down through a pocket and into secret tunnels of dark wood and shade. I lie down and make myself flat, I am a sheet of cold metal that needs help to generate a current. The push of the score board, the little markers to show how this person has this score and this person has that, moving up in multiples of whole numbers, each score an integer that I cannot see. I am not part of their game.

Someone will be putting chalk on their cue now. Walking around the table, looking to see the angles they need to achieve. Stopping, perhaps, for a sip of a drink before leaning down, slow and deliberate under the low light of the billiard table lamp, with its gold fringes that tingle with each pocketed ball, each cue. I wonder who is playing and who is watching now, of the three. They must miss my even number, but I suppose they are getting used to it.

The light will not come in waves anymore; it is in integer particles, like billiard balls, there is one! But it is gone again and between I see only dusk and rain and night. And they are getting fewer, these photons that reach me, as they travel through cloud and more cloud and more, disperse on their journey, or get stolen; I know something about that. I can hear my name but I say that I am studying the photoelectric effect, which is close enough to the truth. I imagine photons so weak they do not have a single quanta of energy big enough to help me, not one single integer to score, and then my wires will go dark and there will be nothing.

December Solstice

Now the sun is throwing dirty ping-pong balls of light my way; they are few, they are flimsy plastic things, they are scattered and easily lost in the grey. The sun is blowing waves of light my way but they are no more than ripples, breath across water, the fading dimples that spread out and blur from a pebble thrown into a pond.

My radio tells me about the outside world on this shortest day of the year, about the millimeters of rain and the temperature of shade and the scarce minutes of sunlight that we can expect today. It plays me music that is named after the seasons and music that is named after the planets, it plays me voices that I come to recognize like friends who I had forgotten and, worse, forgotten that I had forgotten. I sleep.

Then, after midday: a rainbow. Who could have imagined that it would be there, but my curtains have been opened and outside the raindrops are refracting the light like 152 million prisms before a dimming torch. I know that tomorrow the day will be longer. We will have more minutes of light. I count the colours and count them again, looking for the secondary rainbow and I see it – I think – it is paler but perhaps more beautiful than the first.

Periapsis

The earth at perihelion, the closest it ever gets to the sun, but we are pointing the wrong way, here in Bristol in a rented flat overlooking the Downs and everywhere else, too, in the North, and so for us it is still winter. We are making it winter. We are facing away from the light and skulking in the shade. You gonna get up now, yeah? It is Luke, with his sudden movements away from me, like a static shock, and his blond hair, like Zoë's, not that I saw that before, but now in the dark of my room I can notice things. There's no need for this, man, no need. I turn my back and soon enough he is gone and all is quiet, and the waves flatten to nothing and the particles lie still.

I do hear them talking, hushed and concerned, but it only makes them sound more together. In cahoots. That is what I think of them. Luke and Zoë and Christy and the clouds and the axis that is pointing the wrong way and I am left in the middle of it all, holding my hands out in places where no one sees.

We can't do another winter like this. It is Zoë now but I don't know what she wants me to say to that. Look, I know... What does she know? More than me, perhaps, but not all that much. She knows what happens when four people collide like billiard balls, but she doesn't know about diffraction. She doesn't know about interference patterns or how to produce photoelectrons or the threshold below which there is just not enough energy to make things work. We can't do another winter like this, she says. Well then, I say, maybe I should make it my last.

March Equinox

Creeping slowly across my room is the first ray of the real sunlight of spring. I watch it move as the sun rises, over the chest of drawers that hasn't been opened for how long, across the wall making the small bumps and cracks of paint stand out and smile, dipping down to the carpet and up again as it reaches the end of my bed. There have been new sounds from beyond my door, smells that are crisp and fresh like lemon zest and cotton. No one has been in for a while but they are out there, moving about and talking in louder voices, no longer afraid of what I might hear. A song on the radio about tomorrow – don't stop thinking – and later a programme about a ten year old girl who grows her own tomatoes.

I hear some laughter, and there is another ray coming to join the first one, it is coming from under my door and spreading out into my room, across my floor. Particles are bouncing up onto my ceiling, pinging from wall to wall as waves gush in now through my curtains; a blue purple light that comes from my blue purple curtains and mixes like watercolour with the yellow from under the door and the white from the sky outside and then they meet, a rainbow burst above my bed and then hot onto my skin and I know that light is like nothing I have ever imagined. But really, the truth is that it's more amazing than anything I have ever imagined; like nothing and everything, in a million small invisible ways, and I get up and go to find them, Zoë and Christy and Luke, and the blue nail polish and the tang of unfamiliar taste and perhaps we will be okay this time, now that we are all in the light again.

Ali Smith

A & V at the V & A
– taken from Road Stories, *Faber 2012*

Whenever A and V went to the V & A they always ended up going off in different directions and losing each other. The days of mobile phones had made this a problem much more easily solved (though reception could be patchy in certain parts of the V & A). Anyway they were on their way to the V & A now and had been arguing already on the Tube about whether to take the tunnel or the road. Then, walking along the road – V had won – they began another argument. This one was about the first time they had ever visited the V & A together and when exactly this had been.

See, I don't remember that at all, A said.

We did, V said, really early on. When we first knew each other. But it was in the days when you were still being very Scottish about things and full of righteousness –

You think those days are over? A said.

– ha, V said, listen, because when I said I wanted to show you a funny mechanical man being eaten by a tiger you went off on one about how savage it sounded, how like Victorian England, how like imperialism, how you'd no wish to see something like that.

Whenever they went to the V & A or even talked about visiting the V & A they invariably ended up arguing about something, maybe partly because A had had a kind of a fling (10 years ago now) with a rich Kensington girl who'd lived not far from the Conran Shop. There had been a nice deli near this girl's flat and V often taunted A about the burnt broccoli that this deli had sold and that A had particularly liked. It was one of V's subtle ways of getting at A while remaining humorous and benign; it was affectionately done, and in any case the fling hadn't come to anything, had fizzled out well before any difficult verbs were involved. But even so, this would be one of the reasons A was so forcefully disagreeing.

I like Tipu's Tiger, A was saying now. I always have. I liked it as soon as I saw it. It's ingenious. It's a brilliant satire on colonialism and on industrialism. I've always thought that. But I definitely didn't see it till, like, 2001.

Here A faltered slightly, perhaps because 2001 was around the time of the rich girl.

We did, V said.

A was blushing. But a blush was on its way to V's ears too, with what felt like ferocity. What A didn't know was that as recently as last summer V had come to the V & A alone on one of its late-open evenings, to meet a beautiful yellow-haired woman, the kind who turns heads in the street, who when you go to lunch with her gets brought desserts free by smitten waiters in cafés or restaurants, who goes through life casually trailing behind her, like an expensive scarf bought in a shop like the one at the V & A, these and all the other perks of this kind of beauty. They'd had a drink (there was a bar and a DJ – that was what the V & A was like now, nothing like it had been, or any museum had been, when V had been a child); they'd looked at some medieval and Renaissance things in the newer gallery where the light, regardless of what time of day it is, is steadily like Italian summer daylight; they'd gone downstairs and seen some much more ancient stuff made of gold and wood and clay; then they'd drifted out across the late-evening park towards the city, with all the birds on the lake gathered in a secret piece of bird theatre now that the dark was coming down and most of the humans gone.

It wasn't the fact that A didn't know about this, though, that was making V blush. It was the memory, prompted by coming to the V & A again for the first time since, of that beautiful woman's indifference and distraction. They had seen the exhibits and crossed the grass and passed the night birds and it had been as if that woman hadn't actually seen any of it, as if it were all a stage-flat she was passing in front of on her way to some other life entirely, V tagging along, slightly behind, breathless, slightly off to the side.

Luckily A was still holding forth righteously about their own far past:

Because I'd really have remembered something like that, I remember really clearly all the places you showed me in London, all the things we went to see when we were first together, the South Bank and the Hodgkin pictures at the Hayward, and you showing me the Pre-Raphaelite girls coming down the stairs in the National Gallery, but not the V & A, I don't remember the –

Well, maybe we didn't actually go, V said. Maybe it was something I thought we'd do and then told you about and then we didn't do because you said words like savage and imperial.

OK, A said. Well. Maybe.

Now A was off on another tangent, talking about how the thing about the V & A was that it didn't matter where you were in the building, you always had a feeling that there was something you weren't seeing.

Like there's always some secret wing of the building that you're missing out on, A said. Like somewhere there'll be a statue of the Buddha that'll change your life when you see it, or, if you just turn the right corner, a perfect tiny bottle the size of a thumb and shaped like a wise man, that when you see it means you'll understand something you haven't yet understood about life. Or a tiny pair of pink crinkly shoes so small they look like they'd never fit a human foot, that when you see them will let something inside you know how the whole world works.

While A talked on about how, currently, there was meant to be a huge beautiful Madagascan spider-web gold shawl in the V & A, how it was said to be huge and beautiful but how it sounded, to A anyway, like spider slave labour, V walked along not listening, thinking about the 10 minutes that night last summer when the beautiful woman had been taking a call on her mobile in the lobby and V, waiting and polite, had wandered into the new gallery and seen an old Crucifixion figure, a relief, was it? (in the artistic sense of the word anyway) on the wall.

The Christ had had a huge hole in his side, a wound that actually looked like an extra ear. That's clever, V had thought, an ear into the body like that, the appearance of a God with extra unexpected hearing. The figure had also had a hole right in the centre of the chest. The card on the wall next to the figure had said on it: Christ's wounds were a focus for devotion. His side wound was especially venerated, and in prayer it was evoked as a refuge for sinners. The hole in the chest of the figure probably housed a relic.

A refuge – as if you could actually crawl, for safety, inside a wound. But it was the Christ's face in relation to the wounds which had really caught V's attention. The face was full of blank anguish and sadness; all the same the artist had made it look like the Christ figure was holding his side open rather jauntily. The act looked almost camp.

Maybe that was the best way to deal with pain. Maybe it was the only generous way. It would take some doing, to have human form and be so holy – and so holey – all at the same time. The artist had also remembered the nail holes in the hands, and then there was this extra hole, large and circular and untraditional, in the chest, from which the ribs radiated outward. For relics. It looked like it had been made by machine rather than by art. But somehow it made the rest of the piece acceptable, it made the figure even more able to house things other than itself.

Remember? A was saying by V's side.

Sorry? V said.

Made of logs, A said. In the new courtyard. And more and more people, every time we tried to take our photo. So every time we got ready to take one, someone else came in.

I don't remember that at all, V said.

You do, A said. You must do. I don't know, seven or eight years ago. You stood in it and you said: we could live in this. We could be really happy in a house like this one.

Did I? V said.

And then we went through to look at the room that the artist had taken a plaster cast of, that artist who fills things with plaster, the one who did the whole house and then they knocked it down, A said.

I remember seeing that here, V said, the light switches and the skirting boards all white. And do you remember – d'you remember – after the Ossie Clark exhibition when you bought the replica shirt?

At this both A and V started to laugh. They stopped walking because they were laughing so much and they stood just laughing in the street in the noise of traffic. They laughed until they actually had to hold on to each other.

People walked past them.

Oh God. So much money. I know, and we had hardly any. In the wardrobe. Still in the wardrobe. Well, the nipples. Your mother. Never mind my mother, your father. Worth what it cost just to see. Didn't wear it again.

But oh, the moment of buying it. And you'd been so unwell for so long. And your shining face when you did, V said. It was the start of a new time, that shirt.

I'll get it out this summer, A said. I'll wear it anyway. I'll wear it to all the family parties for the next 10 years.

It's such a fantastic shirt, V said. If you don't, I will.

No, it won't fit you, A said.

You didn't even know who Ossie Clark was, V said.

Yeah, well, you and your childhood on the doorstep of the National Theatre, A said, you and your adolescence at the threshold of culture, you and your Pravda, your Julie Covington and David Essex live on stage in Evita.

You and your 'The Kilt is My Delight', V said. You and your Highland museum with the stuffed stag and the stuffed wildcat.

I hope you're not dissing my childhood, A said. And the stuffed wildcat kittens and the mannequin from Burton's Menswear dressed in clan tartan in front of the black-and-white picturewall of the clan burial stones at Culloden Battlefield. Tragic.

In all the ways, V said.

You better not be dissing the museum culture that made me, A said.

Was the wildcat in a glass case? V said. Were its ears flat or pointed?

Of course it was in a case, A said. It's still in a case. You can't touch the wildcat.

How old were you? V said.

Eight, 12, 17, 43, A said. It's still there. They kept it when they upgraded. That means more than just me loved the wildcat.

I like to imagine you at all those ages, seeing it through the glass, V said. Take me to see it next time we're up.

Funny, A said. Because that's what I do every time I come here, I think of that thing you told me about when you were 17 and they let you into the special room somewhere in this building to see the William Morris wallpaper for the research project.

Snakes and grapes, V said. Large grapes, small snakes.

You alone in the room, A said, in this exemplary museum, with that precious wallpaper, touching it anyway though they'd told you not to, to feel the emboss, see what it felt like.

But I was wearing the gloves, V said.

That's what you're like, A said.

Which? The touching the paper or the wearing the gloves? V said.

Bit of both, A said.

I still dream of that wallpaper sometimes, V said.

I still dream of that wildcat sometimes, A said.

They had reached the steps of the V & A. It rose above them like a – a what?

Cathedral? Grand hotel? Railway station? Museum?

We are such stuffed wildcats as dreams are made on, V said, and our little life is rounded with a sleep.

Yeah, A said, well. At least I can honestly say that no dream I've ever had in my life has involved wallpaper.

Snakes and grapes, grapes and snakes; tiny shoes that show what humans are happy to do to their own feet; clay; cloth; wood; gold; a transparent 100 per cent silk shirt; the plaster cast of a gone room; a wise man in the shape of a bottle; the gods; the holes in the gods: it was all ahead of them and all behind them. They went in arm in arm through the big doors. They kissed each other on the cheek. Then they did what they usually did and went their separate ways for a while. V turned right and strolled through to have another look at what was there and what wasn't, and A went straight ahead, maybe to the shop or maybe to the corridor beyond, the galleries of histories of everything from dust-fleck to architecture; or maybe to look again at the man being eternally eaten by the tiger, the machine of nature, the nature of the machine; or maybe just to sit in some of the afternoon sun in the courtyard, who knows? Here in this place named for lovers, this museum of historic fidelities, there'll always be something you know you're missing out on, there'll always be something you'll come back to.

Shane Strachan

Bill Gibb, 1972

Twiggy shook Bill awake. It took him a few seconds to realise where they were – she'd parked her Rolls Royce just off the roundabout in the centre of Mintlaw. He recognised the Kirk Hall nearby and the look of the folk standing at the bus stop outside it. The faces of the youngest were ruddy and wide-eyed, while the oldest among them had hard, weather-worn skin. You didn't see many country folk like this going about back in London. It had taken most of the day to drive up the long, grey motorways from there to this small village.

Can you lend me another fag? Twiggy pleaded with her wide blue eyes. Just need something to keep me going the last bit of the journey.

Aye, nae bother. Bill opened his packet of Players No.6 and passed one to her before lighting one for himself. They rolled down their windows a little to let out the smoke. She started driving again and the fag ash flew around the car with the blasts of fresh air coming in. He caught glimpses of some bairns playing out on the fields either side of the road – the Easter holidays had begun. The pack of bairns reminded him of his own childhood in the farm out by New Pitsligo and he pictured himself running with them through the rows of barley, the stalks high above their heads.

Now that he felt fully awake, he decided to get his sketchbook out the glove compartment. With his favourite black-ink pen he returned to a drawing he'd started earlier in the day of a female figure in a billowing atlas-print coat.

What you working on? Something for the next show? Twiggy asked. Remember, this is meant to be a break.

No no, it's nae for that. I'm just sketching awa. He scratched at his beard. Besides, I'm nae one for breaks. Spare time scares ma.

They both went silent for a while and the sky slowly tinged with red as the sun sank.

Will your mum like me? Twiggy asked when they neared New Pitsligo.

I've never known my mam to nae like somebody, he smiled. Ye'll be fine.

Well I've brought some champagne to help break the ice tonight. I hope they like bubbles.

Bill shrugged his shoulders and laughed. He went back to his sketch and added the last few touches before it was too dim outside: some extra lines on the hem of the coat and a bumblebee brooch on the collar.

Does your... Twiggy began but cut herself off.

Fit? he asked. Fit were ye gan to say?

Oh, it was nothing really. I was just curious – do your mum and that know about you and Kaffe being together?

Bill sighed and closed his sketchbook.

Sorry, she said. I just don't want to put my foot in it, you know?

Dinna worry. It's fine, he said. I think they know. We just dinna spik aboot those sort o things. They widna really understand. He tried to laugh.

They approached his family home on Netherton Farm and he spotted a few folk sitting round the kitchen table. In the low light, he could just make out the rest of the cottage and the surrounding fields. They came to a stop and he got out the passenger door – it felt far colder here than it had been in London that morning.

Billy! his sister Janet called out from the doorway. Come awa in. Ye must be fair jeelt in this caul. His youngest sister Marilyn joined her at the door and he ran to hug and kiss them both. The lobby was warm and had its same familiar smell of pine. He introduced his sisters to Twiggy; they were still in their work pinnies while Twiggy was wrapped up in an old Bonnie Cashin coat that ran down past her knees. Words failed to come to their mouths – all they could do was giggle at the sight of her.

At first, his mam didn't notice him when he stepped into the kitchen; her glasses had steamed up with peering into the open oven. The lenses cleared when she stood up and she flinched at the sight of her son.

Govie dicks! Fit a fear to gie ma loon, she cried, a hand rising up to her chest. She hurried over and bosied into him. Twiggy entered with the bottle of champagne held out before her.

Oh, thank you verra much. His mam took the bottle and squinted at the label. We're nae used to the likes o this. I canna even read thon grand lettrin.

It's nothing special, Twiggy said. Where's your fridge and I'll pop it away to chill for a while?

Bill showed Twiggy around the cottage. She pointed at a picture of a sunlit cove on the lobby wall and asked who'd painted all the landscapes hanging all over the place. He told her about his granny who stayed on a farm nearby and who he'd lived with most of his childhood, how she'd painted for as long as he remembered.

What? Why didn't you stay with your parents? Did you not understand a word they said either? She laughed away at her own joke.

It's just something that used to happen up this wye. Nae much room in this place with aa o us and I guess because I was the aulest.

His mam called through and they sat down at the table, his Dad and brothers already in their seats. Bill turned to the two eldest of his younger brothers, George and Alan, and remarked that, even in their dungarees, they both still looked the marris of Buddy Holly. They sniffed a laugh and said nothing while their mam got on with dishing out the food: cuts of lamb, boiled tatties, mashed neaps and a mountain of Brussels sprouts, all grown on the farm.

Once everybody had sat down, the quines took over the conversation and asked Twiggy question after question. Fit was her real name? Far did she shop at hersel? Fit were English lads like?

George and Alan didn't dare ask her anything, but dichted at their soil-smeared hands with hankies when she wasn't looking their way.

When the conversation finally lulled, Twiggy set her knife and fork down and announced that she was full. There was still a cut of lamb and a pile of vegetables on her plate.

Oh me, d'ye nae like it? Bill's mam said, wide-eyed.

It's lovely Mrs Gibb. I'm just stuffed.

Stuffed! You've only heen a few moofaes.

His sisters scowled at their mam.

A few what? Twiggy laughed. Honestly, it was lovely.

Well, I guess they dinna caa ye Twiggy for nithing, his mam sighed. But we'll seen fatten ye up. They both laughed before the sisters put their own cutlery down and exclaimed that they too were stappit.

Mugs of fizzing champagne in hand, they showed Twiggy through to their old room where she'd be sleeping for the next couple of nights. She'd go in their sister Patsy's bed, who'd moved out the year before after she married. Bill said he was fine to sleep by the fireside in the living room and not take up any of his brothers' space. He got his things out the Rolls Royce – two wooden chemist's chests stuffed with clothes and sketchbooks, and a wee box of brooches – then stowed them away in a corner of the front room. His mam came through with a tartan picnic blanket and a down pillow. She said goodnight with a peck on his cheek. He lay down on the sheepskin rug in front of the fireplace and plumped up the pillow before resting his head on it. In the warmth of the dying fire, he drifted off to sleep.

*

Let It Be was playing somewhere in the cottage when Bill woke up on Saturday morning. After he'd rubbed at his eyes, he shuffled through the lobby to his sisters' room. They were sat on the floor reading the back of the album cover while Twiggy lay across one of the beds on her front. She watched the vinyl spin on the record player he'd given his sisters the Christmas past. He lay down on another bed and listened as the song faded out. Marilyn leapt up onto the bed and unhooked the pink floral-print curtains.

Mind fan we used to dee this? she said. The record player went silent. They all watched as she wrapped the curtain around herself from her oxters down to her knees. Everybody laughed except Bill.

No no no, he said. That's nae fit I did. Ye've created an Ozzie Clark – aa flesh and nae dress. He went over to her and held onto the cloth until she'd spun herself out of it. He wrapped one end round her neck and tied a knot at the back so that it held in place, then he pulled it under her oxters and folded it loosely from her shoulder blades down to her heels. He emptied two purple tartan pillowcases and jammed each one into the halterneck he'd created before tucking them shut round her arms. Marilyn unpinned her fair hair and let it fall down either side of her shoulders, hiding away the join where the curtain and pillowcases met.

Now, Twiggy said. You could put that on a mannequin in Harrods and make a few bob. She turned the record over and placed the needle back down on it.

Well, you sure as hell couldna walk aroon the Broch weering that, Janet said. Imagine!

The bass line of *Get Back* drew their attention to the record player once more. When the cymbals crashed, Bill skipped over to Twiggy and took her in his arms. They writhed against each other slowly, rotating their hips in sync and swaying their heads from side to side. Bill glanced over at his sisters – their mouths were wide open.

Fa taught ye hoo to dunce like that? Marilyn asked when the record finished.

Naebody taught ma. I was born wie them moves! Bill said. Twiggy burst out laughing and only got louder.

I dinna think a man should ever move like that, Janet said. She tutted and left the room.

At breakfast, he sat sketching at the table. He drew various bees on the page, some cartoonish, some lifelike. Crumbs fell onto his sketchbook with each bite of toast. The quines made comments about him being rude at the dinner table.

But it's nae dinner. It's breakfast, he said. Marilyn leaned over his shoulder as she put a teapot down on the table.

Why bees? she asked. She'd asked a hundred times before.

Why nae? he replied, not looking up from the page. She sighed.

The quines moved on to discussing all the films they'd seen recently. Janet was shocked to discover she'd seen more at the picturehouse in the last few years than Twiggy had, even with all the premieres the model had been to. Bill stopped listening and forgot himself as he drew another bee. This time he played with the geometric pattern on each of the wings so that a picture formed across them like stained glass windows. When he was done, he sat up straight and realised the table had cleared and that he was alone. He looked out the window at the fields: it was far brighter than the day before – maybe it was even warm. He felt the urge to go out for a walk. He'd sometimes walk the streets of London at night on his own, but there would just be endless streams of people coming at him from all directions, more and more every time. Here, there was plenty of space out on the fields – a welcome emptiness.

George came into the kitchen and asked Bill if he could give him a hand outside: the milking machines had broken down the week before and now Alan was coming down with the flu. There was so much they needed to get caught up on.

Bill put on his knitted cardigan and followed his brother outside. The sun glared low in the sky as they walked across the large expanse of grass towards the chicken coop. They stepped into the small wire-framed enclosure and George passed him a bucket of chicken feed. He plunged his hand into the pail of grain and relished the feeling of it sifting through his fingers. When he scattered some around the coop, the chickens darted back and fore, running in zigzags and triangles. He studied their different colourations; most were a golden orange with black speckles, except for one that was cream with black zebra-like stripes down the sides of its neck. He imagined a mishmash of these speckles and stripes on one of his dresses. He told George about this idea.

Fit's wrang wie a plain frock? Fit why does it need to hae a chicken on it? George said. Ye'r sic a queer hare Billy boy.

Maybe so, Bill said. He took a handful of grain and threw it up in the air. It showered down on them both and he laughed wildly.

Sic a queer hare, George repeated.

Once they'd collected up the few eggs that had been laid, they headed for the cowshed. Inside, Twiggy was on her knees below Flora, the doziest cow of the fourteen on Netherton Farm. Bill's father watched on from behind as she attempted to milk the creature.

Oh, don't it feel funny? She winced as a thin string of milk squirted out of the teat held between her fingers.

Och, but ye'r deeing just fine ma quine, Bill's father said before winking at him and George. A dab hand compared to Bill here.

George passed Bill a bucket and pointed out all the other cows that still had to be milked.

Nae need to roll yer een, George laughed.

I didna roll onything. I can dee it. I dinna mind deeing it, Bill said quietly. He went over to the furthest corner and, keeping his back to the rest of them, began milking.

It was the warmth of the teat he'd never liked, and the rubbery tautness at the start of the milking, which slowly became soft and flabby over time. The cow stirred every now and then, ambling slightly forward and back in discomfort, but the milk streamed out nonetheless. He knew he could manage fine at this – he'd just never hung around the farm long enough after school to master it all like his father and brothers, but he could do it to some degree.

There was a silence in the shed as milk drummed against each of their pails.

Bill! someone shouted from the direction of the house. Up off his knees, he carried his half-full pail over to George and left it with him before heading out of the cool, dark shed and into the daylight. His mam was leaning out the kitchen window. Bill, there's somebody on the telephone for ye.

It was his manager, Kate. The buyers had been in touch and had decided that the latest designs he'd sent were still too elaborate and costly for the manufacturers to produce. Could he not trim them down? Were the bee buttons really necessary? Maybe he should take a more minimalist approach from now on?

I'll sort it when I get back, he sighed, drumming his fingers on the dining table. His mam watched him as she rolled pastry out on kitchen worktop.

But they need an answer now, Kate said, the line crackling.

I suppose you better give them one then. Just say whatever you think's best but you know I won't be changing the designs either way. You wouldn't paint over the halos in a Rossetti now, would you? He hung up.

His mam placed a floury hand on his shoulder.

Hey now, ye canna be spikkin to folk on the phone like that. That's nae the wye I brought ye up.

Trust ma, ye'd think differently if they were phoning you. He turned from her and headed ben into the living room. He rummaged through one of the chemist's chests and searched out an old tattered packet of fags. Unlike the newer packets, it didn't have a health warning down one side. He quickly whipped out one of the six joints inside of it and headed out the front door. He lit the joint under the shelter of the alcove there.

After the first deep draw he decided he needed to get away from the cottage, even though he'd sore missed the place in the weeks leading up to the visit – he would visit his grandparents who lived a mile or so away at Lochpots farm.

The air was still and cool as he set off down the gravelly driveway and onto the pothole-covered road, smoking as he went. It was quiet except for the twittering of swallows migrating home for summer. In the calm of it all, he felt his face slacken and his head become light and airy.

When he neared the farm, he spotted his dyde out in the fields digging up the earth with a shovel. He studied the distant, jerking movements. The closer he got, the more he was entranced by the rotation of his dyde's arms as he howked into the soil and cast it away – it was like watching a dance that had been practiced for years, a dance that would only end when the earth ultimately won over. How strange it was for a man to do the same thing day in day out, all his life!

Before he got any closer, he smoked the last of the joint and buried the remnants in the ditch at the side of the road. He waved and shouted at his dyde but the old man didn't notice him and kept on digging.

By the time Bill got to the front door of the cottage it already felt like the phone call from London had taken place in the distant past. He chapped on the dark pinewood and his granny answered. In her mid-seventies, she still had the energy and style of her youth; her white hair was pinned up at the back of her head and she floated around the doorway in a lilac nightgown.

William, she gasped. Her glassy eyes were filled with reflections of the noon's sky. I was sair needing to see that face. Come awa in ma loon. They embraced in the lobby before she led him through into the sitting room. Ye've just missed yer auntie. She's awa to the Broch to pick up some eerans.

Is this fit ye'r working on? he asked. He walked over to a canvas that was leant up against the window, a paint pallet lying at the foot of it. The painting seemed to depict thinning tributaries flowing away from a river, or maybe it was a dark blue tree stretching upwards?

Oh, thon? I'm just playing aboot. I'm nae really sure far I'm gan wie it. She examined him with her glassy blue eyes. Fit's this? she tutted, pointing at the flour stain on his shoulder. Before he could answer, she made her way out of the room. He dichted at the stain until it was barely visible.

She returned with a freshly brewed pot of tea and they sat and drank a few cups as they chatted about how things had been on the farm, how his dyde was keeping and what his auntie had been up to. She kept trying to ask him about things down in London but he'd quickly turn the focus back on her life. Eventually she won through and he ended up discussing some of his latest clients: Bianca Jagger, Lulu and Elizabeth Taylor.

I've heard o that Elizabeth fae yer auntie. She's ay at the picterhoose. The other names soond like affa grand folk though. Fit a lucky loon you are to move among such beautiful women, eh? She winked at him with a knowing smile and he couldn't help but smile back.

She stood up slowly and began tidying away their cups and plates. He offered to help but she refused to let him, so he headed through to his old bedroom.

When he opened the door, the air inside smelt musty yet familiar, like putting on an old jacket. It had been a couple of years since he'd last been in the room but everything was the same: sketches pinned up on the walls and bookshelves full of novels and histories. Some still had scraps of paper marking out descriptions of dresses from bygone times. The only thing that felt different was how small it all seemed: his feet would surely overhang the single bed now, and the bookcase would struggle to fit any of the chunky art books he collected back in London.

He lay down on the bed and closed his eyes. He wondered: if given the choice to go back in time – to wake up a bairn in this house once more – would he take it? What did London matter? The only time he'd felt any real joy down there was during his debut show, when all those dresses he'd created were hung on those pretty stalks. One after the other, they'd bloomed before the eyes of the enraptured audience. Then the last model slinked back up the catwalk, the music faded out, and the room emptied. One quick sting and he was left hollowed out – empty for another six months. Is that how he would go on living his life until he was out of fashion? Forgotten?

Groggy headed, he forced himself up off the bed and went back ben to the sitting room. His granny had her back to him as she painted black lines onto the canvas. They might have been grooves in the tree's bark or maybe competing currents in the river.

That's me awa granny. She turned to face him and he kissed her soft, withered cheek.

Ta ta ma loon. Till next time, she said. Her old glassy eyes returned to her art.

He stepped out the front door and scanced the fields: his dyde had disappeared from sight and the sky was empty of swallows. The barley fields swayed in the breeze – how queer it was to see the currents of wind like that! How long had it been since he'd seen that sight? And how long might it again be? He closed the door behind him. Between the silent fields he walked on along the old country road, drifted away from home.

Tat Usher

The Constant Heart

The baker leans against the counter and stares down at yesterday's *Daily Record*. Fiona Kennedy is sitting at the window table reading a Mills & Boon to fat Margaret Blaine and old Mr Slater. They never buy anything, those three – not so much as a bastarding cup of tea between the lot of them. He'd kick them out but he secretly enjoys listening. Fiona Kennedy is from Shetland and she reads beautifully. She sits straight-backed, serious and commanding, holding the book close to her chest, her straggly dark hair falling across her face. Sometimes the baker stops listening to the story and hears only the slow, gentle cadences of her voice washing over him, soothing and erasing him.

Fiona's audience is transfixed: Margaret's pudgy hands are folded in her lap and she has a glazed look. Mr Slater leans back in his chair, his walking stick propped against the wall, his flat cap on the table in front of him. Every so often he fiddles with his hearing aid but other than that he remains eerily still. There have been a few occasions when the baker started to worry that Mr Slater had pegged it mid-chapter. The idea of having a corpse sat in his café made him want to hurl the cash register through the window or set fire to the net curtains.

The current book is called *The Constant Heart* and the cover shows a young, blonde woman in a lilac dress standing in a garden. She is clasped passionately by a dark-haired man in huntsman's regalia. The hunter's white horse looks on, and in the background, slightly blurred, another man loiters beneath a tree and gazes longingly at the couple.

In today's episode, Constance is told by her closest friend, Isabel, that her fiancé, Jack Buchanan, has been untrue. She is devastated.

'The change in Constance was sudden and dramatic,' Fiona reads. 'For days she would not rise from her bed and lay staring into space, her hair a pale swathe across the pillow and slow tears trickling down her wan cheeks. Her clear blue eyes had taken on a bruised, vacant look.

She would see no one and would accept neither food nor drink.'

Margaret sighs, just barely audibly.

A dog barks in the street outside, and there's the faint chime heralding the ferry arrival announcement. '*Thank you for travelling with Caledonian MacBrayne. We hope you have had a pleasant journey...*'

Constance's devoted maidservant, Mabel, tries to tempt Constance with French fancies and implores her to take a little tea at least. The baker glances up at this, but the faces of his three customers are impassive and they do not appear to be inspired to take a little tea at least. He thinks about going into the bakery at the back for a slug of whisky. Instead he turns to another page of his newspaper.

Constance rallies a little, and is advised by a male friend that she has brought this heartache upon herself by showing too much affection towards her fiancé before they were married. She should have saved her love for after the marriage, as a true hunting man needs the challenge of a conquest.

The baker hears the scream of distant seagulls, floating high and cold above the soft flow of Fiona Kennedy's voice.

Margaret sighs again, more heavily this time.

The baker is filled with sudden rage. He opens his mouth to shout, 'Get out mah fucken café, the fucken lot ae ye's!' He closes his mouth, swallows hard and turns the page of his newspaper. There is an article about the trial of a man who attacked a young woman on the seventeenth floor of a highrise flat in Dundee. He gouged out her eye with his fingers and then threw it over the balcony.

'And that's all for today,' Fiona Kennedy announces and closes the book.

Without a word, Mr Slater zips up his grey anorak, claps his hat on his bald head, grasps his walking stick and shuffles out of the café. Fiona puts her coat on, slips the book into one of her pockets, nods at the baker and leaves. Margaret is left alone, staring blankly out of the window at the empty street, her chubby little hands fluttering around her throat, tugging at the neckline of her pink T-shirt, caressing her necklace of large green plastic beads. The baker thinks of the eyeball falling from the seventeenth floor and imagines the little splatting sound it made as it hit the concrete.

The baker stands at his bedroom window looking out at the backs of derelict tenements. He takes a swig of Bell's straight from the bottle. It's been a while since he bothered putting it in a glass. A few yards down the street there's a gap between the houses through which he can see a grey strip of sea. Across it the ferries come and go and the hours are punctuated by the muffled arrival and departure messages. '*Thank you for travelling with Caledonian MacBrayne. We hope you have a pleasant journey...*' He has not left the island in nearly two years. Perhaps he will never leave again. What's the difference anyway?

He turns away from the window and sets the Bell's on the mantelpiece by his fourteen bottles of paracetemol, neatly lined up with the labels all facing to the front. It's Sunday and has been Sunday forever, empty and silent and smelling of unwashed laundry. He will go outside. He will walk the length of the seafront, past the wind-lashed flowerbeds and the crazy golf and the dismal cafés selling chips and ice cream. He will lean on the railing and watch the ferries arriving and departing. He will return home and finish the bottle.

At ten past five on Monday morning the baker lifts his trays of pastry cups from the oven and lays them on the chrome worktop. He's famous for his custard tarts: they're his best seller and he's all but given up bothering to make anything else. He leans against the wall, slides a fresh bottle of Bell's out of his apron pocket, takes a long swig, his eyes closed. The sweet forgiving fire holds him and for a moment he's saved. He opens his eyes and stares at the rows of pastry cups and they seem to him like open mouths waiting to speak. What is it they want to say?

He pulls a roll of rice paper and scissors from a drawer and cuts out a small circle. Now he searches through a cabinet crammed with cake decorating paraphernalia: jars of blue sugar stars, jelly diamonds, marzipan flowers, hundreds and thousands, chocolate shavings, plastic brides and grooms, silk ribbons, bottles of glaze and food dyes. He takes out a bottle of cochineal and a fine brush. His hand trembles as he paints the words on the rice paper circle and drops it into the nearest pastry cup. He makes a little nick in the lip of the pastry. But now they are all saying it: two dozen mouths all whispering over and over, 'It hurts, it hurts, it hurts...' In something close to panic, he hastens to silence them with custard.

The baker watches Mrs Robertson from Kerrycroy select the message-bearing tart, grasping it with the steel tongs, dropping it into a paper bag. He's never liked Mrs Robertson, with her sharp nose and disdainful east coast vowels. As she walks off down the street, he imagines her sitting in her living room, antimacassars on the armchairs and the tart on a willow-pattern plate. She's sliced it in half because she thinks that's more polite:

It   hurts

His pain disappearing between her thin, disapproving lips. She dabs at crumbs with a napkin.

On Tuesday Dougie McFarlane, off the ferry, buys the second tart and has already eaten it by the time he's out the door. Down in one.

On Wednesday Suzie Cameron buys the third tart and a white batch loaf. The baker tries not to appear to be looking at her black eye as she hands him a five pound note, but where the fuck else is he supposed to look?

'Lovely weather we've been having for a change!'

She smiles weakly. 'Aye, it's no been a bad summer, really...'

He wants to take the tart back, exchange it for another one. The poor bitch, married to that drunken bastard and everyone says the we'an's not right in the head.

He grins at her. 'Costa del Scotland, ay?'

The baker leans against the counter and stares down at the football pages of the Daily Record. Kilmarnock beat St Johnson two nil. He hates football. Fiona Kennedy is sitting at the window table reading to fat Margaret Blaine and old Mr Slater. At times the sound of the rain lashing the windows of the café threatens to drown out her voice. No one has bought the fourth tart. It's Thursday and has been Thursday forever.

Constance is to be married to the true hunting man, Jack Buchanan, in spite of his infidelity. As the wedding day approaches, her heart is heavy.

'Constance sat at her dressing table and gazed listlessly at her pallid reflection in the glass. There were bluish circles beneath her dull eyes. The sound of a carriage pulling into the driveway filled her with a cold dread.' There is a note of glee in Fiona Kennedy's voice that suggests she relishes Constance's suffering. The baker wishes someone would gouge Contance's eye out with their fingers and chuck it off a balcony. That'd give her something to whinge about. Mr Slater's hearing aid emits a stuttering high-pitched beep and he reaches up to adjust it.

The wedding day arrives.

'Constance stared resolutely ahead, her face almost the colour of her exquisitely simple ivory silk dress, as Mabel tenderly combed and plaited her flaxen hair.'

The door chings and the baker looks up. It's the Cameron girl – the one that's not the full shilling. She's standing there, dripping on the lino, her school uniform soaked and dishevelled, dark hair plastered to her head and her eyes all wide and blue and starey. The baker thinks of Suzie Cameron with her shiners and shaking hands and he shudders and looks at his watch. Still an hour till closing time.

Fiona Kennedy flicks her eyes at the girl and then continues reading.

'"Smile, my lady," said Mabel. "This is supposed to be the happiest day of your life."'

The girl walks up to the counter. There's something unnerving about her and he takes a step back as she approaches. He wants to tell her to bugger off.

'And what can I do you for?' he asks her in his best Father Christmas voice.

The girl doesn't reply.

The baker coughs and slides his left hand into his apron pocket to touch the reassuring smoothness of the Bell's bottle. He's trying to remember what it is that's supposed to be wrong with the we'an. Watching her ma get battered by a drunken lunatic day in day out would probably be enough to send the lassie a bit loopy, but she has a wild-eyed, feral look to her that makes him think maybe she was born that way.

'Constance sighed heavily. "Oh Mabel," she whispered, "Do you believe that a man's heart can change?"'

Now the girl lifts the hatch and enters the serving area. He backs away from her until he's jammed against the cash register. She takes a step closer. Rain is still dripping down her pale face, or is she crying? Fuck's sake. Maybe he should call the social services or something.

'Mabel applied rouge to Constance's pale cheeks. "A constant heart is a rare thing, mistress," she said hesitantly. "But fate would have it that you found Mr Buchanan and your future is now assured."'

Without warning the girl lunges at him. The baker raises his hands to push her away, but her thin damp arms are already around him and she is clamped to him, face pressed hard against his chest. His hands hover helplessly. Should he attempt to prise her off? Jesus. You can get the jail for this kind of thing. Her hair is creating a wet patch on his apron and it has already soaked through to his skin. A sudden lethargy overtakes him and he lets his arms sink to his sides. The girl continues to cling to him. Fiona Kennedy has stopped reading. He looks over at the window table and sees that she and fat Margaret and old Mr Slater are all staring at him. They look almost frightened. Margaret is twisted round in her seat and is tugging at her green beads. Fiona Kennedy has laid *The Constant Heart* face down on the table. Mr Slater is frowning and has a hold of his walking stick. The baker opens his mouth to say something, but no words come.

'And that's all for today,' Fiona says.

Margaret is up and wrestling with her flowery pink and orange rain mac and manages to beat Mr Slater to the street. In the silence after the door chings behind them, the baker sighs. Fiona Kennedy reaches into her coat pocket, takes out a packet of Marlboros and lights one, leaning her head back against the window and blowing smoke at the ceiling. The baker opens his mouth to say, 'Ye cannae smoke in here.' He shuts it again, and swallows hard. The Cameron girl tightens her grip on him, then releases him, turns and leaves, closing the door carefully behind her. For a moment there is only the sound of the rain. The baker presses a hand to his eyes.

'I'll have a cup of tea, if you wouldn't mind,' says Fiona Kennedy.

Ryan Vance

Gold Star

Corned beef, spam, frankfurters, amazingly all still there, tinned towers of meat gathering dust. Casey doesn't know what to make of this. Even though keeping trim is no longer a vanity – the places you can hide with a thirty-one inch waist! – it shouldn't surprise him the Merchant City left the trans fats 'til last. He pads to the centre aisle and does a quick scout of the supermarket, rows and rows of barren shelves, empty packaging littering the floor.

Then again, it could be a trap. His nearest match was two miles away, but there might be technophobic grey foxes, or hopeless analogue romantics, and of course the roving gangs of lesbians, a constant worry. There's rumours of a hack for the female apps, but there's also rumours that nobody uses them, not even the lesbians. It's probably all nonsense. Casey doesn't know who provides Janice with all this information, but he knows better than to ask. They have an arrangement: food for sanctuary, and no questions about where she goes at night.

So Casey returns to the meat aisle. He tries to inspect the reformed shrine from all angles but doesn't see anything suspicious. Maybe it really is just the last supply of canned dead animal in the city, simple as that. He counts a dozen or so cans. If he doesn't lift anything on the way home he could fit the whole lot in his rucksack, but they're not exactly light. No hope of a clean pass through the business district, he'd have to take a break to catch his breath.

But this is one hell of a jackpot.

He gets three in the bag before pulling the pin on a rape alarm covertly taped to a tin of frankfurters.

He bolts for the exit. Behind him a freezer slams open, the squeak of trainers on tile. Jamming his fingers between the broken sliding doors to prise them open, he risks a look back. Lycra calves, lightweight top, beautiful forearms, a fitness freak, a runner. Shit. There's no escaping this one.

A scuffle in the street, limbs and fists and hard rubber in his face, and somehow Casey's the victor, a dented can of hot dogs in his bloody, white-knuckled grip. He packs the dogs and checks for a pulse – yup, only unconscious – then frisks the body. A set of keys, a sachet of energy gel and a phone with no charge. The energy gel tastes repulsive, but it'll see him back to the flat. The shoes are a steal, too.

In any other situation, he'd drag the stranger into a doorway or a sidestreet, somewhere discreet, but the rape alarm continues to howl and it wouldn't be wise to stick around. He pockets the man's phone, and checks his own. Dorothy loads – sure enough, his nearest match is now one mile away, and closing. No pic, no chat.

As he leaves the Merchant City, bodies of breeders begin to show in the street, gullpecked and grey.

Hey

> *Hey*
> *Good night?*
> *Not bad. Out w friends.*
> *Busy later?*
> *Could be. U up 4 fun?*
> *Got more pics?*
> **pic 1* *pic 2* *pic 3**
> *U?*
> **pic 1* *pic 2**
> *Hott.*

'Why are you,' says Janice, 'looking at that?'

'Gotta get my rocks off somehow.'

'Oh gross, not at the table, pervert.'

Breakfast is coffee and crackers an hour before noon. They split all food equally, and Janice trusts Casey enough to wait until she gets back because this is her flat and he doesn't have anywhere else to crash.

> *Hiya! Good night?*

pic 1 *pic 2* *pic 3* *pic 4* *pic 5* *pic 6* *pic 7*
Yours or mine?

'But no,' she says, sitting down. 'Really. Why snoop through his phone?'

'I need proof. I'm nurturing the hope that not every man in this city is a murderous lunatic.'

'You still have blood under your fingernails.'

He sighs, and makes wet doodles in a coffee spill. 'I just feel there must be somebody else out there who thinks they could survive easier if they weren't...'

Janice snorts. 'Honey, I'm as good as it gets.'

'Wait, yeah, this is great.'

Janice raises an eyebrow.

'Well, not great. I mean it works, I wouldn't have it different.'

This is surprisingly close to the truth. In any non-apocalyptic scenario it might be unreasonable to shoehorn yourself into a friend-of-a-friend's bedsit with little to no warning and stay there indefinitely, long after the mutual connection popped his clogs along with pretty much everyone else thanks to a bizarre and swift sexual plague, but under these specific circumstances, these specific and abominably fucked circumstances, yes, Casey would have to admit it works, and so would Janice. The eyebrow lowers.

'So what's the deal. You suddenly think you'll find romance in a dead guy's dick pics?'

'No, of course not. And he's not dead. I hope. But... it gets quiet at night.'

Hey, nice smile! You look like a young Rennie Mackintosh.

Who?

Hello?

pic 1

Hello?

'Casey, you want to be quiet at night. It's not safe.'

'What do you know.'

Now it's Janice who sighs, and pushes cracker crumbs around a plate, and stares at the grotty ceiling.

'Sorry,' he says. 'I'm being a dick, I don't know why.'

'No, it's fine. Better to flick it than kick it, right?'

'Right.'

Hey.

Hey.

All my friends are dying.

Yup.

I don't know what to do.

Up for fun?

'Well,' says Casey, and sets the phone face down on the table.

'Giving up so easy?'

'He's not my type.'

On days when he doesn't have to hunt, Casey likes to walk around the city. There's little else to do in the flat but sleep, and he has this fear of someday finding solace in inertia, of turning into one of those half-dead people he's come across during residential raids, shrivelled heads cresting mounds of blankets and jumpers, human burritos. The only way you can tell they aren't breeders is how they're not quite as far past their use-by date.

Casey's not proud of how he's adopted the term 'breeder'. He hadn't liked it or used it back when it had a narrower definition, reducing actions of love to functions of biology. Then came the true horror of biology, a plague that cared not for orientation, only heterosexual acts whether fresh or long forgotten, and no excess of love could change a thing. But he wants to define himself as separate from all these corpses, and the alternative – to call himself a Gold Star, a title got for only touching it on the way out - seems unduly congratulatory. So they're breeders, and he's... something else.

So Casey goes for walks, just to prove to himself he's not a breeder and not a burrito, and sometimes it's inadvisable, like right now, racing the length of Sauchiehall Street, ducking and diving between abandoned cars and buses, hiding from a man in possession of a long length of pipe and some anger management issues. From a spot in the middle of the street between two abandoned taxis Casey catches sight of him: sunken-faced, broad-shouldered, a stocky frame turned hard by adversity, a beard which a year ago might have hinted at leather accessories, today serving only as the mark of someone who has understandably just stopped giving any fucks.

Forget Kinsey, this was the new spectrum, apathetic to psychopathic, and if, like Casey, you felt you lay somewhere in between, well, you were kidding yourself. It wasn't real. Given time, you'd choose.

The man starts breaking car windows and howling indiscriminate vowel sounds, intimidation tactics. Casey's registering on his phone as less than 50 feet away. He could sign out, of course, drop off the grid and escape under a cover of non-existence – but then how would he know how close every other creep was? He'd be running blind through the city. He needs a better plan than that.

Time to catfish.

Please be dumb enough for this to work, Casey thinks. He takes the runner's phone from his rucksack, turns it on, loads Dorothy. A bubbly alert sounds out from the hairy man's position; he must have proximity notifications enabled. The alert is light, a creamy yellow tone, the app's unmistakable chime. It says, hi there, stranger, let's be friends, let's get to know each other, let's not fuck on the first date. The man stops smashing cars and checks his Dorothy – it's a threesome, now, the runner's profile just as faceless and empty as Casey's.

A mobile in each hand, Casey makes a quick comparison – heft, durability, battery life – then throws his, overarm, down the street. It bonks off a car bonnet. It's a transparent bait and switch, but he's walked into enough ambushes to know the appearance of a new contender will have his pursuer swithering. After what feels an age, the man sneaks by on the other side of the taxi, tracking the stray signal. Casey holds his breath.

Dorothy updates: less than 100 feet.

He sprints up to Bath Street and ducks into the first building with an open door.

A teal swoosh across the windows underlines the promise of 24 hour fitness. One of those gyms that stays open all night, unsupervised, a mecca for protein-chugging cruisers and the occasional cabbie coming off a night shift. Casey moves quickly upstairs to where the tall windows give a clear view of the street. He avoids looking in the shards of mirror still clinging to the walls. He doesn't like how his clothes flap around his body when he moves, as if dancing to the growls coming from his stomach. Killer cheekbones for a selfie, though.

Hey.

A msg alert rings out in the still of the gym and Casey drops for cover behind a stairmaster, heart rate rapid. Did the man follow him here? He scans the cardio suite for signs of danger, but all he can see are powered-down machines and empty Lucozade bottles

Hey...

You didn't show last night.

The noise comes again from his rucksack – the runner's phone.

Me and the boys waited at The Vic for like a whole afternoon. Where are you?

Fresh communication. Scrolling back through previous chats Casey finds photos of what must either be two cherry midget gems sitting on a rug, or a close up of a man's torso with the flash on. Details unfold of a hookup, developing into semi-regular meets at the weekend. Not much small chat.

He pays closer attention to the new msg. Me and the boys? That means at least three men were waiting, making the runner one of four. Just think. Four men, together, a crew, a posse, four men managing not to bludgeon each other's skulls in a fight over the last existing haggis. In the dark of the dimlit gym Casey pops a semi. *For fuck's sake,* he thinks, *what am I, fourteen?*

How did they all find each other, trust each other, he wonders. It's not unfathomable, of course, that four men in the same city, none of whom had ever slept with a woman, had been friends before everything went to shit. But it's unlikely, at least from Casey's experience of dating which invariably led to coming out stories, and mentions of teenage girlfriends. You didn't get a gold star for nothing. No, he decides, they must have met afterwards. These people chose to support each other. These people exist.

We'll be at Safehouse B tonight. Let me know you're okay.

How should he reply? *I found this phone on the* - no, no, no. Far too casual, hard to believe. *I don't know who your friend is but I'm trying to -* nope. Oh fuck it, what's wrong with *hello*? There's no need to be clever, these days simply being alive was a guarantee of personality. But there's still the fact that their friend is probably now dogfood.

Safehouse B. That could be anywhere. Hell, it could even be here, down among the Smith machines. He remembers the gymrats, how they'd share large handshakes, and stretch their backs and their necks as they swapped technique tips. This probably used to be one of the safest places in Glasgow, everyone walking around inside their very own suit of armour.

Not any more, though. From the second floor he sees the bearded man in the street, checking his phone and looking around for prey. *Don't look up,* Casey thinks, *please don't look up, please, don't look – oh, goddammit.*

Exit, pursued by a bear.

Deli husks proliferate as he nears the West End. Employing the same denial that once propelled him down this street from charity shop to charity shop, he now drops into each artisan cheesemonger, every boutique chocolatier. Ransacked for produce, their minimal chic and roughly plastered walls now appear needlessly sterile.

Ever cautious, he takes a long approach on what used to be an Iranian patisserie. The windows have fogged up, indistinct shapes move inside. It's a gathering. Might he have found Safehouse B by accident? Could it be this blatant? He'd expected a basement, a warehouse, not a coffee shop.

A fifteen minute wait for anything to happen. A middle aged woman, short and stealthy, turns the corner and slides up to the patisserie door. She knocks and is allowed to enter. The shapes behind the glass come together in a series of blurred hugs.

Casey genuinely can't remember the last time anyone hugged him.

He approaches the door, hesitates.

Another woman, older and less stealthy, dressed in grubby country gear and her long hair in a plait, opens the door wide. It's as if she's expecting friends, as if she's having a dinner party. Given the number of women standing behind her, perhaps she is. She looks him up and down, not unkindly.

'Well don't just stand without,' she says.

Voices rise in protest, the door closes, a conference commences. Casey hears snippets of old fears slowly returning.

'Looks harmless enough.'

'I thought this was a safe space.'

'No, I mean a "nice guy" nice guy.'

One outburst seems to settle matters:

'What patriarchy, Hannah? Seriously, what patriarchy? It's gone. It's all gone. Just... just shut up, okay? Let him in.'

He counts six women in total, none of them look over fifty, and that's about all they have in common. They sit Casey down with cold instant coffee and stale bread, then proceed to largely ignore his presence.

'Where's Rosie?' says the older woman.

'Southside,' says the stealthy newcomer. She sounds Polish. 'She's nearly finished with the school hall.'

'It looks really nice,' says the youngest of the group, maybe a few years his junior. 'I think Anne said she'd make bunting, but, you know...'

'I don't want to talk about Anne.'

'What about the bodies?'

'Oh, those, she dragged them out to the playground a few weeks back.'

'Last I checked there were just a few left.'

'Oh, great plan, Rosie, feed the ferals. What good's a community centre with wolves sniffing about the place?'

'Are you a lesbian gang?'

They stare at him.

'It's just, I heard there were gangs.'

The woman sitting opposite, maybe Hannah, he's not entirely sure of names yet, she leans back in her chair. 'Do we,' she says, 'look like a gang?'

'And first define what you mean,' says her neighbour, also possibly Hannah, although there may be two Hannahs, this one sporting an asymmetrical buzzcut, 'by gang.'

'We want to know,' says someone further down the table, 'which sort of gang you think we are.'

'He said already,' says a Hannah. 'A lezzzzzbian gang.'

'Yeah, but gangs usually have, like, a look, y'know?'

'We could all get pixie cuts,' says the woman who doesn't want to talk about Anne. 'Luce could let hers go long and Marie could-'

'No thank you,' says Marie, the older woman. 'I won't let the end of the world undo years of trying to grow it out. Anyway, for whose benefit? Amy, Lara, that lot?'

'Now, that's what I call a gang,' says the youngest.

'But we all know them,' says Marie. 'And they know us. It'd be pretend.'

'More attitude than image,' says the other Hannah. 'Amazonian.'

'Assholian, more like.'

'They were dicks before everything, too, remember.'

And just like that Casey's invisible again. The conversation weaves in and around past betrayals and allegiances, connections and dissolutions. All the stories have been told before to the same crowd, the scant specifics included more or less as decoration, certainly not for his benefit, and he feels loneliness knot inside his chest like a rat king. Then:

'Shh, shh!' Miss Stealth holds her hands up. They all listen; someone's running down the street. Casey pulls out his phone and opens Dorothy – he has three matches, two registering as approximately half a mile away and a third less than sixty feet. That used to be occasion enough to dim the lights and break out the lube.

A body slams up against the corner window, hands smudging blue across the glass. Nobody inside reacts as the figure undresses, shucking upper layers, tossing them away. As he kicks off a shoe he leans against the window to steady himself, leaving a mess of lime green streaks. Off come the trousers, blushing fuchsia. The man, now naked, bolts. Dorothy marks his two pursuers as less than half a mile away.

'Fucking art school kids,' mutters Marie.

Buzzcut Hannah rolls her eyes, 'We're not all-'

'No time, they'll track him here.'

'It's just two guys,' says Casey, hoping it's three. The Vic would be exactly where some fucking art school kids would meet a friend.

'Did your phone tell you that?' asks Luce, zipping up her body warmer, then her army surplus coat. 'Ditch it. Some day those gold star geeks in wherever the fuck the internet lives will die or get bored and you'll be fucked.'

Marie opens the door and gives the street a quick reconnaissance. The lurid result of a paintbomb ambush streaks and spatters up Great Western Road, towards the city centre.

'Let's go.'

'They're outnumbered,' says Casey. He wants to hang around, he wants to say hello. He knows it's a stupid idea but he wants to meet these men.

'There could be twenty of us and one of them and it still wouldn't be worth it,' says Other Hannah.

'*Let's go.*'

The lesbian gang sweep out of the deli and split into pairs. Marie and Buzzcut Hannah run off Kelvinsidewards, Luce and Other Hannah in the direction of Kelvingrove. Miss Stealth and Anti-Anne hang back.

Dorothy reports: a quarter mile.

'Do you live far?' asks Miss Stealth. 'Do you want a chaperone?'

'I... no, I live five minutes away. I'll be - have you heard of Safehouse B?'

'Nope.'

'I never got your names.'

'We know.'

'Does this happen often? Like, meetings? How do I find-'

'It's a small city.'

'See you around.'

'Don't follow us.'

And they're gone, ducking into the subway. Casey hovers and hums and hahs. He should follow them. He shouldn't follow them. He should stay, meet the men at the end of the rainbow. He should run.

600 feet.

Because Miss Stealth is wrong. Sure, everyone's own personal map of the city, before the fall, had been small. His had been a dozen bars and clubs, not many of them strictly defined as gay, although they had gay nights, and a handful of cafes, a bunch of miscellaneous venues where things happened and familiar faces showed up. His map of the city had been the equivalent of a single street, fractured, scattered, knots of common consensus strung along a cat's cradle of acquaintances. But the real city had been unfathomable, a creature too large and too complex and too strange to comprehend by any one group of friends.

Entire social networks had operated alongside each other like blind, gargantuan fish, and to Casey those people who managed to navigate freely between them, whether in person or digitally, by handshakes or winky faces, those had been the strangest creatures of all.

And now everyone's friends were dead, and every door was open.

Casey's palms sweat.

This is just like that time when a guy sent him a message on Dorothy asking if he was hung and if he wanted sucked off and sent him a video in which he put an absolutely massive black dildo to good use and it turned out he was sort of handsome and lived in the building two doors down and it didn't matter that such behaviour to anyone not riddled with loneliness might seem borderline psychotic because Casey never did a damn thing about it and then went travelling and he didn't even get laid once in Malaysia and then when he came back his flat was up for rent and the man with the dildo had been replaced by a pleasant professional couple who went hiking on weekends.

This is exactly like that, he tells himself.

Exactly.

'You're late,' Janice says through a mouthful of boiled hotdog. She hasn't waited in preparing dinner nor in eating his share. This has happened before; her reasoning being if he's dead, he doesn't need sheltered, or fed.

He sits at the table.

'I met some women today,' he says. 'I think they're trying to start a community in the southside.'

'Yeah? Where?'

'A school. I don't know which one.'

'Good luck to them.'

'You aren't interested?'

'Casey, I find it hard enough living with you.'

'The feeling's mutual.'

This economy of compassion is what's kept them alive so long.

Janice rinses out the hotdog can, a hollow clattering. They hang empty cans from the windowsill and collect rainwater, and use them to pee in at night to avoid going down to the garden. They have a his-n-hers collection as a precaution, just in case, although the chances of contamination outside of sex are pretty minimal.

'Don't get me wrong, like you said, it works. It's probably the best combination? Well, it is for me. No... drama. You know?'

'What if I asked you about where you go at night?'

'Well, that would be a precursor to drama,' she says. 'Please, don't push this, Casey. It's a thing I have and it's mine and I don't want to talk about it. You'd only be making yourself more miserable, anyway, if you knew.'

It suddenly strikes him that even in this horrific new world it's still easier for the breeders, even those who haven't bred. He doesn't know how. He doesn't care how.

'Okay. Well. I'll...' He feels like a burlap sack of unnamed kittens being dragged to the river's edge. 'I'm going to bed.'

'It's only half eight.'

'I know.'

He slouches into the living room. A grey depression awaits him in the cushions of the sofa, worn deep and flat over the course of six grim months. He folds his skinny body into a too-tight foetal position, hugging his knees to his chest.

He opens Dorothy, shielding the glow of the screen with a cupped palm. Darren, 5 miles, last online eight months ago. SexBoi, 3 miles, last online three months ago. G---, 11 miles, last online a year ago. Hung4Fuxx, 6 miles, last online two weeks ago. PowerBottomPete, 3 miles, last online one day ago. Twinkdestroyer, account suspended.

He never spoke to these men when things were good, never wanted to make first contact via this ridiculous online zoo, but it's a cruel trick, this longing, this savannah hangover, this readiness for a flash of flesh in the tall grass.

Hey.

Hey. Hey. Hey.

Hey. Hey. Hey. Hey. Hey. Hey. Hey. Hey. Hey.

The messages shoot out into the oncoming night, like flares, or an animal hooting.

Let them come find me, he thinks. Perhaps they're just as hungry.

Casey, 0 miles, online now.

Louise Welsh

The Face at the Window,
the Wave of the Hand

Fiona glanced across Grosvenor Gardens at her apartment. 'I always look up at the window of our lounge when I reach the gardens,' she told the policeman later. 'I'm not sure why. Habit I suppose.' Though it was more than habit, it was the satisfaction at reaching home; the satisfaction of living in Edinburgh's West End; the sight of their flat waiting for her on the other side of the gardens that separated Grosvenor Crescent from its not quite mirror image, Lansdowne Crescent.

She had walked from Haymarket Station, a canvas bag advertising the Edinburgh Book Festival full of groceries, her messages, slung over her right shoulder, her briefcase containing her tablet and the spread sheets she would work on that evening weighing down her left. This time next year, Fiona thought, I won't be burdened with work. And she felt a quick rush of excitement that could have been mistaken for fear.

There was a steak in Fiona's bag which she intended to cook with mushrooms, red wine and shallots for Margaret and her to share. They would eat it with the cold boiled potatoes left over from the night before. Fiona wondered if Margaret had used all of the shallots and decided that if she had, they would just have to do without. It was only Wednesday, but she was Friday-night-tired and there was a headache threatening at the back of her eyes. If Margaret wanted ingings, she could get them herself.

Fiona paused midway along Lansdowne Crescent and looked with satisfaction at the apple blossom on the trees. The branches nodded over the railings of Grosvenor Gardens, too long she supposed, but a shame to get them trimmed now, when they looked so pretty. One white and two pink, like a bride with her bridesmaids Fiona thought, not for the first time. The wind rose and petals gusted across the street, like confetti she thought, and unconsciously bent her fingers so she could feel the pressure of her wedding band.

That was when she looked up at the top floor window of the converted town house where she and Margaret lived and saw the face at the window, the hand raised in greeting. The face was a quick white presence. The hand gave a cheery wave and then the intruder turned and vanished into the darkness of the room beyond.

Later, when Margaret asked why she hadn't waited for the police to arrive, Fiona said, 'You know how slow Edinburgh police are.'

But the truth was that although she dialled nine, nine, nine, asked for *Police please* and gave the operator her name and address, the thought of waiting didn't cross Fiona's mind. She didn't think at all, simply dashed the length of Lansdowne Crescent, cursing herself for leaving the keys to the central gardens at home, passed through the shadow cast by St Mary's Cathedral and ran along Grosvenor Crescent until she reached their building. Fiona unlocked the main door and strode across the entrance hallway, dumping her bags by the table where that day's post waited.

It was only chance that Paul-on-the-ground-floor was leaving his flat at that moment, tousle haired and puffy eyed, like a cartoon of a man suffering from yet another hangover. The two households had been on frosty terms since Paul's friends had spilled into Grosvenor Gardens in the early hours of St. Andrew's Day and let off a volley of fireworks to shouts of *On yersel Rabbie!* As Margaret had remarked later to Murdo and Grant, occupants of the middle landing, 'They were in such a state they didn't know their Burns' Night from their St. Andrew's Day.'

Fiona put a hand on Paul's elbow, steering him towards the stairs in what he later described to Jackie the barman as *a neat dance move* he wouldn't have thought *the old girl had in her*.

'There's an intruder in my house.' Fiona hissed.

'Are you sure it isn't your friend? Dr Gupta?'

'I think I would recognise my own wife Paul. This person was as white as I am. Whiter,' Fiona said.

Paul took out his iPhone and jabbed at the buttons, but Fiona put a hand over his. 'I've already phoned the police.'

'Would you like me to wait with you until they get here?' Paul resisted the urge to glance at his watch. There was a straightener with his name on it waiting in The Cambridge Bar, but as he told Jackie later, the old bird looked a bit green about the gills and he wasn't sure she should be left alone.

It was on the tip of Fiona's tongue to ask Paul if he was a man or a mouse, but she sensed that the question would be counterproductive.

'We could wait all day on the police while whoever it is takes the place apart.' Fiona's fingers tightened on Paul's arm and he had no option but to follow her to the middle landing. She rapped on Murdo and Grant's door, hoping for reinforcements, but it was only just half past five, too early for either of them to be home from work yet, and there was no response. She turned to Paul. 'Do you have a baseball bat?'

'No.' He faltered. 'Football's my game, five asides with the lads every Sunday afternoon.'

'A football's not much of a weapon. What about a golf club?'

'My old man was mad keen on golf,' Paul said. 'It kind of put me off.'

'Useless.' Fiona jogged up the stairs to the door of her apartment and after a moment's hesitation Paul followed her. He whispered, 'I really think we should wait for the...'

But Fiona had already unlocked the door and stepped into the apartment and Paul's only option was to wait outside like a coward or follow her.

'They've got a nice place up there,' he told Jackie later. 'Lots of storage space, nice and clean too, no stoor under the beds. Ask me how I know that.' Jackie the barman obliged and Paul said, 'Because we checked every nook and cranny of that flat. We looked in every cupboard big enough to hold a trained monkey and a few that weren't. Do you know what we found?' Jackie feigned ignorance and Paul said, 'Nada, nothing, not a soul. There was no one there.'

'There was someone there,' Fiona said. She was too shaken to cook the steak and so Margaret made it, trimming the fat before she put it on the griddle, a low calorie tactic that Fiona thought spoiled the flavour. 'The policeman treated me like I was an idiot and as for that waste of space Paul-on-the-ground-floor . . . I wish he'd away and bile his heid.'

Margaret laughed, but her forehead creased with concern.

'Thank goodness Paul went with you. Imagine if there really had been someone there.'

'There *was* someone there.'

'It was probably sunshine hitting the window.' Margaret lowered the gas beneath the grill pan, crossed to where Fiona was sitting and put her arms around her. 'God knows that's a rare enough sight in Edinburgh to confuse anyone. You glimpsed the sun's reflection and your overworked brain decided it was a person at the window.'

Fiona's shoulders stiffened.

'I saw a person. They were as white as a ghost. I was too far away to make out their features, but somehow I could tell that they were smiling. Whoever it was raised their hand and waved at me.'

Margaret said, 'You don't believe in ghosts.'

The steak was beginning to burn, but neither of them made a move to turn it.

Fiona said, 'Whoever it was was real. But they were prison-white. Like someone who had been kept indoors a long time.'

Margaret stroked Fiona's hair. 'It was just a trick of the light', she whispered.

The second time Fiona saw the face at the window, the hand raised in a cheery wave, she didn't bother to call the police or knock on neighbours' doors. She took the stairs two at a time, her heart hammering as if it was trying to escape her chest. Fiona locked the door of the apartment behind her, so the intruder couldn't escape, and went swiftly from one empty room to another.

'There's no point in hiding,' Fiona shouted, but though she spent the next hour searching she found nobody.

'What on earth is going on?'

Margaret stood in the doorway of the flat looking at the contents of the walk-in cupboard in the hall, the glory hole, strewn the length of the lobby.

Fiona emerged.

'Remember the cupboard in *Rosemary's Baby*? I wanted to check there wasn't an entrance into next door hidden behind all this stuff.'

'And why in the name of the wee man would you think there might be?' Realisation dawned on Margaret's face. 'I thought we'd agreed that this ghost you thought you saw was just an optical illusion.'

Fiona pressed the heel of her hand to her forehead. She had a headache, tiny lights pulsing behind her eyes.

'You decided it was an illusion. I know there was someone here, a real person, not a ghost. They had the damn cheek to wave at me again. I'm going to find out who they are, if it kills me.'

September stripped the leaves from the trees in Grosvenor Gardens and October hardened the ground, strangling the last of the flowers. Fiona and Margaret strolled along Lansdowne Crescent arm in arm swathed in winter coats.

'I hate this time of year.' Margaret's voice was muffled by the scarf wrapped around the lower half of her face. 'No colour, everything dead.'

'Your red coat is pretty bright,' Fiona teased. Her hat was pulled low over her eyes, but the cold air was pine needle sharp and her sinuses stung. 'Anyway, I like winter. No life without death. And it means we can light a nice fire when we get in.' She glanced up at their flat and suddenly she was running.

This time Fiona had almost been able to make out the features of the person waving from the window. It was someone she had met before, she was sure of it. She tore off her gloves, turned the key to the building with numb fingers, dropped her bag and ran up the stairs.

'Fiona!'

She could hear Margaret on the landing below, but Fiona didn't slow her pace. She reached the third floor, flung open the door of their flat and descended into the blackness her mother had always said would claim her. The moon white face from the window sailed towards her as she fell into the dark and Fiona recognised it as her own.

The oncologist was unsure how long the tumour had been nestling against Fiona's brain, but she was certain that Fiona was, '... a very fortunate woman. If your friend hadn't...'

'My wife', Fiona corrected.

'Your wife.' The oncologist smiled. 'If your wife hadn't insisted on a CAT scan, the outcome might have been different. As it is, I think we caught it in time.'

Fiona stood at the sitting room window watching the trees in Grosvenor Gardens dip and swoop against the breeze. It had been the recurring hallucinations as much as her blackout that had alerted Margaret, though she still berated herself for not noticing the tumour's symptoms earlier. Silly, Fiona thought. She would never have got such a quick diagnosis without Margaret's persistence. She smiled, remembering the uncharacteristic way Margaret had insisted on using her professional title, *Dr Gupta*, and the quick responses it had prompted.

Fiona looked beyond the trees, to Lansdowne Crescent and saw Margaret walking towards home, a bag of shopping in each hand. She looked lithe and strong despite her five-plus decades, her hair tied back from her face revealing the cheekbones that had helped to snare Fiona over thirty years ago.

I am lucky, Fiona thought. And the prognosis is good. We could have another twenty, even thirty years together. Some people live to eighty and beyond, why not us? She stepped closer to the window so that Margaret might see her from the street below, raised her hand in a cheery wave and then turned away, into the dark.

Nicola White

I Live Here Now

'Have you met *the boys*?'

Hilda says it with the kind of heavy emphasis that suggests euphemism.

We're standing on her lawn and the bright grass is up to our ankles, but the mower won't start. Every spring, the same game. My shoulder aches from pulling the cord, and I would like Hilda to go away.

'They're called Douglas and Mark, and Mrs Anderson says they're civil *pah-tners*. Isn't it exciting? They've bought the house at the top of the brae. Douglas is a musician and Mark is Canadian.'

'A professional Canadian?'

'Well, I think it's great. Stimulating. Kinlochbuie drags itself into the twenty-first century.'

'What about me?' I say, 'I've been here for years.' And Hilda shakes her head and gives a little laugh, almost says something. I can tell by the way she sprints away to deadhead the puckered daffodils that she is embarrassed.

Hilda has forgotten that I am one of them. Or maybe she thinks lesbians don't really count. Buggery being so much more vivid. Or could it be that I don't count because I'm on my own. If you don't have sex with anyone, maybe your orientation becomes academic, like Latin or Middle English, fallen out of use.

I pull the cord, quick as I can. The mower farts and dies.

I live here now, in a village at the head of a loch, encircled by hills. I ran from the city and a bad relationship that took Houdini skills to escape. My first priority was to be unseen, and I found a cottage with high hedging, and so only got to know the populace gradually. They are discreet, wholly Caucasian, unanimously straight. As far as I can tell.

I never lied about myself. I made the effort to come out early and come out often. 'It's *Mizz* actually' and 'My former partner, *she* always/never...'

First Christmas, my immediate neighbors asked me to a drinks party. It was mostly their retiree friends, bridge players and golf enthusiasts. We drank gin and tonics, ate cheese footballs. Men wore blazers with shiny buttons. The kind of gathering that in my old life would have passed as a retro theme party.

I was pushing my chit chat about when a woman in a gathered skirt and spangled cardigan said to me. 'And what does *your* husband do?' First question. Not my name or dwelling place or even my own job.

'I don't have a husband,' I said with too much volume, too much velocity. We stared at each other, silence spreading thick. I have no fear of silence.

But you get worn down. When a plumber or bank teller calls me Mrs Kearns now, I let it go, tell myself it's just an honorific, like *madame*. And you know, here in the outlands of middle age, we women start to converge. I become *Mrs*, wear the odd floral pattern. They cut their hair shorter, wear lower shoes. We can see each other well enough, but in the eyes of men and the young we mist and we blur.

I still love it that no windows look into my windows, no footsteps squeak over my head, no troubling screams break the night, bar the owls and foxes. But I found that the more space and silence I created, the louder grew the voice of me, prattling away in my head, by turns dull and neurotic. No getting away from her.

I took up gardening work to root myself in something. A trite metaphor but a potent one. It makes me steady. I have genteel clients like Hilda Trench and Delphine McEwan, and the Doctor Fowlers, Iain and Jan, eccentric people with rhododendron-ringed gardens and ramshackle Victorian villas. The kind of Scottish houses once run by cheap servants. Pinterest boards on 'shabby chic' have nothing to teach these folk. They deeply understand the expressive pointillism of mould, the sun-tattered curtain lining, the *duende* of peeling wallpaper.

Despite the fact I garden slowly and don't understand machinery, people hire me. I am easy to have about the place, and I know the difference between a weed and a beloved plant. For the heavy stuff, the drainage ditches and the annual hedge cutting, they call in Kyle-from-the-garage with his big muscles and demands for mid-morning coffee and bacon rolls.

As I travel my route of mossy lawns and knotweed-lined burns, people tell me news of the 'boys'. They have thrown themselves into village life, I hear. Douglas is giving free fiddle lessons to the primary school children, and Mark the Canadian has been prominent in the campaign to keep the little library open.

One bright evening I'm driving along the single track road that rims the far side of the loch when I see them out walking together. Douglas, dark and stout in a mossy green tweed jacket, Mark slim and dressed in jeans and thick jumper. Between them, a red setter strains at the lead, a shine like water running over her coat. I slow the van and start to edge past, rolling down my window.

'Lovely evening!' I call. They agree and move past. I want to say more than that. I want to give them the secret sign that I am not like the others. I stop the car and look at them in the wing mirror. They keep walking away, into the low sun with their beautiful dog. They don't notice I've stopped. I switch my eyes to the shapes the wind makes on the water surface.

At home, I uncap a bottle of beer, and walk down the garden to the hammock, my blanket under my arm. I bought the hammock thirty years ago. Thirty years, the very phrase seems impossible. On a trip to Mexico with Marlene, first girlfriend. Ochre striped cotton with tassles. I brought it from flat to flat with faith that one day I would have somewhere to hang it. When I first saw the garden here, a pair of perfectly spaced trees were like an omen.

I had reckoned without the midges. But they're not biting yet. Spring is my hammock window. Rolled in the blanket, I lie back and look up at the branches of the two trees intermingling over my head, the spurt of new leaves.

I think about Douglas and Mark. The differences between them and their sameness. I remember the way relationships unbalanced me. The idea that in couples one will be messy and the other neat, one gregarious and the other less willing, one slim, one plump. The distorting pull and push of it. I sip at my bottle, suspended in the dusk, and listen to the birds falling silent.

The 'boys' are at the pub quiz at the Lochbuie Arms Hotel. Hilda has recruited me for her team, because Sheena is in Fort William 'for her op.' We are called The Disparate Housewives – I don't want be under the banner of any kind of housewife, but that is the name they have had for three years now, and Delphine, who is at least seventy, has told me to 'lighten up'.

I catch the eye of Mark the Canadian. He has a long face, and brushed back fair hair. His skin is lightly marked with the traces of teenage acne. He smiles quickly with teeth that are very white and even. I nod back and try to make an expression that will convey a surreal amusement at our predicament. He frowns. Does not get me.

They're sitting with a small group of teachers from the primary school, and one leans forward to whisper in his ear, glancing back at me while she does. The quiz starts.

Under the bonhomie and banter there is a ferocious competitiveness. None of the many things I have in my brain are useful for the kind of things they want to know – questions about how many medals Team GB won at the Sochi Olympics or the name of Elizabeth Barret Browning's spaniel. I do know the main ingredient of guacamole, but so does everyone else. I find it hard to believe they do this every week, for pleasure. The stress makes me thirsty. Hilda is buying wine by the bottle.

Up at the bar, Kyle-from-the-garage surveys the room with scorn, his elbows propped back on the counter, one boot hooked up on the rail. He is not a quizzer. He would not give anyone the chance to call him a fool or a dunce.

He smiles and nods at me when I go up, though, because we have business dealings. We are almost pals.

'Enjoying yourself?' he asks, as I wait to be served.

'I wouldn't go that far.'

He tips his chin in the direction of the table that the 'boys' sit at.

'See that lot? Sitting with the teachers. Hear they're volunteering with the young ones. Hope someone's keeping an eye on that. Know what I'm saying?'

'I'd be very careful what you're saying, Kyle.'

Back at the table, my pulse starts hammering, a delayed reaction. I can't listen to the questions being asked, I'm too busy in my head finding better words to face Kyle with, words to crush and reprogramme him.

When Douglas and Mark leave, I find myself checking that Kyle is still up laughing with his mates, is not going to follow or approach them. Hilda keeps asking if I'm alright.

At home, I take out a pad of paper and start writing them a letter. I'm thinking they need to be warned. Writing is difficult. I suddenly notice a mechanical thrum outside the house. I don't know how long it's been there for. I go into the unlit front room and peep out the window. Through the half-leafed hedge I can see the beams of a car's headlights stopped on the road by my gate, idling.

I've never felt scared in this place before. I lock the front and back doors, though I normally don't bother. I check the windows too. When I look out again, there are no lights. I strain my ears for the sound of the engine, but the wind blows harder now. I can't be sure it's not still there.

I wake parched and hungover. No sign of a car in the road. On the kitchen table, beside the whiskey bottle, are my attempts at a letter:

This place may seem friendly, but there are people with narrow minds. Perhaps teaching children is not the best idea…

I use the pages to light the range. Everything is benign in the new light. Kyle is an ignorant prick, but I've no grounds to think him violent.

I got carried away. Carried myself away, indeed. Too ready to believe the Gestapo are lurking in the back lanes of Argyll.

Today is the Spring Fling. They have set up a marquee by the public car park. There will be bric-a-brac stalls and hoopla and an afternoon ceilidh. Douglas's fiddle club will be giving a recital. I hope Kyle is too busy at the garage to attend.

I am wheeling a barrowload of pots down the brae to re-stock the plant stall. Halfway down I stop to admire the marquee by the waterside, fluttering with little flags. The potency of cheap bunting. And suddenly I remember another marquee, the women's dance tent at Pride in Brockwell Park in the nineties, the amazement of stepping inside the warm fug and seeing wall to wall girls, dancing the grass into blackness. More lesbians than I had ever set eyes on. And right beside my nervousness and excitement was parked another feeling. *They'll get us for this.* Nothing so good can go unpunished.

Like last night. The tendrils of my Calvinist upbringing, returning, never quite vanquished.

Someone says my name, and I turn to see Mark catching me up.

'Are you going to the fair?'

'The fling. I am. You're Mark, aren't you?'

We shake hands formally, and I can tell by the way he looks at my face, the way he takes me in, that someone has told him. I feel seen.

'Can I go down with you?' he asks, 'Douglas is the sociable one. I get a bit nervous with crowds. You're laughing at me. You think I'm a big baby.'

'Not laughing,' I say, 'not that. Where's your dog?' I pick up the barrow handles and we walk side by side down the lane.

'She's at home. Can't keep her paws on the ground. I blame the owners. Can I ask you something?'

His eyes are serious.

'Have you been happy living here?'

'That's a big question.'

A family I know, a five-link line of teens and adults pass by, shout 'Hiya!'

The day is sunny and giddy with it. The family look with open interest at Mark. He gives a little half-bow in response, clicks his heels. One of the young girls laughs, but it's not mockery. It is only delight.

'Happy enough,' I say, but I'm thinking, *happier now*.

Christopher Whyte

Unfamiliar Rooms

– an extract from work in progress

Raymond dials a number and starts talking. Thomas soon realises the person at the other end of the line is his employer, the owner of the restaurant. Again he feels scared. His papers are not in order. In fact, like fifty per cent of the people he deals with every day, and two thirds of those working in the restaurant, he has no papers at all, no legal basis for being in France or working there. Normally the police would see no point in interfering. But this guy knows the owner's number, and makes nothing of calling the man long after midnight!

Raymond passes the receiver to Thomas, who cups it in his hand, takes a deep breath, then brings it close up to his ear.

'Just tell him everything you know, Thomas,' he hears. 'Don't hide anything, and don't feed him false information. Got it? That's the best thing you can do.'

Thomas says nothing, looking across at Raymond, who is stubbing out the remainder of his cheroot. His boss is afraid, too. The note in his voice is unmistakable. Thomas is unsure what to do with the receiver. Raymond nods in the direction of the wall, so he replaces it. He cannot remember how long it is since a call had such a big effect on him. All he usually has to deal with are enquiries about the day's menu or the availability of a table, news from the fish market of a specially lucrative haul, or else that surplus goods are being sold off cheaply now the buying day is coming to an end.

'Why don't you take me upstairs?' says Raymond.

It sounds like a request but is effectively an order. The detective realises he has an erection, but chooses to take no account of the fact. It does not get jotted down in that ever so useful mental notebook. Unforeseen erotic reactions are not part of the scenario he has planned. For the moment he prefers to ignore their implications.

(I should interject that, if I have dedicated what may seem an unjustifiable amount of time to specifying what each man smokes, this is because I am concerned with the taste of their kisses, the aroma and flavour they will encounter when their lips open and they mingle their saliva. Of the two, Thomas registers olfactory data more directly. He will very quickly identify the particular fragrance of Raymond's skin but, beyond that, will explore a whole symphony of different scents, in his armpits, at his crotch, the fact that his hair smells differently on the crown of his head, at his sideburns, around his balls and, notably, in the carefully trimmed beard that has only recently started being flecked, prematurely, with grey. Because it is already May, and the hot season has started, their exertions will cause them to sweat profusely. Thomas will understand, each time his nose comes into renewed contact with Raymond's body, how long it is since he last washed, whether or not he has perspired within the last few hours, and the extent to which the sweat has impregnated his skin. During pauses in their lovemaking he will lick, with scholarly deliberation, whatever stretches of Raymond's body are damp, glistening and available. Fresh perspiration has a different flavour. But always, behind it, like the long drawn out, sustained background chord in an orchestra, is the odour he will recognise as this man's, sufficiently strong for the others never to overpower it.)

Without thinking, Thomas pours himself a cognac once they get upstairs. More slowly, he then takes a second glass, pushes it to Raymond's side of the table, and brings the bottle closer. Raymond gives a nod of assent and, with the thumb and index finger of his right hand, indicates the quantity he will accept.

'You want to know about Déodat and René, right? Everything?'

Thomas is waiting for Raymond to produce a pencil and a notebook, where he will note things down. He does none of this, merely looking meditatively at the new cheroot he has lit, then back at Thomas. Raymond is no fool. He is not just interested in what Thomas is going to say. He will be attentive to each intonation of his voice, to the emotion behind the phrases. He has to decide how much credence to lend, which information is unvarnished, what is merely stuffing, intended to put him off the track long enough to give his interlocutor time to develop a strategy, and what unadulterated lies are woven into the general fabric.

(Ages. I have said nothing about ages. Raymond can be thirty-four or thirty-five, though he looks, and acts, a little older. When he was younger, he regularly practised sport, swimming and cycling. Now all he does is take a relaxing spin on his bike on Sundays. Thomas will detect a layer of flab on his tummy, around the belly button, thick and pervasive enough for him to tug playfully at the point near Raymond's hips where the pelvis starts. Thomas, by contrast, is frighteningly lean. When he goes to the beach to swim at the height of the summer, he does so alone. Women catching sight of him experience an irresistible urge to feed him, to take him home and stuff him with rice or else the fluffy, white bread they have in Marseilles, so useful for mopping up sauces, and the remainder of soups, from the bottom of a dish. But it would all be to no purpose. Thomas can be twenty-eight or twenty-nine. The man he will talk about, Déodat, is a couple of years younger. The distance in age between the two should be no greater. René was in his middle forties when he met his end.)

'Déodat was into cocaine. That was the start of all his troubles.'

Thomas draws nervously on his cigarette. Raymond is privileged. Nobody ever sees this. As I have said, Thomas is what you might call an invisible smoker. Now he is acting as though the tobacco he draws into his lungs could supply the courage, indeed, the audacity needed for the story which he has to tell.

'His family lives up by the park. You ought to know.'

Raymond nods, but offers no corroboration. He is fully informed about Déodat's background. His chief is concerned because Déodat's father occupies a position which will allow him to obstruct the prosecution of his son. There are plenty of strings he can pull in the city administration.

'Three servants, and an apartment ten times the size of this room. His father wanted him to become a lawyer, maybe still does. He started having sex with a cousin when he was twelve. In some cases specific tastes emerge early on. For the cousin it was a passing phase, but not for Déodat.'

'And the cocaine?' Raymond puts in. 'Is taking cocaine common practice among law students?'

'You have to understand what it was like for him. He always had plenty of money in his pocket, quite a lot more each month than I earn here. No lodgings to pay for, ample food laid on at the family table whenever he cared to put in an appearance. His elder brother went straight into the business. Déodat is, or was, his father's pet, the apple of his eye. They have aristocratic origins. Blue blood in his veins. But they moved to the city two generations past. The revenues from the lands they left behind wouldn't be enough to keep them clothed, never mind supply them with food and drink. The older brother had to make sure the money kept on coming in. Déodat was an indulgence for his father, a luxury. Much brighter than his brother, or so the father thinks. Maybe he's right.'

'Get to the point.'

'I want you to understand the strains that he was under. His cousin lost interest and moved on to a girlfriend. Déodat had to look for something else. He's not someone who can do without for long. If nobody is available, he will jerk off two or three times in the course of a day. But that won't satisfy him.'

'So where did he turn?'

Raymond is stubbing out his cheroot in the ashtray. Suddenly his hands loom into close-up for Thomas, who is struck by the care and delicacy with which they carry out this mundane task. He is in the habit of reading hands. Not the way a clairvoyant does, more like someone cast alone into the world, who needs to exploit every survival skill he has. He believes they tell you infinitely more than a face. After all, we use them in ways we never use our faces. What he perceives in Raymond's elegantly shaped, yet slightly stubby fingers, in the wrist which is larger and more articulated than you would expect, can be summed up in one word. Goodness. Here is a good man. Deciding this for Thomas is like finding in the larder of an untended house a longed for food he has never been able to afford. All he wants to do is sink his teeth into it. Will he be discovered? Can he indulge himself without fear of retribution?

'There are places where you can pay. Don't laugh, please, if I say I've never visited them. I've never felt the need. I am more patient than Déodat. If something is there for me, then I enjoy it. If not, I can wait.'

Raymond is hard again, so hard it is uncomfortable. The edge of the table hides the lower part of his body from Thomas, so he puts his hand to his crotch and strokes his sex with his palm, as one might do the head of a dog, settling it, soothing it. The touch is reassuring and comforting. It will not be enough for much longer.

'So he began a double life. As long as his cousin was the only man Déodat slept with, he had no no need to rove beyond the confines of the world where he grew up. Receptions, family parties, the occasional concert or theatre. Two summer months up in the hills, where they have a holiday home. Inviting fellow students round in the afternoon, ostensibly to cram for an exam, kids from respectable families whose fathers and mothers all know each other. Now he began alternating that with visits to this part of the city, to the port.'

'So that is where he met René?'

'How little, or how much, do you want to know? Would you rather put the questions, while I answer them?'

Raymond makes a gesture of deprecation with the hand he has lifted from his crotch. He is good at his job. Thomas has no basis for feeling riled. Questions are Raymond's way of participating, registering his presence. Also of directing the flow of talk, as gently as he can, into the channels that concern him. I, too, need to remind myself of Raymond's presence, of the intensity with which he listens. His whole body is tense. His interjections could be a way of trying to reduce that tension.

'In those places he met a different sort of people. The private rooms are upstairs, or at the back. If a client is in a hurry, or knows who he wants to be serviced by, he loses no time. But rushing is regarded as bad form by the people who work there, as well as by the ones that run the place. Even in the sex trade, manners are important. Generally you sit downstairs, before and after, passing the time of day with the other clients, and with whatever members of the staff – let's call them "staff" – aren't actually working. They organise parties, too. If you go, then you get invited to other parties, in more sumptuous surroundings. Private parties.'

'So that's where they got together?'

'I told you, if you try to rush me, we'll get nowhere. I don't want to mix things up. And in the end I can take all the time I need, can't I? Or am I a suspect, too?'

Raymond wants to reach across and cup Thomas's cheeks in his hands. He loves these spurts of insolence. At this point he acknowledges to himself his double motivation for being there. He, no more than Thomas, wishes Thomas to make short work of his testimony. What is more, he does not want the Slavic man to give himself too easily. If Raymond has already yielded, there has been no external evidence of the battle going on inside him. Does Thomas guess? He thinks not.

'Those visits were a learning curve for Déodat. Parallel to what was happening at the university, if you like. More interesting, and more engrossing. Let us say, he acquired a more refined and rarefied kind of knowledge. Erotically, what went on between him and his cousin had been pretty limited. Now he got the chance to extend his repertoire. Déodat is an inveterate talker, much like me. Though I'm more frustrated than he is.'

Thomas gives a laugh, which illuminates his features. A Czech peasant looks out of Thomas's eyes at such moments – a strapping lad got up in traditional costume for a feast day riding out, with a peacock feather in his cap, overjoyed to have everybody gazing at him. He rides as part of a cavalcade down the centre of the unpaved village street. The light of the June morning is sharp and angular, every part of his homeland being high above sea level. Though the lie of the land may be flat in some places, in fact it is hill country, mountainous in parts. Thomas does not say what is in his mind, namely, that in the situation they have created, he can indulge his penchant for talking to the full. Grateful to have found a listener at last, he looks up at Raymond, still smiling. What he sees in Raymond's face is not what he expects. Choosing not to stop and think about it, he pushes ahead with his story.

'So one thing was his conversations with the staff. Sex and talking, talking and sex. That has always been his way. The man whose body he was paying for would explain some of his own experiences. Those people are not often listened to, you know. Their mouths tend to be full when they are working. How could they manage to say much? And for them, talking makes a change from having sex. Déodat paid by the hour or the half hour. Nobody took care to check exactly how the time was spent.'

'And all he did was listen?'

'Of course not. He hadn't much experience of his own to share. But he had ample fantasies. Déodat has an incredibly rich imagination. Rich, and perverse. He should have been a novelist, I often think. And I can't help wondering if some of the things he talked about got back to René, if René concluded that here was the man he had been looking for, waiting for, year after year, without ever managing to find him.'

'So René knew about Déodat before they actually met?'

'I can't be sure. I'm merely speculating. In those establishments people gossip endlessly. Most of the gossip is about sex. What people do, what they have done, what they would like to do. They are discreet enough, in their own fashion, where the world beyond those doors is concerned. Absolutely trustworthy, I would say. Secrets circulate within the tribe, not elsewhere. But among members of the tribe, no holds are barred.'

'And Déodat was a member?'

'Fast on the way to being fully paid up. It was foolish of him to talk so openly. And to several different people. The men who listened never imagined they were being asked to fulfil the roles which he described. But naturally it would occur to them to wonder who might, and when. Not everyone is capable of distinguishing fantasy from reality. That could be how word got back to René. But you should remember I have no basis for saying this. They're just thoughts that come to mind.'

Raymond thinks about saying, keep strictly to what you know. But then he decides any embroideries Thomas may add constitute helpful information in themselves.

'As I said, if Déodat had not started on cocaine he could have maintained the balance for much longer. Controlled the slide, so to speak.'

'What were his sources?'

Thomas gazes at him in disbelief.

'Do you take me for some kind of fool? You can find anything you want to in this part of the city. Prices vary dramatically, as does the quality. But the supply is constant.

'When Déodat first set eyes on René, he'd been off the drug for a while. After that meeting he went back on again. Déodat's father knew something was going on. If you ask me, he had a very shrewd idea of the circles his son had got mixed up in. Actually putting it into words would be too painful. That meant they could never talk about it. He began reducing the amount of money he gave Déodat. Later on it was René who paid. That created a further bond between them.'

'René didn't take drugs himself?'

Thomas shook his head, and smiled, as if Raymond's suggestion could not have been more ridiculous.

'A man in René's position had to have his wits about him. Have you any idea how many deals he had on the go at one time? How many pulses he had to keep his fingers on? He was as sharp as they get. A brilliant intelligence. That was one of the things I admired about him.'

'So you knew him personally?'

This question has placed him in difficulty, and Thomas pauses. Various possibilities flash through Raymond's mind – that they were lovers, that there was a threesome, that Thomas rejected René, or the other way round, or the simplest explanation of all, namely that Thomas was jealous of Déodat. Thomas has removed the cigarette from between his lips, and is turning it between his thumb and his forefinger. Watching closely, Raymond notes a black patch beneath the nail of the thumb. Has Thomas hit himself with a hammer? Or caught it in a door, or something?

'I saw him. Once. I never spoke to him.'

'Why not?'

'He was too – dangerous for me. Talking would have been a bad idea.'

'You're not attracted by dangerous men?'

Thomas lifts his gaze and surveys Raymond coolly, defiantly.

'No. They're not my thing.'

'You never took cocaine yourself?'

Thomas looks straight at him. Again a smile plays round his lips. As he listens, Raymond realises how unusual it is for him to be awake at this late hour. Yet he feels no tiredness.

'I have a job to do. You cannot not know how far I am from home. If I make a slip, if anything happens to me, who am I to turn to? I have no-one but myself. And if I gave them a reason for taking me out, no-one would be any the wiser. Your department wouldn't show an interest, whatever happened to my corpse. I'm not René Simon. I could swear you weren't even aware of my existence till this evening.'

This is far from the truth. Raymond, however, does not trouble to contradict him. What he has already said about the months during the previous summer when Thomas shared a flat with Déodat suggests precisely the opposite. But in the end it is better if people imagine the police department knows infinitely less than is in fact the case. If Raymond feels awkward, his disquiet has a different basis. Thomas has not noticed, but Raymond realises, in retrospect, that the question expressed concern. That is alien to the business which they have in hand. The annotation belongs in a different notebook, one whose pages have been effectively empty for several years.

'Go ahead,' he says. 'Sorry I interrupted.'

The apology is out of order, motivated by the awkwardness which I have just explained. Thomas pauses, gazing at the policeman with undisguised suspicion. The expression on his face is grimmer now. At the same time, his penis has gone hard. Thomas has a predominantly playful relationship to this part of his anatomy. You could say it plays Sancho Panza to his Don Quixote, were it not that Thomas gives his penis much more credence than the idealistic knight ever accorded his manservant.

This is the point when Raymond moves into action. What happens next admits of two explanations. There and then, Thomas does not have time to think about it. The question does not occur to him until the following day when, in the afternoon, once the restaurant has been cleared after lunch and the waiters have disappeared on their various inscrutable errands, he gets time to reflect. All of a sudden, without any warning, Raymond is leaning over Thomas. He is gripping the back of Thomas's chair, which has tipped away from him. His feet are on the floor, or rather the front part is there. The heels are lifted, perhaps because every section of his body is straining. Thomas's knees are spread wide. Raymond is standing between them. He lowers his head. Without being fully convinced he ought to, Thomas enjoys the pressure of Raymond's lips. He has not had contact of such a subtle nature with another man's body since the previous summer, when he and Déodat shared a bed. His encounters in the intervening months have been furtive, hurried, clumsy, but never brutal. Differently from Déodat,

Thomas is not interested in brutality. He is trying to decide whether or not to part his lips. He does not want to move too quickly. Though impatient to welcome Raymond's tongue into his mouth, he is at the same time caught up in the feeling of timelessness that not infrequently intervenes when making love.

At this point the chair falls over. Or rather, some part of it snaps. It turns out afterwards to be beyond repair. When Raymond comes upstairs to continue their conversation the following night, he notes the difference between his chair and Thomas's. Thomas will be using the one Raymond sat on, having filched a new chair from the restaurant to accommodate his guest.

But back to the incident with the chair. Is it all calculated on Raymond's part? Thomas hears the sound of splitting wood. But he cannot decide if that causes the collapse, or is provoked by it. Suddenly his body is no longer supported. Instead of falling backwards, he feels Raymond's arms catch hold of him. The detective jerks himself upright, bringing Thomas along. Neither has opened his lips. Within a moment, Thomas regains his balance. Raymond gives no sign of being disconcerted. Clutching Thomas tightly, he tucks his chin into the hollow of the other man's left shoulder, so that he can barely move his head. Thomas reflects, with an internal laugh, that if this is what being taken into custody is like, it could be enjoyable. Meanwhile Raymond manoeuvres both of them towards the bed. Thomas makes a show of resisting, but it is only a show. His face has broadened in a smile. His lips are parted. There can be no mistaking the intensity with which Raymond presses his crotch into Thomas's, seeking, burrowing. As their trousers are securely buttoned, no more intimate contact is possible as yet.

When they collapse on to the bed, Raymond rolls over onto one side. He still holds Thomas close. Already they are kissing. His right hand tugs at Thomas's shirt, freeing it from the belt. Now at last he gets access to his skin. It is smooth, and practically hairless, as he was hoping. The discovery exhilarates him, giving an added vehemence to movements he already has difficulty keeping under control. Raymond moves his hand backwards and forwards. Sometimes it is his palm that comes into contact with Thomas's skin, sometimes the back of the hand. The two sensations are distinct, but equally satisfying in the information they supply. He investigates the belly button, the place where Thomas was cut free from his mother. He would like to kiss it, nuzzling in with his lips and with his nose, letting the beard along his chin tickle the flesh of Thomas's abdomen so he chuckles and complains, begging him to stop. But for Raymond to do so would be like jumping ahead in a book. He prefers to proceed in order, not caring how long the plot takes to unfold, how much time is needed for each intricate knot to be unravelled.

Anyone observing the two from a corner of the room would have problems deciding whether they are making love or fighting. Having once ceased to resist the impulses flooding through him, Raymond renews his aggression minute after minute, not knowing how it is going to end, when he will no longer need to do this. Each aggression is transformed because, rather than harming, it provokes pleasure, a further opening on Thomas's part. The process fascinates Raymond, so that he makes attack upon feigned attack, always producing the same result he cannot quite bring himself to believe. Thomas's movements, as before, are caught between warding off and welcoming, but more and more the welcoming predominates. The two men's mouths are gulping, gobbling at each other. It may look frenzied, but neither hurts the other's tongue, nor do their teeth collide. That shows the quality of their concentration. The puzzled onlooker would find an unequivocal answer to his doubts in the smile that has spread over Thomas's face, as for a minute he turns his head aside, his mouth gaping as he takes in air. It is the smile of a man who has found precisely what he wanted.

Having recovered from his surprise, he is no longer uncertain what is happening, or how he should react. He accepts Raymond's embrace, his closeness, his need to adhere with every possible limb, with the extremity of every limb. Slipping his left hand between their two bodies, Thomas neatly snaps the button fastening his trousers open so as to release his sex from the constraint. Understanding, Raymond laughs as Thomas's fingers tease at his belt, pulling to and fro until the metal tongue slips out from the hole punched in the leather. Raymond grasps Thomas's trousers at the sides, so as to free his hips and buttocks. One would be hard put to say whether two bodies are helping one another, or if a single entity endowed with four hands and two heads struggles to free itself from the cocoon that has imprisoned it.

Raymond has not lost his urgency. With a touch of roughness, he manoeuvres Thomas's body around so the back is to him. One of his hands goes to the buttocks, caressing the cleavage between them. Thomas's face is turned to one side, away from Raymond, resting on the pillow. Very quickly he pulls open the top drawer of the battered cabinet. He is barely within reach, but dexterous enough to flip the top off a small jar inside. Falling to the floor, the top wobbles crazily, before settling flat with a resounding clatter. Thomas holds the jar up to Raymond who, bemused, sniffs. An odour of coconut. Understanding, he dips two fingers in, taking a generous quantity of the ointment.

Everything proceeds more slowly now. Raymond has understood that care and caution are required at this point. He anoints the hole that is the focus of his concentrated attention, pushing in a little with his finger. Now the tip of his penis is where his finger was, hunting for the place that will receive it. Thomas digs his chin into the pillow, enjoying the way that hardness moves up and down the cleavage, as Raymond's hand did only a few moments ago. Then Raymond locates the spot, and settles. The time has come for Thomas to breathe regularly and deeply, closing his eyes in the effort of relaxation, and letting his body do the rest. It, not he, will decide when release comes. Thomas is foolish enough to be pleased things are not easy, because this might lead Raymond to think he had been penetrated only the day before, which is not quite the truth. Raymond, for his part, enjoys this prelude more than he could say, the unrelenting hardness of his sex and the premonition of how warm, soft and enclosing the place it is destined to end up will be.

When at last he does enter, Thomas utters a murmur. Raymond pulls back, thinking he has hurt him. But Thomas shakes his head. His left hand seeks out Raymond's left buttock, settling there with the gentlest of pressures, which is nonetheless explicit. Entry is easier the second time. Raymond's sex goes deeper. This time it is he who gives a grunt. Having ascertained the nature of the place he has arrived, he begins to thrust, first tentatively, then regularly.

Jeff Meek

Afterword:
Scotland's Queer History

Only in recent years has Scotland's 'queer history' attracted much interest. Arguably this has been due to the tendency amongst those investigating the treatment of non-heterosexuals historically in the United Kingdom to view legal proscriptions in unified terms. However, this ignores the fact that Scotland has its own independent legal system, as well as independent religious institutions. Scotland, of course, did not decriminalise male homosexual acts between consenting male adults in private until the passing of the Criminal Justice (Scotland) Act in 1980, thirteen years after similar legislation was passed in England and Wales. This inequity poses the question: why was Scotland different?

Men who engaged in homosexual acts faced the same problems as their English and Welsh counterparts during the period up to the mid-twentieth century. Although trials relating to homosexual acts were rare in Scotland up to the 19th century, there is evidence that men convicted faced a grisly fate. John Sawn and John Litster were both strangled at the stake and their bodies burned for engaging in sodomy in 1570, while Michael Erskine faced a similar fate in 1630. Legal commentators of the period believed that such crimes were rare in Scotland due to the scarcity of existing legal records, however, some evidence exists that summary executions were undertaken, which left little trace in legal archives. However, compared to the volume of legal activity witnessed during the 19th and early 20th centuries, the early modern period witnessed relatively few prosecutions for same-sex intimacies.

Scotland did not have an 'Oscar Wilde' moment; an event which brought same-sex desire into the public realm. That is not to say that same-sex intimacies were absent from Scottish public discourse; queer men, and women, were just much more circumspect. There is certainly plenty of evidence of 'romantic friendships' between Scots, such as the intense relationship between poet David Gray and writer Robert

Buchanan. Buchanan, in his 1868 text *David Gray & Other Essays*, described his relationship with Gray:

> ...there was in Gray's nature a strange and exquisite femininity – a perfect feminine purity and sweetness. Indeed, till the mystery of sex be medically explained, I shall ever believe that nature originally meant David Gray for a female; for besides the strangely sensitive lips and eyes, he had a woman's shape – narrow shoulders, lissome limbs, and extraordinary breadth across the hips. Early in his teens David had made the acquaintance of a young man of Glasgow, with whom his fortunes were destined to be intimately woven. That young man was myself.

Such 'men of letters' or artists – for example, Robert Colquhoun and Robert MacBryde – largely escaped suspicion and legal action, perhaps due to their status, but during the late 19th and early 20th centuries other 'ordinary' Scots were not quite so fortunate.

Specific legislation penalising same-sex intimacies emerged in the late 19th century; Section 11 of the Criminal Law Amendment Act of 1885 widened the legal proscription to *all* acts short of sodomy, whether conducted in public or private. This act, also known as the *Labouchère Amendment*, applied in Scotland. What is apparent from these legal sanctions is that almost every eventuality was covered: any sexual intimacy between males whether conducted in a public park, a private bedroom or a public convenience was prohibited. Notably, the *Labouchère Amendment*, like almost all legal proscription, ignored sex between women. Various myths have emerged regarding the absence of legal proscription against lesbians in the 19th century, mostly relating to Queen Victoria's sexual naivety, but women's sexuality had historically been reduced to matters relating to procreation and exploitation. Even by the late 20th century the issue of sex between women was dismissed by Scottish legal authorities. In a letter from Stanley Bowen, the Crown

Agent for Scotland to the Scottish Minorities Group (Scotland's foremost homosexual law reform organisation of the period) in 1970, detailing the legal proscriptions against homosexual acts, Bowen comments: 'so far as female perverts are concerned, they have never been a problem to this Office'. While authorities in Scotland were loath to discuss male homosexuality there was a consistent silence with regard to female homosexuality. However, this silence was not representative of tolerance and many Scottish institutions saw female homosexuality as pernicious as male homosexuality.

While the Scottish police and legal authorities had no interest in pursuing cases relating to sex between women, men who engaged in homosexual acts often felt the full force of the law. This was particularly true of queer men during the late 19th and early 20th centuries. There were close to 100 High Court cases relating to sodomy or attempted sodomy during this period, and the majority resulted in guilty verdicts. A further 240 or so cases were investigated, and either dealt with at a lower court or not pursued. The average sentence handed down at a High Court trial was around 3 years with or without hard labour.

What is notable about the vast majority of prosecutions in Scotland is that they related to homosexual acts committed in public spaces, including parks, tenement closes and public toilets. Only a small fraction of offences prosecuted occurred within private residences. Indeed, during the post-war period there were virtually no prosecutions undertaken for private, adult, consensual sexual acts, and certainly none from the 1960s onwards. Indeed it was an unwritten policy in Scotland that successive Lords Advocate followed, not to prosecute in those circumstances. However, one mustn't assume that this policy was related to a more tolerant climate towards homosexuality in Scotland. In fact, the thorny issue of corroboration under Scots Law played a significant part in this decision: failed prosecutions during the earlier part of the century revealed just how difficult securing a prosecution in these circumstances could be.

This is in stark contrast to events in England during the post-war period. There, police actively sought out men who had sex with men, whether the offences were committed in public or private. The police force's prurient interest in the bedroom activities of queer men led to controversial legal cases such as that concerning Peter Wildeblood, Michael Pitt-Rivers and Lord Montagu of Beaulieu. Wildeblood's prosecution centred on letters to his lover Edward McNally (a Scot), and McNally's evidence for the prosecution. During the 1950s police raids at dawn on the homes of suspected homosexuals in England was not uncommon, nor was the spectre of queer men being forced to name other men of their acquaintance.

While the legal powers and politicians were aware of the anomaly of the law in Scotland ignoring consensual homosexual acts committed in private, the vast majority of queer men were not. Housing conditions in major urban centres such as Glasgow and Edinburgh meant that for many non-heterosexual men private sexual relations were impossible. Working-class Scots were much more likely to find themselves appearing in court charged with sodomy, attempted sodomy or gross indecency, than their middle or upper-class counterparts. From the mid 19th century onwards particular public spaces in urban centres became a locus for homosexual activity: Nelson's Monument on Glasgow Green; Kelvingrove Park; and Queen's Park, all featured prominently in prosecutions in Glasgow, while in Edinburgh, Calton Hill, Arthur's Seat and various leafy parks featured. Additionally, heightened interest in the activities of queer men led to criminal investigations into certain leisure venues in the Scottish capital. The prosecutions relating to prostitution undertaken against management and owners of the Kosmo Club led to similar vice squad activity at Maxime's Dancehall, where male prostitutes entertained paying guests and undertook organised trips to public spaces where queer men lingered. Glasgow too saw increased legal interest in the activities of the city's notorious 'whitehats' who plied their trade around theatres, cinemas, and railway stations. Prosecutions which focused on public spaces, and prostitution, hit their peak in the interwar period before falling away following World War 2.

There have been a variety of reasons forwarded as to why Scotland was omitted from the Sexual Offences Act 1967, which brought the limited decriminalisation of homosexual acts between consenting male adults in England and Wales. Reasons forwarded include: fierce resistance from Scotland's main churches; overwhelming public opposition; a lack of appetite from Scottish politicians; and Scotland's abrasive culture of homophobic masculinity. However, the manner by which Scots Law dealt with homosexual offenders was a key determining factor. The resultant low level of prosecutions and the refusal to prosecute private, consensual homosexual acts led to Scots Law being valorised in debates after the publication of the Wolfenden Report in September 1957. If Scotland did not prosecute consensual private homosexual acts then why change the law? Crimes that were being prosecuted north of the border would still be crimes in England and Wales beyond 1967.

What this ignored of course was the injustice that non-heterosexual men were effectively denied legal recognition or rights. An unwritten rule followed by one Lord Advocate might have been rejected by another and non-heterosexual men still lived under the threat of legal intervention; they were effectively criminals by default. This situation of legal limbo was initially supported by Scotland's main church, the Church of Scotland, which had not attended the deliberations by the Wolfenden Committee, and had repeatedly decried any attempts to legalise homosexual acts north of the border. Their resistance was supported wholeheartedly by James Adair, the former procurator fiscal, and member of the original Wolfenden Committee. Adair had disagreed fundamentally with the recommendations of the committee (to offer limited decriminalisation) and produced a minority report warning of the dangers, particularly to the young, of relaxed laws regarding homosexual acts. The Scottish press too, particularly the tabloid press, was resistant to calls for legal equity between Scotland and its southern neighbours.

It was not until the appearance of the Scottish Minorities Group (SMG) in the late 1960s that homosexual law reform in Scotland became a real possibility. The group, initially comprised of middle-class men, sought to challenge the status quo by underlining both the existing legal anomaly – that a law existed that was rarely enacted – and the legal inequity between Scotland, England and Wales. The fight for law reform would take just over a decade of campaigning and the assistance of prominent, and persistent, politicians such as Robin Cook, who enabled the passing of the Criminal Justice (Scotland) Bill 1980, which brought legal equity with England and Wales. Along the way the SMG had garnered support from some of the Scottish institutions which had decried attempts for law reform; including the Church of Scotland (the SMG also received support from the Roman Catholic Church).

Scotland's queer population, historically, had to grapple with a culture of silence regarding same-sex attractions; a legal system which was forced to apply only elements of laws governing homosexual acts, by necessity rather than design; and publicly hostile institutions. The legal inequity between Scotland, England and Wales was only challenged once an organisation was willing to step out and campaign for law reform, and required the assistance of committed and persistent politicians. Scotland *was* different but it has travelled far towards a nation that is liberal, enlightened and consistently strong on issues of social justice, inclusivity and equality.

Bibliography

Cant, Bob (Ed.) *Footsteps and Witnesses: Lesbian and Gay Lifestories from Scotland*, 2nd Edition (Edinburgh: WP Books, 2008)

Davidson, Roger & Davis, Gayle, *The Sexual State: Sexuality and Scottish Governance, 1950-80* (Edinburgh: Edinburgh University Press, 2012)

Dempsey, Brian, *Thon Wey: Aspects of Scottish Lesbian and Gay Activism, 1968 to 1992* (Edinburgh: USG, 1995)

Jeffrey-Poulter, Stephen, *Peers, Queers, and Commons: The Struggle for Gay Law Reform from 1950 to the Present* (London: Routledge, 1991)

Meek, Jeffrey, 'Scottish Churches, Morality and Homosexual Law Reform, 1957 to 1980', *Journal of Ecclesiastical History* 65 (2014)

Meek, Jeffrey, *Gay and Bisexual Men, Self-Perception and Identity in Scotland, 1940 to 1980*, PhD Thesis (University of Glasgow, 2010)

Settle, Louise, 'The Kosmo Club Case: Clandestine Prostitution during the Interwar Period', *Twentieth Century British History* (February 2014)

Weeks, Jeffrey, *The World We Have Won: The Remaking of Erotic and Intimate Life* (London: Routledge, 2007)

Contributor Biographies

Janette Ayachi (b.1982-) is an Edinburgh-based poet who graduated from Stirling University with a combined BA Honours in English Literature and Film Studies, then from Edinburgh University with an MSc in Creative Writing. She has been published in over fifty literary journals and anthologies, edits the online arts/literature magazine *The Undertow Review* and reads her poetry at events around Scotland. She lives with her two young daughters, likes whiskey and wild women, and is the author of *Pauses at Zebra Crossings* and *A Choir of Ghosts*. She is currently working on her first full poetry collection, *Hand Over Mouth Music,* and a series of non-fiction shorts *Collecting Women Like Dolls.*

Damian Barr is a journalist, writer and salonier. *Maggie & Me*, his memoir of growing up in 1980s Lanarkshire, won him Stonewall Writer of the Year, Sunday Times Memoir of the Year and Politico's Political Humour and Satire Book of the Year. It was Radio 4 Book of the Week and has been optioned for television. He lives with his husband and their chickens in Brighton.

Paul Brownsey is a former newspaper reporter and a former lecturer in philosophy at Glasgow University. He has had more than 60 short stories published in magazines and collections in Scotland, England, Ireland and North America. He lives in Bearsden with his partner, Jim McKenzie.

'My stories often centre on characters who are gay but the stories are not usually *about* being gay. This has sometimes prompted the question: Why, then, do you make your characters gay, if you're not making a point about homosexuality? Things will be as they should be only when this question is never asked.'

Jo Clifford is known as one of Scotland's leading playwrights. She has written about 80 performed scripts in just about every dramatic medium, some of which have been performed all over the world. She wrote many of these plays when she was still living as a man, and known as John Clifford. The plays she wrote for the Traverse in the eighties are among those that revived that theatre and made it internationally famous. Since transitioning to Jo, she has also re-discovered herself as an actress and performer. She has just written a 'Dear Scotland' monologue for the National Theatre of Scotland, is reviving JESUS, QUEEN OF HEAVEN for the 2014 Fringe, and the opera made from her INES DE CASTRO is about to be revived by Scottish Opera. She is the proud father of two amazing grown up daughters; and an even prouder grandma. More information and her blog on **www.teatrodomundo.com**. Follow her on Twitter **@jocliffordplays**.

Toni Davidson is the author of *Scar Culture* (Canongate, 2000); *The Gradual Gathering of Lust* (Canongate, 2007); *My Gun Was As Tall As Me* (Freight, 2012). **www.tonidavidson.com**

'Sexuality has always been part of my writing. As an undercurrent, as an overtone, for moments of anger, despair, confusion and unbridled joy.'

David Downing lives amongst the three-billion year old rocks and deep sea lochs of Scotland's northwest Highlands. His writing has featured in *Gawp and Gaze, People Your Mother Warned You About, Eros At Large, Gazebo* and *The Best of Gazebo*. He is currently editing the Highlands' first LGBT magazine, *UnDividingLines*.

'The Quilt' was inspired by the public hall at Strathnaver, Sutherland, and its unimposing rootedness in time, landscape and community. However, the setting of the story, including its hall, can be found only on the map of the author and reader's imagination.

'Writing is my defining means of engagement with the flux and flow of the world around me. Every aspect of who I am enters into this dialogue, but it is my sexuality that offers the most rewarding source of inspiration and understanding.'

Carol Ann Duffy is the first female Poet Laureate of Great Britain. Her most recent book of poetry is *The Bees,* winner of the 2011 Costa Poetry Award and the 2011 T. S. Eliot Prize. In 2012, to mark the Diamond Jubilee, she compiled Jubilee Lines, 60 poems from 60 poets each covering one year of the Queen's reign. In the same year, she was awarded the PEN/Pinter Prize.

After being anointed as Laureate in 2009, she said: 'Sexuality is something that is celebrated now we have civil partnerships and it's fantastic that I'm an openly gay writer, and anyone here or watching the interviews who feels shy or uncomfortable about their sexuality should celebrate and be confident and be happy. It's a lovely, ordinary, normal thing... Poetry comes from the imagination, from memory, from experience and from events both personal and public. I will write what needs to be written.'

Jenni Fagan's debut novel *The Panopticon,* was received to great critical acclaim and she is currently completing the script for Sixteen Films. She was selected for the once-a-decade Best of Young British novelists list and has been shortlisted for the James Tait Black Prize, Dublin Impac, Solerno Book of Europe and Desmond Elliott, amongst others. She has written for *The New York Times, The Independent* and *Marie Claire.* Jenni's poetry has won awards and seen her twice-nominated for The Pushcart Prize. She is currently Writer-In-Residence at Edinburgh University and her second novel *The Sunlight Pilgrims* will be published next year.

'I am not aware of my sexuality affecting my writing but of course it probably does, just as everything else in my life and psyche becomes part of my work. I am interested in what makes individuals who they are internally – often in contrast to how they are externally defined.

Nearly all of the main young characters in *The Panopticon* were bisexual or gay, this was not contrived – that's just who they were and it wasn't a focus of the narrative. I often have lines that are blurred sexually within the characters I create and I sometimes like to write characters that could be either male or female and not create definition, really to value the internal space of being rather than the imposition of gender values created by outmoded patriarchal structures. While I personally don't think about whether my sexuality affects my writing – I have often been told I write like a man. By that I think they mean I write about sex in a way that is forthright, stark and realistic, I write about female sexuality as something that is complex and driven – personally, I don't think that's male either, I think it's just accurate.'

Ronald Frame is the author of sixteen nooks of fiction, six of which have appeared in the US. His novel, *The Lantern Bearers,* was Scottish Book of the Year 2000, and received a Stonewall citation from the American Libraries' Association.

'As a writer of fiction, I become all my characters – or rather, they all already live inside me: male, female, old, young, middle-aged, dementia-raddled or (as a child) shaping up to the world.

I take an initial decision, although it's really instinctive: is this person I feel compelled to bring to life and put into words a 'she' or a 'he'? The rest will then follow from that.

I consider my mind to be androgynous.

Alone at the keyboard or with a sheet of A4, I'm nothing in particular, and I am also – have to be – everything.'

Roy Gill is the author of two YA novels – *Daemon Parallel* and *Werewolf Parallel* – that follow the adventures of a teenage boy across an alternate Edinburgh.

He is also a scriptwriter, whose work includes a feature-length special 'The Prime of Deacon Brodie' for Big Finish's drama series *The*

Confessions of Dorian Gray. He was a 2010 Scottish Book Trust New Writers Award Winner, and has been shortlisted for the Kelpies and Sceptre Prize.

He is currently working on more scripts and a third novel. Find out more at roygill.com or follow him on Twitter **@roy_gill.**

'Does my sexuality inform my writing? Like most writers, my *identity* informs my writing, the interests I have and the stories I try to tell. I couldn't and wouldn't be able to subdivide my sexuality from that.'

Kerry Hudson is the author of *Tony Hogan Bought Me an Ice-Cream Float Before he Stole My Ma* and *Thirst*. She was born in Aberdeen. Growing up in a succession of council estates, B&Bs and caravan parks provided her with a keen eye for idiosyncratic behaviour, material for life, and a love of travel. She has identified as queer for thirteen years and feels her queerness or 'otherness' allowed her to see the world from a different perspective and informed her choice to write about sections of society that often get overlooked in literary fiction.

Jackie Kay was born and brought up in Scotland. *The Adoption Papers* (Bloodaxe) won the Forward Prize, a Saltire prize and a Scottish Arts Council Prize. *Fiere*, her most recent collection of poems, was shortlisted for the Costa Award. Her novel *Trumpet* won the Guardian Fiction Award. *Red Dust Road* (Picador) won the Scottish Book of the Year Award, and the London Book Award. She was awarded an MBE in 2006, and made a fellow of the Royal Society of Literature in 2002. She is Professor of Creative Writing at Newcastle University.

'I suppose that everything that I am influences my writing in some way – being black, being a mother, a daughter, a lesbian. I'm always interested in the truth being somehow multiple and in creating characters where what they are is not necessarily what they are about.'

David Kinloch was born and brought up in Glasgow. He studied French and English at Glasgow and Oxford Universities and worked for many years as a teacher of French. He is currently Professor of Poetry and Creative Writing at the University of Strathclyde and is the author of five books of poetry. He has edited a number of literary magazines, including *Verse,* which he co-founded and edited with Robert Crawford and Henry Hart, and he has received a number of awards for his poetry including the Robert Louis Stevenson Memorial Award and an Arts and Humanities Research Council Fellowship. In recent years he helped to found the Scottish Writers Centre and to set up the Edwin Morgan Trust. He came out as gay in his late twenties and since then his poetry and prose has often addressed the twin themes of gay and Scottish identity. His first book, *Paris-Forfar* (Polygon, 1994) took the form of a sustained elegy for a generation of gay men who lost their lives to AIDS. *Un Tour d'Ecosse* (Carcanet, 2001) was a highly satirical look at the pleasures and dangers of growing up gay in Scotland which culminated in a mad bicycle tour of Scotland in which the yellow jerseys were worn by versions of Walt Whitman and Federico Garcia Lorca. *In My Father's House* (Carcanet, 2005) commemorated an affectionate and difficult relationship with his opera singing father and featured a long poem about a gay relationship set in 17th-century Turkey. His most recent collection, *Finger of a Frenchman* (Carcanet, 2011) contains many poems about Scottish paintings that were influenced or modelled on French examples, as well as a historical epic that features a disappointed 17th-century English cleric on a grand tour of Europe. His next collection will feature a distressed giraffe stranded by the Paris flood of 1910, a long poem that recounts a visit by Dorian Gray, Oscar Wilde's anti-hero, to the Falls of Clyde, and a sequence of lyrics and prose-poems that respond to an exhibition of art by 20th-century American gay and lesbian artists.

Kirsty Logan is a professional daydreamer. Her first book is *The Rental Heart & Other Fairytales* (Salt, 2014); her second, *The Gracekeepers*, will be out in the UK, US and Canada in early 2015. She lives in Scotland with her girlfriend, and has a semicolon tattooed on her toe. Say hello at **kirstylogan.com**.

'All of my writing is queer. Sometimes it concerns characters who consider themselves LGBT, sometimes it doesn't. But I like to twist, to subvert, to upend, to go to uncomfortable and truthful places. However I approach my life or my writing, there's always a touch of queer.'

Marcas Mac an Tuairneir was born in 1984 and educated at the University of Aberdeen, where he graduated, in 2008, with an MA Hons in Gaelic and Hispanic Studies, and in 2010 with an MLitt in Irish and Scottish Literature. He then completed an MA in TV Fiction Writing at Glasgow Caledonian University with the support of MG Alba. He currently resides in Inverness where he is Internet and Informations Officer at Bòrd na Gàidhlig. His début collection, *Deò,* was published in 2013 by Grace Note Publications and his début novel, published by Acair, is expected in 2015 as part of the Aiteal series. Marcas writes poetry, prose songs and drama for theatre and television. He is also an actor and sings with Inverness Gaelic Choir. For more information, please visit **marcasmac.co.uk**.

'I wouldn't say that I go out to write explicitly about homosexuality per se. I definitely write about my experiences as an out gay man. I have also discussed the political situation around gay rights in Britain and how homosexuality is viewed in a specific Gaelic-speaking context. The latter is perhaps the most important issue to me, personally, in that in this speech community the boundaries of LGBT issues are not so clearly defined, the lexicon is not completely developed. These issues and identities are still seen as English-language concepts, to a certain degree. Perhaps the reason I write is to change that, but that said, I write about what I know and what I feel and these issues crop up in my work as frequently as the other themes I identify with and embrace. I am uncomfortable with the monicker of 'Gaelic LGBT Trailblazer' as one critic called me. I don't write in order to foist dogmae on people, but I do hope that people of many backgrounds can find resonance with their own lives in my work. In today's Scotland it is still a political act to speak Gaelic. It is still a political act to express an LGBT identity. That the combination of the two might be seen as controversial is unfortunate, but it is out of this kind of friction that, historically, some of the best work has come and if that is my road into the Gaelic canon then so be it. I am who I am and am prepared to stand up and be counted. I am proud of that.'

John Maley was born in Glasgow in 1962. He has written two award-winning short films, Daddy's Girl and My Daughter's Face, and published a book of short stories, *Delilah's*. 'The Thatcher Years,' his poem about life under Thatcher in the 1980's, has been published in *New Writing Scotland, Mungo's Tongues* and most recently in *Scottish History In Verse*. John is also a playwright and work includes *Daylight Robbery, Witch Doctor* and *Greenock Central*. His most recent play, *Close Mouths,* features the haunting voices of former tenants of a demolished Glasgow council estate.

'I once heard someone on a chat show say Tennessee Williams was Blanche Dubois. But I found myself wondering who was Stanley Kowalski? Brick in *Cat On A Hot Tin Roof*? Chance Wayne in *Sweet Bird Of Youth*? Big Daddy? The best writers can write well beyond their comfort zone and write not just about themselves, but about the society they inhabit. Does being gay influence my writing? Of course, but so does the kindness of strangers and a million other things.'

Val McDermid has published 28 novels, as well as short stories, non-fiction and childrens' fiction. Her books have been translated into more than forty languages and she has won many awards including the

Stonewall Writer of the Year, the Cartier Diamond Dagger, the Portico Prize for Fiction and the LA Times Book Prize. She grew up in Fife and read English at St Hilda's College, Oxford, where she is now an Honorary Fellow. She is a regular broadcaster on BBC Radio 4 and her books have been adapted for radio and TV. She lives in Edinburgh with her partner.

'I always wanted to write books that portrayed the whole landscape I inhabit. So that meant including GLBT characters as a matter of course, rather than to make a point. I'm proud to have created the first British lesbian detective, Lindsay Gordon, but her adventures were never about being gay – that was integral to her life but incidental to the mysteries she solved. My sexuality is important to my writing. But so is being a woman, being a mother, being Scottish and having a political consciousness.'

Katherine McMahon is a spoken word poet. She performs across the UK, as well as running OUT:SPOKEN, an Edinburgh-based queer spoken word show. She recently co-edited *Naked Among Thistles*, an anthology of creative writing about LGBT+ identities and mental wellbeing, produced by LGBT Health and Wellbeing and published by Elephant Juice (an imprint of Stewed Rhubarb). Her first pamphlet, 'Treasure in the History of Things', is also published by Stewed Rhubarb. She likes swimming in unlikely places, baking elaborate desserts, and growing things. You can find her at **katherinemcmahon.bandcamp.com**.

'My sexuality and gender identity have informed my writing in a number of ways, but the deepest is that the experience of being marginalised has made me treasure and cultivate connection, community and solidarity - all things that writing can create in a powerful way. The writing of other queer people has been so important to me because at key times it has made me feel less alone - and in doing so, illustrated that what I have to say has value because it can do the same for other people.'

Paul McQuade is a Scottish writer and translator currently based in upstate New York. He is working on his first novel, a collection of short stories, and finding the time to do all of the above. He is the 2014 recipient of the Sceptre Prize for New Writing.

'It's hard to say how my sexuality has informed my writing; it is such a small part of me, yet remains an important factor in how my life intersects with the social and the political, alongside race, class, and language. What interests me, what I write about, is always queer to the extent that it is affected by that intersecting, that queer play of forces that shapes our lives.'

Jeff Meek

I am an historian of gender, emotion, sexuality and relationships based at the University of Glasgow. My research has focused on the development of queer identities and same-sex intimacies in Scotland from 1850 – 1980, as well as examining wider discourses of sex, romance and family. Undoubtedly, my own queer identity has informed my research directions. As a young man growing up in rural Scotland during the late 70s and 80s, the mysteries of sexuality and the culture of silence regarding sexual diversity left their mark and played a significant role in shaping the mind and interests of my future self.

Alison Napier lives in Perthshire and works for a local charity. Her fiction and non-fiction have appeared in anthologies, national newspapers and literary magazines and her debut novel, *Take Away People*, is currently seeking a discerning publisher. Many things inspire her fiction, including a love of wild and rugged land-sea-and-sky-scapes, and telling the stories of the traditionally 'invisible and voiceless'. Viewing the world through the prism of heterosexism simply adds a further dimension to her writing and to the intriguing experience of being alive at this point in history. She can be contacted via her website at **www.alisonnapier.com**.

Allan Radcliffe was born in Perth and now lives in Edinburgh. He has worked as a journalist for twelve years and is now the theatre critic for The Times in Scotland. His short stories have appeared in Markings, Elsewhere, Gutter, ImagiNation and New Writing Scotland among others. He is a previous recipient of a Scottish Book Trust New Writer's Award.

Elizabeth Reeder is originally from Chicago but now calls Scotland home. Her short writing has been widely published in journals and anthologies and has been broadcast on BBC Radio 4 as stories, drama, and abridgements. Her debut novel, *Ramshackle,* is published by Freight Books and was shortlisted for the 2013 Scottish Mortgage Investment Best First Book Award, the 2012 Saltire First Book Award, and longlisted for the 2013 Author's Club Best First book. Her second novel, *Fremont,* is published by Kohl Publishing. She teaches on the Creative Writing Programme at University of Glasgow.

'Being a lesbian affects everything and nothing at all about my writing. It's simply integrated into who I am, who I love, how I view the world and the choices I make, and how I define and create family; and it's completely common and everyday and makes no difference at all.'

Berthold Schoene is Professor of English and Associate Dean for Humanities and Social Science Research at Manchester Metropolitan University. His books include *Writing Men* (2000), *Posting the Male* (2003), *The Edinburgh Companion to Contemporary Scottish Literature* (2007), *The Cosmopolitan Novel* (2009) and *The Edinburgh Companion to Irvine Welsh* (2010). He has edited two recent journal issues on 'Texting Obama: Politics, Poetics, Popular Culture' for *Comparative American Studies* and 'Cosmopolitanism as Critical and Creative Practice' for the Open University's *Open Arts Journal*. In 2012 Berthold was Distinguished Visiting Professor of British Literature at the University of Connecticut.

Helen Sedgwick is a writer, editor, publisher and former scientist. She has won a Scottish Book Trust New Writers Award and her work has been published internationally and broadcast on BBC Radio 4. As a writer, she is represented by Johnson and Alcock. As a publisher, she is joint managing director of Cargo Publishing. As a scientist, she studied non-equilibrium states of matter. Say hello at **helensedgwick.com.**

'It can be subtle or explicit, a sharp focus or blurry undercurrent, but it's always there.'

Ali Smith was born in Inverness in 1962 and lives in Cambridge. Her books have won and been shortlisted for many awards. Her latest books are There But For The (2011), winner of the Hawthornden Prize, Artful (2012), winner of the Foyles / Bristol Festival of Ideas Best Book 2013, and, forthcoming, the novel How To Be Both (2014).

'The thing about the imagination is that it has, simultaneously, no gender or sexuality, and all genders and sexualities. Nothing human is alien to us. The thing about being gay is that it means you always inherently question the norm, and if you're an artist of any kind, and happen to be gay, then this is a bit like inheriting French windows. On horseback. In a very small living room. Flooded with sunlight and the squawks of the exotic jungle birds and no visible ceiling on the room or roof on the house. You know that things can be different, and you know it without having to learn it.'

Shane Strachan was brought up in Fraserburgh and Peterhead, and is currently working on a collection of short stories related to the decline of the Northeast fishing communities as part of a PhD in Creative Writing at the University of Aberdeen. His work has appeared in *New Writing Scotland, Northwords Now, Causeway/Cabhsair, Metazen, Leopard* and various other publications, while another story, 'Starnie', is forthcoming in *Stand* magazine. He also writes for the stage and has had work performed in Aberdeen's The Lemon Tree and His Majesty's Theatre.

'Although I rarely set out to write a story specifically about sexuality, it has naturally recurred in my work and has often made me reflect on being gay in this day and age, as well as in the past. Writing 'Bill Gibb, 1972' made me appreciate that, while I may have found growing up gay in a close-knit fishing community a struggle at times, to have been born just a few decades earlier would have been a completely different minefield altogether.'

Tat Usher wanted to be a writer as soon as she learned to read, and her love of 'making stuff up' has remained. Growing up gay gave her an awareness of social margins and 'outsiderness' – themes that persist in her work. She sees margins as places of creative freedom and aims to celebrate all that is 'out there'. Tat completed a Creative Writing MA at UEA in 2007 and received a New Writer's Award from The Scottish Book Trust in 2009. Her short stories have been published in anthologies, magazines and online and in 2010 her short story 'Fifty-One' was dramatized for Radio 4.

'As soon as I learned to read, aged 4, I decided I wanted to be a writer. My idea of what 'being a writer' is changed slightly over the following 38 years, but the love of making stuff up remains the same. Although I haven't been drawn to explore sexuality in my writing, I think that growing up gay gave me an awareness of social margins and 'outsiderness', and these are themes that are present in all of my work. I tend to see the margins as places of creativity and freedom rather than alienation, and I aim to celebrate what's 'out there'.'

Ryan Vance is a writer and freelance designer based in Glasgow. He edits *The Queen's Head,* a literary zine that champions the weird, the unlikely and the hysterical. More of his work can be seen at **www. ryanvance.co.uk,** but when he's not collecting projects like so many stray cats you'll find him on a dance floor, any dance floor at all.

'Aside from simply wanting to see more LGBT stories told through horror, fantasy and sci-fi, I'm also interested in the potential those genres have to explore queerness, not as the misunderstood, standing in opposition to the world, but to question it on its own terms from within, with its own fears, mysteries and wonders.'

Louise Welsh is the author of six novels, most recently *A Lovely Way to Burn* (John Murray 2014). She has written many short stories and articles and presented over twenty programmes for BBC Radio, most recently 'Bannockburn' for BBC Radio 3, produced by Louise Yeoman. Louise was writer in residence for The University of Glasgow and Glasgow School of Art 2010 – 2012. She has received several awards and international fellowships, including an honorary fellowship on the University of Iowa's International Writing Program (2011) She lives in Glasgow with the writer Zoë Strachan. **www.louisewelsh.com @louisewelsh00**

Nicola White's first novel, *In the Rosary Garden* (Cargo), won the 2013 Dundee International Book Prize and acclaim from writers such as AL Kennedy who called it 'A moving, intelligent and courageous book' and Val McDermid who described it as 'mesmerising'. Her short stories have been widely published in anthologies, journals, as stand-alone booklets by Artlink (Edinburgh) and broadcast on radio. Originally from Dublin, Nicola moved to Scotland to work as a curator in Glasgow, then as a producer of arts programmes for BBC Scotland. She lives on the Clyde Coast, near the submarines.

'I think sexuality affects my writing as much and as little as my gender, age, upbringing, nationality and quirks of personality do. That is, it affects where I stand, my point of view, but not necessarily what I choose to look at.'

Christopher Whyte has published four novels in English. The third, *The Gay Decameron,* offers the widest-ranging panorama of gay life so far attempted in Scotland or, indeed, anywhere in Europe. His fifth collection of poems in Gaelic, *An Daolag Shionach* (The Chinese

Beetle) appeared in 2013. Some 180 poems translated from the Russian of Marina Tsvetaeva are to be published in New York as *Moscow in the Plague Year* in summer 2014. He abandoned a successful academic career in 2005 to write full-time, and now lives between Budapest and Venice.

'I wouldn't say homosexuality has influenced my work, so much as the suppression of homosexuality. The oppression I grew up with meant taboo after taboo had to be broken. But for a writer to have a new subject, something never written about or not written about enough, is an immense advantage. It gives you a head start. Nowadays, while gay situations and gay experience may be my point of access when writing about love and sex, my treatment of these topics goes far beyond issues concerning the gender of those involved. Or so I hope!'

Acknowledgements

'The Female Husband' by Carol Ann Duffy first appeared in *The Bees* (Picador, 2011).

'Orta St Giulio' by Carol Ann Duffy first appeared in *The Bees* (Picador, 2011).

'You' by Carol Ann Duffy first appeared in *Rapture* (Picador, 2005).

'Quickdraw' by Carol Ann Duffy first appeared in *Rapture* (Picador, 2005).

'Grace and Rose' by Jackie Kay first appeared in *Reality, Reality* (Picador, 2012).

'The Road and the Miles to Dundee' by Val McDermid first published in 2005 by Flambard Press.

'A & V at the V & A' by Ali Smith first appeared in *Road Stories* (Faber, 2012).